KISS OF DEATH

HELL ON EARTH SERIES, BOOK 3

BRENDA K DAVIES

BRENDA K. DAVIES

ALSO FROM THE AUTHOR

Books written under the pen name
Brenda K. Davies

The Vampire Awakenings Series

Awakened (Book 1)

Destined (Book 2)

Untamed (Book 3)

Enraptured (Book 4)

Undone (Book 5)

Fractured (Book 6)

Ravaged (Book 7)

Consumed (Book 8)

Unforeseen (Book 9)

Forsaken (Book 10)

Relentless (Book 11)

Coming Fall 2020

The Alliance Series

Eternally Bound (Book 1)

Bound by Vengeance (Book 2)

Bound by Darkness (Book 3)

Bound by Passion (Book 4)

Bound by Torment (Book 5)

Bound by Danger (Book 6)

Coming 2020

The Road to Hell Series

Good Intentions (Book 1)

Carved (Book 2)

The Road (Book 3)

Into Hell (Book 4)

Hell on Earth Series

Hell on Earth (Book 1)

Into the Abyss (Book 2)

Kiss of Death (Book 3)

The Edge of the Darkness

Coming Summer 2020

Historical Romance

A Stolen Heart

Books written under the pen name
Erica Stevens

The Coven Series

Nightmares (Book 1)

The Maze (Book 2)

Dream Walker (Book 3)

The Captive Series

Captured (Book 1)

Renegade (Book 2)

Refugee (Book 3)

Salvation (Book 4)

Redemption (Book 5)

Broken (The Captive Series Prequel)

Vengeance (Book 6)

Unbound (Book 7)

The Kindred Series

Kindred (Book 1)

Ashes (Book 2)

Kindled (Book 3)

Inferno (Book 4)

Phoenix Rising (Book 5)

The Fire & Ice Series

Frost Burn (Book 1)

Arctic Fire (Book 2)

Scorched Ice (Book 3)

The Ravening Series

The Ravening (Book 1)

Taken Over (Book 2)

Reclamation (Book 3)

The Survivor Chronicles

The Upheaval (Book 1)

The Divide (Book 2)

GLOSSARY OF TERMS

- **Adhene demon** <Ad-heen> - Mischievous elf-like demon. Corson and Wren are the last adhenes.
- **Absenthees** – Center of the Abyss and its main focus of power.
- **The Abyss** – The Abyss is another plane. The jinn can open a doorway into the Abyss and enter it. Absenthees is at the center of the Abyss and main focus of power in the Abyss.
- **Akalia Vine** <Ah-kal-ya> - Purple black flowers, orange berries. Draws in victims & drains their blood slowly. Red leaves. Sharp, needle-like suckers under leaves. Behind the 6th seal.
- **Barta demons** <Bartə> - They were locked behind the 55th seal. Animal of Hell. Now part of Lucifer's guard.
- **Calamut Trees** <Cal-ah-mut> - Live in the Forest of Prurience.
- **Canagh demon** <Kan-agh> - Male Incubus, Female

Succubus. Power thrives on sex but feed on souls on a less regular basis than the other demons. Their kiss enslaves another.

- **Ciguapa** (see-GWAH-pah) – Female demon with backward feet.
- **Craetons** <Cray-tons> - Lucifer's followers.
- **Crantick demon** – Crazy. Often run head first into walls and throw themselves off ledges for fun. Howl in a pack. Like to fight but mostly innocuous.
- **Drakón** <Drak-un> – 101st seal. Skeletal, fire breathing dragons. They now protect the varcolac's Chosen.
- **Erinyes** (furies) <Ih-rin-ee-eez> - demons of vengeance and justice. 78th Seal.
- **Faerie/Fae** – Empath demons who were slight in build, fast, and kinder than the other demons. The fae bloodline still exists in mixed demons but the purebred fae died out thousands of years ago.
- **Fires of Creation** - Where the varcolac is born.
- **Forest of Prurience** <Proo r-ee-uh nce> - Where the tree nymphs reside. Was also the original home of the canaghs and wood nymphs.
- **The Gates -** Varcolac demon has always been the ruler of the guardians of the gates that were used to travel to earth before Lucifer entered Hell.
- **Ghosts -** Souls can balk against entering Heaven, they have no choice when it comes to Hell.
- **Gobalinus** (goblins) <Gab-ah-leen-us> - Lower level demons, feed on flesh as well as souls. 79th seal.
- **Hellhounds -** The first pair of Hellhounds also born of the Fires of Creation, with the first varcolac who

rose. They share a kindred spirit and are controlled by the varcolac.

- **Jinn (Singular form is jinni)** – 90th seal. Beautiful creatures. They'll grant a wish, make it more of a nightmare, and tear out their victim's heart as payment. Feed on the life force of others as well as on wraiths.
- **Lanavour demon** <Lan-oh-vor> -The 3rd seal. Can speak telepathically and know people's inner most secrets and fears.
- **Leporcháin** <Lepor-cane> - Leprechaun looking creatures. Half on Kobal's side, the other half are on Lucifer's. Only ten in existence.
- **Macharah** – 103rd seal. Creature with 30 plus tentacles at the bottom.
- **Manticore** – 46th seal. Body of a red lion, human/demon head.
- **The Oracle** – The oracle is a lake of fire, deep in the bowels of Hell, where earth could be looked on. Few made the journey as the lake was also the central focus of all the heat in Hell.
- **Ouroboros** - 82nd seal. Massive, green serpent.
- **Palitons** <Pal-ah-tons> - Kobal's followers.
- **Púca** <Poo-ka> - 80th seal. Shape changers which can take on animal or human form. Could also be the source of vampires as they drain their victim's blood.
- **Skellcins** <Skcl-ccns> - Guaidians of the Gates.
- **Spiny Clackos** – demon who is known to have spikes in every part of their anatomy.
- **Tree Nymphs** – Live in the Forest of Prurience. Men and women. Striking and very free sexually. Smaller than wood nymphs and live in the trees.

- **The Wall** - Blocks off all of Washington, Oregon, California, Arizona, New Mexico, Texas, Louisiana, Mississippi, Alabama, Georgia, Florida, South Carolina, North Carolina, Virginia, Maryland, Delaware, New Jersey, Connecticut, Rhode Island, Massachusetts, Vermont, New Hampshire, and Maine. Blocks parts of Nevada, New York, Pennsylvania, and Arkansas. Similar wall blocks off parts of Europe.
- **Wraith -** A twisted and malevolent spirit that the demons feed from. On earth they only come out at night.
- **Varcolac demon** <Var-ko-lack>- Born from the fires of Hell. Only one can exist at a time. When that one dies another rises from the Fires of Creation. Fastest and most brutal of all the demons. They are the only kind that can create and open natural gateways within Hell as well as close them. They control the hellhounds.

Demon Words:

- **Mah lahala** 'Mɑ: <la-hall-a> - My Love.
- **Mohara** <Mo-har-ah> – Mother
- **Paupi** <Pow-pea> - Father.
- **Unshi** <Un-she> – Uncle

CHAPTER ONE

Hawk

I rubbed at my eyes as we crested a hill and the wall came into view. The fatigue clinging to me like a second skin vanished as the prospect of drinks, a shower, and friends caused excitement to race through me.

This journey back to the wall had been especially exhausting. The last truck we possessed gave a loud groan and belched smoke before dying on the side of the road three days ago. We'd continued on foot, but most of the humans looked about to collapse as they walked with their heads bent and their shoulders slouched forward. Some of the demons didn't look any better.

We'd left half our troops in the Wilds with Magnus, Amalia, and Shax to command our growing number of soldiers there. It had been over a year since River succeeded in closing the gateway, and during that time, we'd cleared most of the Wilds and were reclaiming the land from the demons seeking to destroy us.

If we could only find and destroy the rest of the horsemen and angels, we might succeed in ending this war, but they'd been scarce since Amalia and Magnus battled them in the Abyss. That was in February, and it was now October.

We'd run into them, even fought with them a couple of times, but the few times we encountered them, they retreated. For the most part, it was as if they'd ceased to exist. There were sightings of them, but there hadn't been any solid leads in a month.

Able to travel on the air, Death could be anywhere, and the same with the angels, but the other horsemen had to be somewhere in the Wilds. They wouldn't get past the wall without us knowing. However, where they were was a complete mystery, and one I could take a break from trying to solve for the next few days.

The dust rising in the distance indicated the approach of vehicles from the wall; someone must have spotted us, and they were on their way. A massive shadow passed overhead and swept over the land. It was so big it blocked the sun before turning sideways and sweeping over the earth.

Shielding my eyes, I tilted my head back as the enormous drakón nearly touched the land with the tip of a wing. The hundred-foot-long, fire-breathing dragon soared over the ground while the blue flames enveloping its body flickered on the air.

Most of its frame was skeletal, but strips of tattered flesh covered some of the bones making up its wings. When its head turned back to look at us, I glimpsed the blue fire in its eye sockets as it released a roar that shook the ground. The beast was letting us know, if we tried anything, it would torch us where we stood.

I didn't know if this drakón was Flint or Blaze as only River could tell them apart. I also didn't know how long it stalked us before deciding to reveal itself. For such large creatures, they were stealthy.

I was glad it was a friend; otherwise, we would be nothing but ashes as they were extremely loyal to River. After Lucifer forced River to break the seals in Hell, the Drakóns—which were locked behind the hundred and first seal—had followed and

KISS OF DEATH 3

protected her. They were her guards, and they took the job seriously.

The cloud of dust drew closer until a white pickup rose over the hill; an assortment of other vehicles from the wall followed it. When another shadow passed overhead, I looked up as the angel, Raphael, soared overhead.

I turned my attention back to the vehicles and almost let out a shout of joy at the prospect of finishing the rest of our journey in one of those vehicles. I started walking faster and wasn't surprised when Corson and Wren kept pace with me. We'd had enough of this endless walking, and I was tired of feeling like Frodo with the ring.

The pickup pulled to a stop fifteen feet away. Two demons climbed out of the cab of the vehicle while more exited the bed. It was impossible to miss Kobal, the six-foot-nine King of Hell, when he stepped out of the back of the truck.

Bare-chested, except for a piece of cloth slung over one shoulder and around his chest, the black markings on his arms, upper chest, and upper back were mostly visible. Flames, with intricate symbols, marked Kobal's right arm. Since becoming a demon over a year ago, I'd learned some of the demon's symbols, but I didn't recognize many of Kobal's.

On Kobal's left arm were two hellhounds surrounded by flames. I'd seen those two hellhounds leap out of his body and tear into anything threatening him or River. The King of Hell was a formidable figure with many secrets.

He possessed so much power that my skin prickled as he strode toward us with a broad smile and what I swore was a twinkle in his black eyes. The blackness of Kobal's eyes took up the entire eyeball, but when he was infuriated, his eyes became more human in appearance and turned an amber color like a wolf's.

I was at the wall for nine years before River arrived, and I'd never seen Kobal smile before then. Of course, he often moved around and was rarely at our camp, but the few times I saw him, there'd been nothing inviting about the imposing demon.

He held his hand out to Corson, and the two nearly embraced as they clapped each other on the back. Bale hugged him next, but it wasn't until Lix approached and a tiny hand rose over the cloth on Kobal's chest that I realized the King of Hell was carrying a baby.

"River had the baby," Caim murmured.

I detected a hint of pride in the fallen angel's voice, and his raven eyes, with their rainbow-hued flecks, were filled with awe. He glanced at me before straightening his shoulders and ruffling his ebony wings.

Like his eyes, rainbows of color danced through his wings, but midnight blue was the most prevalent color amongst the feathers. The silver spikes sticking out of the top of his wings were nearly a foot long, as were the ones on the bottom.

"I am an uncle again," he stated proudly.

I didn't know how River would feel about him declaring himself as such. She'd always hated that they referred to her as their niece and Lucifer had considered her his daughter. However, at one time, the angels all considered themselves brothers and sisters. Descended from Lucifer and Michael, the other angels saw River as their niece.

"Congrats," I muttered to Caim as Kobal and Lix shook hands.

When the small fist continued to fly, Bale took the tiny hand and smiled when it gripped her finger. I stepped closer to get a better look as she asked, "What's his name?"

"Braxas," Kobal said.

"He can draw on life," Bale commented.

"Just like his mom," Kobal said. "He's extremely strong."

I'd only seen that look on Kobal's face when it came to River, but as he gazed at his son, the love and pride he felt for his child were as evident as the markings on his arms. A twinge of longing tugged at my heart. Before becoming a demon, I'd planned to eventually settle down. My family was gone, and I could never replace them, but I wanted to experience that love again.

And now... well, now I couldn't kiss a woman without enslaving her and ruining her life, and I couldn't have any children unless I found my Chosen. That was a possibility, but with the angels and horsemen still out there, starting a family wasn't an option. There was a war to fight, and after...

Who knew what after held? I was trying to stay focused on one day and one battle at a time. I could think about a Chosen and a family when the fight was over.

I stepped closer to Bale so I could see the baby and smiled when he gazed up at me with the same amethyst eyes as his mother. The child didn't have his mother's black hair, but he did have his father's dark brown coloring.

Because the fires of Hell forged Kobal, he couldn't pass his abilities on to his son, but I sensed a lot of power in the boy as he jerked on Bale's finger. But then, his mother was a mighty force.

"Come on," Kobal said. "You must all be exhausted, and River is looking forward to seeing you. We've got showers, mjéod, and beds for you."

"Those all sound fantastic," Corson said as he wrapped his arm around Wren's waist.

With the sun filtering over him, Corson's black hair shone with blue, and his orange eyes sparkled with amusement. The silver bird he wore in the tip of his pointed right ear spun in the faint breeze. Wren gave him the bird earring when she became his Chosen.

Wren wore the matching earring in her left lobe. The bottom of the earring brushed the braid of pale blonde hair she'd draped over her shoulder. When Wren became Corson's Chosen, he turned her into an adhene demon to save her life and grant her immortality. Like Corson, she now possessed talons that burst from the backs of her hands, but hers were shorter than Corson's foot-long spikes.

"Let's go," Caim said and transformed into a three-foot-tall raven before taking flight.

His shadow passed over me as I trudged to the back of the pickup and climbed into the bed. I plopped down and draped my arms over the sides while I took in the warmth of the sun. I didn't pay the others any attention as I savored this chance to relax.

It happened so rarely now, and it wouldn't last long.

CHAPTER TWO

Hawk

"Hawk!" River cried as soon as I stepped into the hall.

I grinned as she rushed toward me with a radiant smile on her pretty face. Her amethyst eyes sparkled when she threw her arms around me, and her black hair tickled my cheek as she hugged me.

"How's it going, queen bee?" I asked.

She chuckled as she stepped away and brushed a strand of loose hair away from her face. "The little prince rules the roost now. Did you meet Braxas?"

"I did. Congratulations."

She radiated happiness as she bounced on her toes. I'd seen her use her powers to destroy things, but she looked as threatening as a kitten now.

"Thank you. He's amazing," she breathed. "But enough of that." She looped her arm through mine as she led me through the large hall. "How have you been?"

"I can't complain."

"Any sign of the horsemen and fallen angels?"

"There have been sightings, but we haven't fought them since they broke Vargas's leg."

Almost three months ago, we encountered Envy and Famine; they fled the battle, but not before Envy broke Vargas's leg. After the fight, we brought Vargas back to the wall to heal, and Erin decided to stay with him.

That was the last time we returned to the wall. Now we were supposed to pick up Erin and Vargas along with supplies for the humans, more vehicles, and fresh troops to join us in the search for our elusive enemies.

"I think they may have left the country," I admitted.

"How?" River asked.

"I don't know, but it's like they've vanished."

River's fingers tapped my arm. "They're up to something, and I don't like it."

"Neither do I."

When River grew quiet as she led me through the hall, I turned my attention to the building erected for the king and queen. The demon symbols covering every inch of the walls were stained with River and Kobal's blood and thrummed with power.

At the far end of the hall, the king and queen's thrones sat on a raised dais. River's brothers, Gage and Bailey, sat on the steps of the dais watching the demons and humans in the room. When they spotted me, they smiled and waved; I returned the greeting.

"How are Erin and Vargas?" I asked.

River grinned at me. "They're great. Vargas's leg is healed."

"Good."

I'd missed them since they left the Wilds. Like myself, Erin and Vargas volunteered to leave their families and towns behind to journey to the wall when they were only sixteen. My human status may have changed while theirs remained the same, but we'd trained together, battled Hell creatures, and had each other's backs through some horrible shit. They were more like family than friends.

The crowd in the hall parted to reveal Erin and Vargas strolling toward us.

"Hawk!" Erin cried as she ran at me and threw her arms around me. "You're safe."

"Of course," I replied as I hugged her before setting her on her feet.

Her black hair, usually cut below her ears, hung to her shoulders. Her almond-shaped, dark blue eyes shone when she smiled at me, but there was something sad in her gaze.

"Is everything okay?" I demanded.

"It's great."

She said the words, but uneasiness lingered about her. Before I could question her further, Vargas approached and held out his hand. When I accepted his hand, he pulled me close, and we slapped each other's backs before stepping back.

Vargas looked like he'd put on a few pounds, probably due to inactivity and not being able to train. His black hair, cropped close to his head, emphasized the broad cheeks and olive complexion of his Peruvian heritage. His eyes were so dark a brown they were nearly black, but they held flecks of a paler, golden brown in them.

"How's the leg?" I asked him.

"Much better," he said and emphasized this by stomping his foot. "How have you been?"

"I'd like to say busy hunting the horsemen, but things have been quiet."

"That can't be good."

"No, it can't," I agreed. "But we have wiped out a fair amount of lower-levels demons and escapees from the seals since I last saw you. We've also cleared a large portion of the Wilds, and we're holding that ground. By this time next year, we might have everything secured."

"That would be amazing."

"What about the horsemen and angels?" Erin asked.

"We don't know where they've gone."

She bit her bottom lip as she exchanged an uneasy glance with Vargas and River. Vargas took her hand in both of his and gave it a reassuring squeeze. Their entwined hands didn't surprise me. I'd noticed them growing closer for a while now, and Erin had insisted on staying at the wall while Vargas recovered. What did surprise me was the pang of longing that accompanied the comforting gesture.

I'd never felt anything remotely romantic toward Erin. She was pretty, but we'd never been anything more than friends. However, this comforting gesture made me long for a family again.

I tore my eyes away from their hands and focused on the hall as Daisy, one of the ghosts who'd come to the wall after the gateway closed, floated up to hover near River's shoulder. Daisy waved at me, and I waved back.

The first time I encountered ghosts, they irritated the shit out of me. Due to things they'd done while alive, or because they feared moving on to the afterlife, the ghosts were trapped in Purgatory on Earth. They couldn't move on to Heaven until they served their time here.

They were pretty selfish beings, who were afraid of the dark, but Daisy was far less selfish than most of her ghostly counterparts. The ghosts were offered a home at the wall in exchange for their help in keeping things lit around here. They couldn't do much, but they could produce small amounts of light, which became stronger when enough of them got together.

When Kobal arrived at River's side, she beamed at him as he bent to kiss her head. Grasping a piece of the wrap Kobal wore, she pulled it back to reveal the peaceful, sleeping face of her son.

I focused on the wall as they shared a private moment. I tried not to think about the fact that if I did find my Chosen, I would never be able to kiss her, and I'd feed on her every time we had sex.

KISS OF DEATH   11

I could only imagine how thrilled so many women would be to find themselves bound to someone like me.

The idea of feeding on anyone made my stomach twist, but at the same time, hunger churned through my veins. I dragged a hand through my hair and tugged at the ends of it as I tried to regain control of myself. I needed to feed, but even with the pleasure it gave me as it eased my hunger, I *loathed* doing it.

But I couldn't stay here.

"If you don't mind, I'm going to take a shower," I said abruptly.

"Oh, of course," Erin said. "I put some clean clothes in your room and washed the blankets. We'll walk home with you."

"No, stay here," I said. "Enjoy the party. I'll be back."

Before she could reply, I hugged her again and turned on my heel, leaving the hall.

CHAPTER THREE

Hawk

I examined the buildings and homes in the town as I walked through it. Everything was much as I remembered it, if only a little more weather-worn, but then, so was I. Stopping outside of the house Vargas and I used to share with a couple of other male soldiers, I studied the chipping white paint and sagging shutters.

I tried to recall what it had been like to live here as a human; had I worried about death? I'd thought about women a lot and brought more than my fair share back here, but things were simpler then. That was before I was a demon, before I accidentally ruined Sarah's life by kissing her, before I entered Hell, but mostly, it was before I lost my family.

When I volunteered to come to the wall, I knew there was a chance I'd never see my mother and sisters again, but there had always been the hope of *one day*. One day it would end, one day the wall would come down, and one day I could go home to them, but none of that hope remained.

I recalled the last time I'd seen them. It had never happened before, but Kobal ordered the families of those who would be traveling to the gateway with him and River to come to the wall. None of us had expected to discover our families waiting for us when we went to the school, but there they were in the cafeteria.

My mom refused to let go of me as she sobbed into my shirt. My sisters all talked eagerly over one another as they peppered me with questions while gushing about the details of their lives. I couldn't tell them what was really going on here, but it hadn't mattered. All that mattered was being with them again.

I'd been nervous about the journey, but seeing them solidified why I was making the mission. There wasn't anything I wouldn't do to keep them safe, and I'd failed. We succeeded in closing the gateway, but not before Lucifer escaped and killed them and so many others.

Now, they were gone, and I remained. And I would do everything I could to see this through to the end. They'd deserved better, and so did so many others. I didn't mind continuing the fight; it was all I had left besides my friends, but sometimes, even with all of those friends, it was so lonely.

I bent my head and trudged up the steps of the house. I didn't know what happened to the other soldiers we'd lived with; they'd either moved on to another section of wall or died, but only Erin and Vargas resided here now.

There was enough daylight left that I didn't bother with the lights as I climbed the stairs and strode down the hall to my room. I flicked on the switch to discover my room as I'd left it, but it didn't smell stale from being closed; instead, the fresh scent of laundry from the line permeated the air.

I smiled when I spotted the framed picture on my nightstand. It hadn't been there before, but as I approached it, I saw it was a polaroid of me, River, Erin, and Vargas taken the last time I returned to the wall. I didn't know where River found the ancient camera or the film, but she'd given it to Kobal, told him to hit the button, and joined us for the photo.

Though Vargas was lying in bed due to his broken leg and we had to make room for River's belly, we were all smiling as we huddled together. I thought Kobal was going to crush the camera as he fumbled with it, but he snapped the picture without destroying it.

I lifted the photo and smiled at the group of us. It had only been a few months ago, yet I felt so much older, or maybe just more exhausted. Setting the picture down, I removed my weapons and set them on the bed before turning away to gather clothes from my dresser.

I showered before dressing in a pair of brown pants and a black sweater. I sat on the bed, shoved my feet into my boots, and tied them before rising to put my gun holster back on. Lifting my rifle, I slid it onto my back, then placed my two handguns in the holsters.

The sun had set while I was in the shower, so I turned the lights on as I went downstairs where I spotted the homey touches Erin and Vargas had added to the house. Flowers sat in a vase on the dining room table, and there was another polaroid of the two of them standing by the wall on the table near the door. I suspected Erin knitted the colorful blanket draped over the back of the couch.

I recalled the sadness in her eyes in the hall and had the sinking suspicion they wouldn't be returning to the Wilds. They'd made a home here, and they had each other, so I didn't blame them if they decided to remain here. They could have sent word to us, but we would have returned anyway to gather supplies.

I glanced around the house again and realized it was the home of a family. That awful loneliness tugged at my heart as I smiled while resting my hand on the blanket. There was so little happiness in this world, and two of my best friends had managed to carve a piece of it out for themselves.

I made my way out the front door and jogged down the steps. Pausing at the bottom, I inspected the sleepy town before turning my attention to the immense wall looming over it. The blinking red lights on the wall cast an eerie glow over its concrete surface, the soldiers patrolling it, and the town.

In the Wilds, the screams or call of some animal or demon often drifted over the land, but here, the only noise was the low hum of the electricity powering the wall and the distant flow of music coming from the hill where the demons resided. I turned my attention to the hill and the tents there.

I'd never gone to the hill as a human. I knew others who had, but I was content with the women in town. As a demon, I'd been there once on one of my trips back to the wall. I usually avoided it, not because it was mostly demons there, but because it was my punishment.

I ruined Sarah's life when I kissed her; I hadn't known I was a canagh demon at the time or that my kiss could ensnare another, but I'd ruined her life. If Sarah hadn't died, she'd still be a mindless creature, helplessly following me around. Because of that, I deserved to suffer. I also worried it might accidentally happen again.

I shuddered at the possibility as the material of the tents rippled in the gentle breeze. The flames of the bonfire located in the middle of the tents rose higher into the air. Sparks danced like fireflies as they floated on the currents before going out. If the wind picked up, they would put out the fire, but for now, the demons would be gathered around it as they played music, danced, and screwed.

My body tensed at the image, and my earlier hunger blazed back to life. I should return to the hall, but I couldn't get my feet to move in that direction. The tents and fire called to me like a siren to a sailor, and I couldn't resist the call.

I hated myself more with every step I took up the hill. I should be with my friends. I should be strong enough to resist my instincts, but my excitement grew as I walked.

I scented the enticing, musky aroma of sex on the air. My

nostrils flared, and I gritted my teeth against my arousal; I could resist this. But why had I come here if it hadn't been to satisfy the canagh demon clawing ravenously at my chest?

I hadn't wanted to acknowledge it when I started up the hill, but I'd known I couldn't resist anymore. I was going to join those at the bonfire and lose myself to the pleasure they'd provide me.

I'd gone far longer than I should have without sex, and my body craved the release it would provide. However, I refused to be a slave to my impulses, and after what I'd done to Sarah, I deserved to suffer by depriving myself of the sex canaghs required to survive.

Since Sarah, I went for weeks without sex and only caved when I feared I might accidentally hurt someone. I'd also stuck mostly with nymphs who had experience handling canagh demons.

Arriving at the top of the hill, I passed Kobal's old tent and continued toward the fire. With every step, I willed myself to turn away, but I stalked onward. The sounds of ecstasy drove me onward as my heart raced and my mouth watered.

It had been almost three weeks since I was last with a woman; it was such a short stretch to be proud of, but it was my longest one since becoming a demon. It may have been *too* long. I felt out of control in a way I never had before. I had to restrain myself from running toward the fire, but I could still control myself at least *that* much.

Most canagh demons had sex every day and often multiple times a day, but I hated that I'd become such a slave to a desire I controlled when I was a mortal. I despised that every time I slept with someone, I put them at risk and left them depleted. Even the nymphs with their canagh experience always stumbled from my bed after I absorbed some of their energy. It probably wouldn't be as bad if I fed more often, but I couldn't stomach the idea of feeding off someone daily.

I emerged from between the tents to stand at the edge of the circle surrounding the bonfire. In the center of the clearing, the fire crackled, and the scent of burning wood filled the air, but it was the demons and humans gathered there who held my attention.

Some of them wore skimpy clothes that left nothing to the imagination, but most were naked. A small, redheaded demon sat on a tree stump as she played the lute; the instrument's haunting strains were out of place with the rough rutting of the three demons only five feet away from her.

More demons and humans were scattered around the edges of the clearing, while others were in the shadows of the trees. Two women were on their knees between the legs of a demon with two penises.

I could walk into the clearing and approach any of the female demons, and they would probably let me take them. Demons viewed sex as casual and fun until they bonded with their Chosen. They were with countless others before then, but once they met their Chosen, there was never another for them.

All demons sought was the pleasure sex offered; it was all I wanted too, but whereas I couldn't get my feet to stop before, they wouldn't move now that I was here. I wished I could be one of those demons who didn't require sex to survive. I hated the help-lessness that came with this compulsion the most; I lost control of my body when I became a demon.

The self-hatred coiling inside me kept me frozen. I had no doubt my feet would eventually move, or one of the women would approach me, and I would give in to my weakness.

It was going to be an endless immortality if this cycle of self-hatred and denial continued.

Sighing, I ran a hand through my hair and tugged at the ends of it as my eyes fell on a woman standing across the clearing. She had her arms crossed over her chest and a red cup in hand. An amused smile curved the corners of her lush, pink lips when her brown doe eyes met mine.

The fire danced in her irises as she surveyed me. The movement caused her chocolate hair to sway around her shoulders. The slight up tilt at the end of her slender nose made her more alluring.

She took another sip of her drink and licked the wetness from her lips. I hadn't considered it possible, but I hardened further as lust hammered through my veins. I forgot all about trying to deny myself as I imagined grasping her hair as I pulled her close for a kiss....

No!

Not a kiss. That could never happen, but I could hold her hair and slide its silky depths through my fingers while I peeled away her clothes to reveal what lay beneath. Unlike everyone else here, she wore a pair of brown pants and a navy blue sweater that fit snugly across her breasts.

Somehow, the clothes were sexier than if she'd been wearing nothing. But then, once she was naked, I probably wouldn't agree with that anymore.

Extremely beautiful, she looked entirely human, but the raw sexuality oozing from her screamed demon. If she was a human, I couldn't have her. Demons could handle what I did to them if I kept it in control, but I would never risk being with a human again after Sarah.

The idea of not possessing this woman caused my nails to bite into my palms until they bled. I'd hate to turn her away, but I would if it was necessary.

When she set her cup down on a table by a tent, I braced myself as she sauntered across the clearing toward me.

CHAPTER FOUR

Aisling

The man caught my attention the second he emerged from between two tents to stand at the edge of the circle. The other demons didn't often smile when they came to the bonfire, but they were relaxed and eager to plunge into the hedonism openly offered here. This man looked tormented and lost as he stared at the others with a clenched jaw and sweat beading his brow.

He looked like he was waging war with himself, but what kind of battle could he possibly be fighting? This was a place for fun. Even the humans who came here did so because they were eager to experience the ecstasy the demons so readily offered.

I didn't know what to make of this guy as I sipped my mjéod and studied him taking in the activities with a look of disgust and yearning. Usually, such a tortured soul would have me walking away. I didn't have time for someone who didn't know what they wanted, and if they sought anything more than sex, I had less time for them.

I found myself strangely captivated by this guy as a range of emotions played over his face. Maybe it was because he was gorgeous with his short brown hair and chiseled jaw. About six inches taller than my five-eight height, he was broad through the shoulders and chest. He wore clothes, but the way they hugged him emphasized the layers of muscle beneath.

When he turned his head and his eyes met mine, I sucked in a breath at the vibrant, indigo color of them. His eyebrows rose as he surveyed me. I shifted when I found myself growing aroused by the intensity of his gaze.

I sipped my mjéod as I tried to decide what to do. Tormented wasn't my thing when it came to men, but this one had my curiosity running wild. Curiosity killed the cat, but was she purring when she died? Because I had a feeling this guy could make me purr, and though a part of me was screaming *run*, the biggest part of me was ready to let him pet me all over.

I'd never seen him before, which meant either a new group of soldiers had arrived at the wall, or he was part of the group from the Wilds who was supposed to return today.

He had a soul; I could see it. It was a beautiful, shimmering white light with golden edges that radiated warmth, but there was also a streak of red going down the back of it. I didn't take the red as anger; I'd seen the souls of angry people, and that anger was a festering *thing* inside them.

This red was more a steel rod of strength running down his spine. Without speaking to him, I guessed he was kind and strong and possessed the spirit of a warrior. The soul meant he had to be human, but power oozed from him in a way it *never* did from humans.

I forgot all about purring as I tried to figure this man out. Who and what was he? Was he like me—a human who later learned they were part demon—or was he something more? One thing was certain, I'd never get the answers to my questions by standing here and staring at him.

Deciding that tormented could be my thing for a night, I took another sip of mjéod, set my cup down, and strolled across the clearing toward him. His shoulders went back as his gaze dipped to my breasts. I couldn't stop myself from smiling; he may look like he preferred to be somewhere else, but I had him.

I didn't stop when I reached him; instead, I trailed my fingers across his chest and back. Slowly circling him, I admired the breadth of his shoulders and the way his pants hugged his firm ass. I couldn't wait to sink my nails into that ass as he thrust within me.

"Do you like what you see?" I asked as I stopped before him.

"Yes."

When he said the word, I spotted two upper fangs. *Not human, but what is he? And how can he have a soul and fangs?*

"Do you like what you see?" he inquired.

"You've made me curious."

"Curious about what?"

I smiled at him as I rose on my toes to grip his shoulders and turned my head so my lips brushed his ear while I whispered, "As to what your mouth is going to feel like between my thighs, because you *are* going to tongue fuck me until I say you can stop."

He growled as I smiled at him. When my hand brushed his, heat flared through me, and I nearly yanked my hand away to gawk at it. I learned I was part demon when I stopped aging two years ago and developed the ability to produce fire. Since then, I'd screwed numerous male demons, and a couple of humans before then, but I'd *never* experienced anything like that.

It scared me, but at the same time, I found myself yearning for more of him as my toes curled in my boots. I was part demon, but I wasn't into the exhibition many of them enjoyed. However, that didn't matter as I was close to pulling his pants off and taking him right here.

The obvious bulge in the front of his pants wasn't helping to keep me focused on finding somewhere private to enjoy him. Suddenly, the hundred feet to my tent seemed like miles.

"Come," I murmured, and taking his hand, I led him into the maze of tents.

"Are you human?" he asked.

I glanced at him over my shoulder. "Do I look human?"

"Yes."

"Do I *act* human?"

He hesitated before responding. "I'm not sure."

I laughed and squeezed his hand. "Do you want me to be human?"

"No," he grated in a voice that did funny things to my insides.

"Then I'm a demon."

I wasn't expecting him to come to an abrupt halt before pulling me around. My eyebrows shot up, but my protest died when I saw his hooded eyes and the serious expression on his face. A vein in his forehead stood out as he stepped closer to me. I held my ground against him, but that might have been worse as his chest pressed into mine and fire spread through my veins.

What was it about this guy that kept me here? If any other man acted like this, I'd walk back to the fire and find another or go home alone, but I wanted to ease his tension. I used my free hand to stroke his arm; I smiled when he shivered and his eyes closed halfway.

"It's important I know what you are," he said.

"And why is that?"

"Because I'm afraid I'll hurt a human."

Those words were like a cold bucket of ice over my head. "Are you violent then? Because I'm up for many things, but I don't mix violence and sex. I already taught one demon that lesson when he decided slapping me was the way he liked to get off. From what I heard, it took him a week to regrow the balls I tore off him before burning them."

His eyes widened before narrowing. I fully expected him to

walk away after my admission, and good riddance, because I was not about to deal with that again.

"Is that demon in this camp?" he demanded.

The anger in his voice surprised me, but it must have surprised him too as he blinked before shaking his head. We didn't know each other, but I suspected if I said yes, he would hunt the bastard down and make my castration of him look like a party.

"No. I think he's still in Virginia, but I'm not sure," I said. "Either way, I'm not into violence."

He clasped my hand and turned it over. He ran his fingers over mine in a caress that was so out of place with demons, it took my breath away. I'd enjoyed a lot of sex over the years, but I couldn't recall the last time someone touched me with such tenderness. It made my knees wobble as my desire for him grew.

Damn it, what was this man doing to me, and why was he so different than all the other demons?

"What are *you*?" I inquired.

He gave me a sad smile. "I'm a demon."

"Hmm," I said, but I didn't entirely buy it.

Either way, I didn't care. Sex with him might not be the best decision I'd ever make, but I'd made it.

"I'm a demon," I said and tugged his hand as I started toward my tent again.

CHAPTER FIVE

Hawk

I admired the sway of her hips as she walked, but I had to utter the words that might chase her away. "What's your name?"

She shot me a playful smile over her shoulder as she released my hand and removed her shirt. My breath sucked in when she revealed her pale skin and black bra. Her full breasts nearly spilled out of the bra as she reached up to drape the shirt around my shoulders. When she gave both ends a little tug, I caught the scent of something sweet and realized it came from her.

As much as I admired her lithe body and ample breasts, I wanted to cover her with the shirt so no one else saw her. I glanced around, but no one was nearby.

"Does my name matter?" Her voice held the faint hint of a Southern accent.

With most of the women I'd been with, no, it didn't matter. Tonight... "Yes."

"It's Aisling, but you can call me whatever you want." She stopped outside a small tent and pulled back the flap to reveal the shadowed interior. "Here we are."

I ached to go in there, but she had to know the truth before this went any further. The knowledge of what I was had scared away some demons before, and I didn't know what I'd do if she turned me away, but I'd vowed not to keep what I was from any of my partners.

The idea of returning to that fire and finding another made my stomach twist with nausea, but if I didn't feed soon, then I would become a risk. I wanted her more than I could ever recall wanting another, but I forced the words from my throat.

"I'm a canagh demon, Aisling."

She frowned as she released the flap. I glanced at the tent behind her; I assumed it was hers if she'd led me here, but she seemed confused. Didn't all demons know about the canaghs?

I supposed it could be possible not to know about certain types of demons as there were hundreds of different species, but the canaghs were numerous and deadly. Every other demon I encountered had known what I was when I said it, so why didn't she?

"Is that your tent?" I asked.

"Yes."

"Do you know what a canagh demon is?"

"No. What is it?" she asked.

"Have you heard of an incubus before?"

"Yes."

"Canagh demons are where the legend of the incubus and succubus came from in the human world. Just like them, I feed on sexual energy."

"And you're going to feed on me if we have sex?"

"Yes."

Her gaze ran over me as she placed the tip of her finger on her lip and nibbled it. "Will it hurt?"

"It might weaken you, but I won't take enough to cause any permanent damage."

"And can you cause permanent damage?"

I refused to lie to her. "Yes, but I don't do that."

She removed her finger from her mouth to run it down the front of my shirt. "And how do I know I can trust you?"

"If I meant you harm, would I tell you this? I could have kept it from you."

"Good point," she said as she tapped her fingers against my chest. "So why didn't you keep it from me?"

"Because I refuse to feed on someone without their knowledge."

"How noble of you," she murmured as she traced the line running down the center of my stomach. "Will I like it when you feed on me?"

"You probably won't know until it's over, but I promise you'll experience a lot of pleasure."

"I'm going to hold you to that promise."

She turned away, pulled back the flap, and swept inside the tent. I stood for a second before following her inside. The rustle of the flap falling back in place was the only sound in the small tent. I searched for her in the darkness, but it was as if she'd melted into the shadows.

Then a flame emerged as she lit a lamp and turned it up until it revealed a cot against the wall and a small table in the center of the room that had one chair pushed into it. A trunk sat at the end of the bed; the open lid revealed the neatly folded clothes inside. Another trunk was against the far wall, and though the top was closed, I suspected it housed weapons.

The golden glow of the lamp she set on a small nightstand near the cot danced over her skin as she sashayed toward me. She stopped in front of me and ran her hands down my stomach before resting them on my waist.

"I don't think you need this," she said.

Her deft fingers undid my holster before pulling it away. She lowered my guns to the ground before tugging her shirt off my shoulders and tossing it aside. Unable to stop myself, I grasped a piece of her hair and let the silken strands slide through my fingers. She removed the rifle from my back and set it against the wall of the tent.

Tugging her hair free of my hand, she turned away and undid her bra. My teeth ground together as I admired the sway of her breasts while she walked. She undid her pants and kicked off her boots. Stopping before the table, she turned to face me as she slid her pants down her round hips and long, shapely legs. She pulled them off one leg before using her toes to kick them off the remaining leg.

The flame danced over her skin as she sat on the table and slid back a little. Spreading her legs, she gave me a good view of the brown curls between them. Hooking her finger, she beckoned me toward her. I obeyed her command as the enticing scent of her arousal fanned my hunger into an inferno.

When I was only a few feet away from her, she pointed down and smiled at me. "You're going to feed on me in more than one way," she said. "It will be easier if you're on your knees."

I quirked an eyebrow as she gave me a sultry smile. Over the past year, I'd become accustomed to demons knowing what they wanted and asking for it, yet there was a challenge in her sparkling eyes. I was more than ready to answer that challenge.

I didn't know how many others she'd been with, but she would never forget me or this night. Stopping before her, I rested my hands on the table next to her hips. She leaned further back and planted her hands behind her; the movement caused her hardened nipples to rise toward me.

"So that you know—" I skimmed my knuckles down the valley between her breasts before bending to tease one of her nipples with my tongue. "—I expect to see that beautiful mouth of yours on my cock tonight too."

∽

Aisling

Confusion tickled at the edges of the passion he so easily stoked to life within me. I somehow managed to keep my smile in place. Demons didn't talk about beauty; hell, they didn't talk.

Any other demon would have followed me in here and been banging me already. They wouldn't be staring at me with that ravenous look while they caressed my breasts and teased me until I was on the verge of begging for mercy.

At eighteen, I volunteered to go to the wall, but I hadn't started messing around with demons until I was twenty-three. That was when my body suddenly started going through all kinds of changes; the biggest being the astonishing ability to create small balls of fire in my hand, but I also found myself moving faster, seeing better, hearing better, and feeling more sensitive to things like touch and the world around me.

When they learned what I could do, the demons brought me into their fold, and I discovered I was a descendant of one of the demons who walked the earth over six thousand years ago—a time before the angels fell from Heaven. Before the gateway opened, I might never have experienced any changes, but with the gateway open, I was more one of them than a human now. And I was immortal.

At first, I dug my heels in and refused to believe it, but it didn't take much time for me to accept what they were saying. The sudden balls of fire helped with that, as did all the other changes my body was going through. I didn't eat, go to the bathroom, or sleep as much.

My sex drive amped up, and at first, I was hesitant about being with a demon, but once I decided to try it, I discovered how much I enjoyed it. No matter how casual it was with a demon, they always made sure I found my release too.

I'd slept with a couple of humans before becoming a demon, but they never quite fulfilled me. I realized why when I discovered I wasn't entirely human; I'd needed a beast to make me come.

However, this man wasn't acting like a beast, and I found myself aching for him in a way I'd never ached for another. I clasped the bulge in his pants and squeezed it. "Is this the cock you want me to suck?"

"Keep teasing me, and I'm going to turn you over and fuck you now."

There was the demon I was more familiar with, and though I yearned for his mouth between my thighs, I almost rolled over and spread my legs for him. I'd never wanted a man inside me as badly as this one.

I stroked his erection as his eyes darkened and a vein appeared in the center of his forehead. "You're not getting inside me until you go down on me." And then, because I sensed I might have pushed him too far, I murmured, "Please."

His hands gripped my thighs, and his eyes held mine as he jerked me toward him. I gasped as I found my ass almost off the table, but before I could react, he knelt between my legs. My heart thudding against my ribs was a drumbeat I was sure he heard.

"Don't forget your promise," I whispered.

He smiled at me, and my eyes remained riveted on him as he bent toward me. Helpless to do anything else, I leaned forward to watch his head between my thighs. When his tongue licked my clit, little bolts of electricity raced over my skin.

My hands gripped the edge of the table as he parted me with his fingers and thrust his tongue inside me. My body became boneless, and though I wanted to keep watching him, I fell back against the table.

Grasping my ass, he lifted it in his palms and pulled me closer to him as he feasted eagerly on me. The sensation of his tongue, his hands, and the scrape of his fangs against my flesh had me panting for air as my hips rose and fell with the rhythm he set.

I couldn't breathe. I couldn't think. I needed... needed him to....

He took one hand away from my ass to rub my clit as his tongue delved into me.

That was what I needed!

My back arched off the table as a cry erupted from me. I kept waiting for the waves to crest, but they pounded through me as every nerve ending I possessed came alive. When they finally eased, I collapsed onto the table and gazed at the ceiling as I tried to get my bearings. I *loved* sex; I relished in the sensuality of it, but I'd never experienced anything like that before, and I craved *more*.

I somehow restrained myself from tearing off his clothes when he rose over me. However, the mindless impulse vanished when I saw the ravenous look in his eyes.

"I'm a canagh demon, Aisling." When he first uttered those words, I hadn't cared what he was. I'd been with plenty of demons, and some of them were more than a little frightening, but they all ended up being fun.

The look in his eyes was anything but fun. It was more than torment, more than starved. It was almost pained as he undid his pants and pulled them down his hips. He tugged his shirt off to reveal his rock-hard pecs, chiseled abs, and the V of his hips pointing toward his thick erection.

What are you doing? This man is going to feed *on you!*

The part of me that still identified as a human was prepared to leap off the table and run screaming. The wilder part of me had embraced my demon side, and it clamored with excitement as it told my human side to *shut up*. Unable to stop myself, I caressed my breasts before running my hand down my stomach while I admired his exquisite physique.

Years of training and battle had honed this man into a mouth-watering specimen who was going to be inside *me*. My thighs parted further in anticipation of him stepping between them. This man was mine for the night.

As I'd anticipated, his gaze latched onto my hand and followed it. "Did I fulfill my promise, Aisling?"

The huskiness of his voice caused me to shiver in anticipation. "I'll let you know once I learn how good you fuck."

He caught my hand when I went to dip it between my legs. "I'm the *only* one who will be inside you, *owning* you."

The human part of me contemplated punching him in the face for that comment; *no* one owned me. But I couldn't deny I *wanted* him to own me.

What is wrong with you?

I didn't have an answer, but *none* of my experiences with demons had ever been like this. Raising my arms over my head, I wiggled as I smiled at him. "I'll be the judge of who owns me, but I think it's time to back up all your talk."

His smug smile should have warned me, but I was unprepared for him to grab my hips and flip me over. I cried out as I found myself gazing at the table, but the sound quickly became one of excitement as he parted my thighs with his leg and guided the head of his cock to my entrance.

My muscles clenched around him, and I bit my lip as I stretched to accommodate his size. I took him deeper until he settled inside me. His body pressed against my back as he rested his hands on the table beside my head.

The sensation of his skin against mine as he lay deep inside me was almost too much; I had to fight the inexplicable urge to start weeping. He felt right in a way nothing ever had before. I belonged here, with him.

Once the silly idea worked its way into my head, I couldn't get rid of it, but I had to, or I would get hurt. Demons saw sex as a passing fling, and so had I for the past two years; I couldn't let that change now.

But when he bent his head to nuzzle my ear and his breath warmed my cheek, the urge to cry hit me all over again. *This is just for fun! Get your shit together. You don't even know his name.*

When he lifted his hands and pulled away from me, I waited for him to pound out his release within me, but he remained unmoving. Then, his fingers traced my spine to my ass in a caress that undid me more than the orgasm he'd given me.

CHAPTER SIX

Hawk

As soon as I entered her, I knew something was different. No, I'd known something was different while I was feasting on her and absorbing her energy. But now that I was *inside* her, a change crept over my skin and seeped into my bones. Her skin was like silk beneath my hand as I ran my fingers over her back.

She's mine.

I didn't know where the idea came from, but as soon as it hit me, I knew it was true. This woman was mine. She was created for *me*.

Slowly, I pulled out of her and slid back in. When she groaned, I tenderly enclosed my hand on her throat and lifted her head as I bent over her. I couldn't kiss her lips, but I could taste her flesh. I kissed her ear and then her cheek as I inhaled her scent while feasting on the energy she exuded.

When she turned her head to kiss me, I pulled away. She blinked as if shocked at herself before giving me a playful smile. I would explain why I couldn't kiss her later, but I was too lost in her to form words right then.

I carefully pulled her further off the table so I could run my hands down the front of her. I cupped one of her breasts, and it filled my hand as I gave her nipple a gentle tug. She moaned in response, and when I did it again, she wiggled her hips against me.

As I moved in and out of her, the energy she created drifted into the air on waves. This was a common phenomenon when I had sex with others, but I wasn't used to the strength of the waves or seeing color in them. Usually, they were clear ripples that stirred the currents of air, but Aisling's had a faint orange hue to them as they flowed into my skin, seeped into my cells, and filled me in a way nothing ever had before.

When she arched into my touch and cried out, starbursts of energy filled the air as her climax generated more power. My gaze latched onto her neck as the impulse to sink my fangs into her shoulder rocked me.

I *had* to brand her and make it clear she was mine.

Aisling

My fingers clawed at the table as an even more intense orgasm rocked my body. I collapsed onto the table and tried to catch my breath, but he didn't let me go as he continued his relentless possession of my body.

And it *was* a possession. He'd been right; he owned me in a way no one had before, and my body responded to the demands of his again.

"Don't stop," I panted, though I was sure I'd bitten off more than I could chew with this demon. "Don't stop."

His low growl gave birth to butterflies in my stomach and something else. I poked at my incisors with my tongue as a strange tingling started in them. And then they lengthened at my prodding.

I almost shrieked when two tiny fangs emerged where none were before.

What the...?

I didn't have a chance to figure it out before he pulled out of me and rolled me over. I forgot all about my new fangs when my gaze met his. Those beautiful, indigo eyes were bright against the shadows surrounding him. He'd looked tormented before, but his face had eased, and he almost looked *vibrant* as he clasped my wrists and leaned over me as he pinned them to the table.

He was gorgeous, and he was mine. My tongue touched those fangs again as he entered me once more.

Hawk

The power of her orgasm lingered on the air; I wanted to continue feasting on her and absorbing all she had to offer, but I had to shut down my ability. I would injure her if I kept feeding on the vast energy she emitted, and though it still wavered on the air between us, I didn't take any more.

I admired her exquisite body as she moved against me. Years of training at the wall had left her lean and fit, but she still had curves in all the right places. I couldn't get enough of gazing at her and watching her reactions while I moved within her.

An odd yet familiar pressure filled my shaft when her back bowed. As a human, I'd known the pressure of my semen, but once I became a demon, I stopped experiencing the sensation as my body changed.

Now it was back, and I nearly bellowed with the joy of its return. The male demons didn't know what they were missing by not being able to ejaculate until they found their Chosen, but I *had* known, and no matter how much I still enjoyed sex with my partners, I was always left with an unfulfilled feeling afterward. But not this time.

Lifting her off the table, I gripped her nape as I braced my legs apart. Her nails dug into my back as she rode me, and when her eyes latched onto my neck, I saw the glint of fangs that hadn't been there before.

Mine. She's mine.

The thought kept racing through my mind as she lowered her head to my shoulder. Her lips brushed my skin before her fangs pierced my flesh, and she released a muffled cry as she orgasmed again. Helpless to do anything but follow her over the edge, I sank my fangs into her shoulder.

My cock pulsed as I came in a rush and almost collapsed onto her. Holding her against me, it took all I had to stumble to the cot and collapse onto it with her. We lay in a tangled heap on the small bed. My mind raced with the implications of what just transpired while her breathing gradually returned to normal.

"You kept your promise," she murmured.

I chuckled as she nestled against me, and after a few moments I brushed back her hair to discover she'd fallen asleep. I ran my fingers across her cheek as I studied her, making sure she was all right. Because she filled me more than anyone I'd ever been with, I'd taken less energy from her than I usually took from others, but it might have been too much.

Her skin color remained good, and her breathing steady. When I cupped her face, she smiled in her sleep. I hugged her as I closed my eyes and relished the feel of my Chosen in my arms.

CHAPTER SEVEN

Aisling

Exhaustion clung to me as I cracked my eyes open to discover an arm draped around my waist. I tried to recall who that arm belonged to and why they were still in my tent. It was only good demon manners to take your ass home when you finished with someone. And if the soreness between my legs, my tiredness, and the limpness of my bones was any indication, someone had finished with me in the most amazing ways.

And then I recalled the indigo-eyed, dark-haired stranger who did the most wonderful things to my body. It may have been good manners to leave when someone fell asleep, but I was ready for more of what he'd given me last night. If it was still early enough, we could get in another round or two before I had to be on the training field.

He could leave after I finished with him; I ignored the twinge to my heart such a prospect created. I didn't want him to go.

Don't be a human about this!

I gritted my teeth as I steeled my resolve. We would move on, as demons always did and I'd enjoyed it over these past two years.

Arriving at this camp had given me a new assortment of demons to choose from, and there were some I'd still like to try. I'd take my mind off this strange demon with one of them.

I ignored the nausea twisting in my stomach at the idea of another demon. And then, when I thought of *him* with another demon, my teeth ground together and my fingers dug into my palms.

It was time to take a break from sex. When I first learned what I was, I hadn't seen a reason not to indulge myself. I was more demon than human now, and I couldn't get pregnant or carry a disease. I may be immortal, but that didn't mean I couldn't die, and life at the wall was dangerous, so I grasped what little joy there was here and cleaved to it.

Plus, I wasn't ready to settle down, and I loved sex, so why not indulge in it?

I had my why not reason lying against my side. His warm breath tickling my nape made me doubt things that were so simple yesterday. And what kind of a demon was he? What demon had a soul, fangs, *and* could ejaculate?

I'd never heard of anything like that before, but I'd felt the pulse of his shaft when his sperm filled me. *Maybe he's like me and was a human who found out they were part demon.*

My brief hope over this died away. When I became immortal, my reproductive system transformed into a demon's, and I stopped getting my period. But just because that happened to me didn't mean it would happen to every human who learned of their true heritage by becoming immortal.

A loud siren began to wail; it echoed over the land and reverberated around the tent. *What is that?*

I was so caught up in my thoughts that I couldn't register what was happening. Footsteps thundered past my tent and shouts rang through the air, and then I realized *what* the sound was. My heart lodged itself in my throat, and before I could toss the arm aside and bolt from the bed, someone thumped against the side of my tent. The canvas rippled from the blows.

"If you're in there, Ash, get your ass up!" Zanta shouted. "We're under attack."

The panic in my friend's voice rattled me more than the siren and shouts. Zanta had taken me under her wing when I learned I was a demon and showed me the ropes of my new world. She'd faced countless enemies before, but I'd never heard a hint of panic in her voice.

I tossed the man's arm aside and leapt to my feet at the same time he sat up and shoved himself off the cot. I yanked a pair of pants up my hips and buttoned them before putting on my bra and tugging on a shirt.

I put on my socks and shoved my feet into my boots before lacing them and tying my hair into a bun. Rushing over to my weapons trunk, I threw open the lid and removed my holster; I pulled it on before inserting two handguns and a trench knife into it.

I slid my hand through the brass knuckles making up the handle of my other trench knife. I could create fire, and my ability had gotten stronger over the past two years, but it wasn't my best defense. Bullets wouldn't kill a demon, but they would wound one enough I could cut its head off before it recovered.

When I turned to the front of the tent, I discovered the man was gone. I ignored the stab this inflicted to my heart as I ran for the exit. Flinging open the flap, I plunged into the night and almost smacked into the back of him.

He caught my wrist when I stumbled back and helped to steady me. One of the drakón swept overhead and down the other side of the hill as it headed toward the training field and woods beyond it. A burst of blue fire erupted from its mouth as it scorched the earth.

The glow of its fire illuminated thousands of enemy troops

spilling from the woods and racing toward the wall. And those were just the ones I could see as they continued to flow from the woods. I understood the panic in Zanta's voice now as countless demons poured toward us.

"My God," I breathed.

I was far from the gateway when it opened and unleashed Hell on Earth, but I suspected it looked much like this as the freed demons overtook everything in their way. The craetons—those demons who once fought for Lucifer and now followed the remaining fallen angels and horsemen—seemed infinite in their numbers as they spread across the land.

I ducked and covered my head with my hands when the wings of the second drakón swept so close to my head it nearly tore my tent from its moorings. When they kicked up from the ground, dirt and rocks pelted me in the face as some of the tents tore free and tumbled away.

I lowered my hands as the second drakón unleashed a wave of blue fire before sweeping high to follow its mate. The first drakón was already dipping down to scorch the earth again, but as its fire consumed our enemies, more flowed around their bodies as they charged forward.

"I don't suppose I could talk you into going to the hall," the man said.

The hall was where the children, some of their mothers, and those unable to fight would shelter, but it was *not* where I was going.

"No, you can't," I told him.

He looked strangely disappointed for someone who had known me for less than six hours.

"I didn't think so," he said before grasping my arm and pulling me forward. "We have to go."

I staggered after him as we plunged through the tents. I'd been in fights before, nothing to this extent, but I could do this. I *would* do this. I was a soldier, a demon, and I had no other choice.

Gunshots and explosions rent the air as screams echoed through the night, but the tents blocked my view of what was happening. I ran faster, eager to break free of here so I could see what was happening and fight.

We were almost out of the tents when a lumbering beast staggered out from between the tents. Its yellow eyes landed on us, and it charged. The man released my wrist and ducked as the eight-foot-tall creature swung a lobster-like claw at his head. Judging by its foot-long snout, crustacean-like hands, and armored plate on its chest, this was a lower-level demon. It wasn't as powerful as the higher-level demons, but the thing looked like it could squish an elephant.

When it stalked toward the man, he threw a knife at it, which embedded in its throat. The thing didn't hesitate before it seized the guy by the throat, lifted him, and flung him away.

No! My heart lodged in my throat as I watched the man fly thirty feet through the air before crashing into a tent. He disappeared when the material collapsed around him. He was a demon, that wouldn't kill him, but he'd flown further than anyone ever should fly outside of an airplane.

It hadn't killed him, but was he wounded?

I had no idea why the possibility of such a thing infuriated and scared me as much as it did. When the beast started stalking after the man, I knew I couldn't let anything more happen to him.

I ran in low as I raced at the beast. It turned and swung its claw at me; I avoided the blow and sliced my knife across the back of its knee. The creature howled like a dog, and its legs buckled, but it didn't go down. A breeze blew against my cheeks when its other hand, the size of a sledgehammer, arced toward my head.

Throwing myself to the ground, I managed to avoid having my skull bashed in, but when its hand kissed the top of my head, I saw stars. I tried to rise, but I couldn't get my legs to cooperate. With no other choice, I rolled across the ground. Vibrations quaked the earth as it stalked after me.

Shit!

My back came up against a tent, and I looked up to discover the beast towering over me with its claw raised to smash me to pieces.

Turning on my side, I sliced a hole in the canvas of the tent as the man leapt onto its back, and I breathed a small sigh that he was okay. He cinched one arm around the beast's throat and yanked backward before driving a knife into the creature's ear and brain—if it had a brain.

When the thing's yellow eyes focused on me again, I realized it wasn't done with me. I yanked back the pieces of the tent I'd sliced open as it lifted its claw high. I squirmed into the tent and pulled my feet inside as its falling claw dented the earth.

I stared at the indent before jumping to my feet and pulling my other knife free. With the armor plating on this thing's chest, a knife wouldn't do much good, but neither would a bullet, and my knives wouldn't ricochet and hit me instead.

The man stuck his finger in one of the beast's eyes as I lunged forward and sliced its Achilles tendon. The creature howled again as its leg bowed out to the side, but unlike when I cut it before, it couldn't hold itself up as it tilted to the side before falling to one knee.

The man yanked his knife out of the demon's ear and drew the blade across its throat while he pulled back on its black hair. I slashed my knife across its other Achilles tendon before rising. The man succeeded in sawing the demon's head off and tossed it aside as its body slumped forward and hit the ground. I gazed at the hole where its head was with grim satisfaction; the head was the only body part a demon couldn't regenerate.

I didn't know if I was fortunate enough to have this regenerating ability too. I was immortal, but I wasn't a full demon, which was why I still occasionally used the bathroom, ate, and drank things. However, there wasn't one part of me that I was willing to cut off to see if it would regrow.

"Are you okay?" the man demanded.

"I'm fine. Thanks."

He didn't reply as he stalked toward me and grasped my arm. "We have to go."

As much as I appreciated his help with that *thing*, and as relieved as I was to see him unharmed after his unscheduled flight, I had training to follow. "I have to find my team. They're expecting me."

"They'll be on the field."

He was right, but I had to get to them. We broke free of the tents, and my mouth dropped when the field outside the town came into view. At this time of year, it was normally a sea of grass where we trained and ran drills, but now it was awash in fire and bodies littered the ground.

Troops poured out of the town and away from the wall to clash with those still emerging from the woods. They'd met each other closer to the wall than the woods. The flames of the drakón illuminated the thousands of fighters and bathed them in a blue light as they slashed, stabbed, and shot their way through the enemies.

My team was somewhere down there, but I'd never find them. In this chaos, all our training had been tossed out, and only a battle for survival was left. If we lost, these things would get past the wall, into the towns, and destroy what little remained of the world that existed before the gateway opened.

My body felt encased in ice as the screams of the injured and dying echoed over the land. Death was marching toward us, and there was a good possibility I wouldn't see the sunrise today. It was so strange that I'd passed out last night with the knowledge I would wake up, go to training, wash my clothes, and take my turn at night-shift on the wall.

Instead, I'd woken to a different world, and all those things might never matter again. Somehow, I found my hand in the man's as we ran down the hill and toward the battle.

If we somehow won this, would someone let my parents know if I died here today? My poor mom would take it the hardest. Before I learned what I was, she was already questioning why she hadn't aged a day in fifteen years. My father had gray hairs, laugh lines, and put on a few pounds, but my mom still looked like she did at thirty-four.

When I also stopped aging at twenty-three, and my ability to create small balls of fire awakened, the demons told me what I was. Upon this discovery, they also brought my parents to the wall in Virginia, where it became clear my demon heritage came from my mom. She never manifested any physical abilities, as I did, but it was clear she'd stopped aging.

To say she was stunned was an understatement, but her sadness was the worst part. My parents loved each other deeply; they'd expected to grow old and die together, but now my mom would watch my father become an old man while she remained the same. And she would stay on this earth for centuries after he passed. Her only consolation was that I would stay with her, but if she lost me too...

A lump clogged my throat, and I shut down all thoughts of my parents. They were strong; they would get through this, and they were the reason I fought these things. If we didn't win tonight, none of it would matter, because these things would destroy everything in their path as they swept across the rest of the wall and the country.

The screams intensified, and smoke from the fires clogged the air as both drakóns turned and soared low over the land. Chunks of dirt and flaming bodies flew into the air as they released more blue fire and wiped out a row of attackers, yet they didn't make a dent in the army spilling from the woods.

"What's your name?" I panted as we ran.

In the grand scheme of things, it wasn't important, but if I was going to die tonight, then I'd like to know his name.

"Hawk!" he shouted over his shoulder

The name tickled something in my memory, but it didn't matter. The only thing that mattered was making sure this army from Hell didn't make it beyond the wall.

CHAPTER EIGHT

Hawk

I kept hold of Aisling's wrist as we raced toward the battle. I couldn't let her go; I'd just found her, and I would *not* lose her. Some of the smoke cleared enough to reveal Corson and Wren slicing their way through a horde of lower-level demons. I bent to scavenge a sword from the headless body of a fallen demon. I rose and plunged the blade into the belly of the next one who lunged at me.

With no other choice, I released Aisling's hand to yank the blade from the demon's belly. I glanced back at Aisling as she ducked a demon lunging at her before plunging her knife into the eye of another.

"Stay close to me!" I shouted as I reclaimed her hand and carved my way toward Corson and Wren.

All around us, steel clashed against steel and demons and humans fell. Blood already stained the ground and ran in rivulets over the land as the bodies piled up. But as the dead fell, more rose to take their place.

My hand tightened on Aisling's when she tugged on mine

before pulling me to a stop. I turned when she released my hand to pry a dead demon's hand away from its spear. When a demon lunged at her, I swung my sword out and sliced its head off. Aisling pulled the spear away and rose beside me.

"Thank you," she said.

When her haunted eyes met mine, I saw she was far paler than she'd been earlier in the night. I wanted to draw her into my arms, kiss her forehead, and shelter her from all this, but that would only get us both killed. I wished she'd gone to the hall, but I'd known she would refuse when I suggested it. Demons and soldiers didn't walk away from a fight, and they especially didn't leave their friends behind.

I would keep her safe; it was the only option. I kept Aisling at my back while I hacked my way through more demons to reach Corson and Wren.

"Where have you been?" Corson demanded as he sliced the head off a lower-level demon with his talons.

He scowled when I pulled Aisling in front of me, but his scowl vanished when he saw the bite on her neck. His gaze flew to me, and his mouth closed.

Aisling's forehead furrowed as she studied Corson, but a squealing shout drew everyone's attention to the horde of gobalinus rushing toward us. I'd seen the two-foot-tall, hideous creatures while in Hell, but I'd hoped to never see the flesh-eating monsters with their yellow eyes, warts, piranha-like teeth, and leathery skin again.

One of them launched itself at Aisling, but I snagged it out of the air and snapped its neck before tearing its head away. She lunged forward to spear three of them while Corson and Wren took out a few more. Three of them leapt at me. I caught one and threw it aside and stabbed the other, but the third grasped my leg and started clawing its way toward my thigh.

I grabbed it as Aisling tossed her spear aside, pulled out a knife, and stabbed it. I kicked it back before cutting its head off. I took down another demon before throwing Aisling my sword and claiming the sword of the demon I killed.

"Where are River and Kobal?" I shouted to Corson.

Before Corson could reply, a pack of hellhounds burst through the fighters. The two at the front of the pack were Crux and Phenex, the hounds that resided within Kobal. The hellhounds looked like wolves with their vivid amber eyes, but they were easily twice the size of a wolf, and their claws could eviscerate someone with a single swipe of their paw.

When I kicked another gobalinus, it soared over the heads of the crowd as I stabbed the next little monster. A sudden breeze ruffled my hair, and I glanced up as three repulsive creatures swooped overhead.

"What are those?" Aisling asked.

"Don't you know?" I asked her.

"No."

I'd assumed all demons knew what the other types of demons were, but I must have been wrong. Maybe she was young for a demon, or maybe because a seal locked the erinyes away for thousands of years, she'd never learned about them.

"They're erinyes." I recognized the ugly women from when I first entered Hell with River. These things were fleeing Hell as River and I headed deeper into it. "They're better known to humans as furies."

Aisling gulped as one of the erinyes dove into the crowd and rose out again. Two humans dangled from her hands as she streaked upward. The snakes of her hair waved about her face when she stopped to hover over the crowd before releasing the humans.

The erinyes dove for another victim when a drakón snatched her out of the air and swallowed her whole. "I'm getting so I like those things a *lot* more," Corson said.

I was too, and I was *really* glad they'd decided to throw their loyalty River's way instead of toward what remained of the fallen angels. More erinyes swept overhead, but when they went to dive toward the crowd, a brilliant blast of golden light slammed into their chests and tore them apart.

The crowd parted to reveal the golden angel, Raphael, with his feet braced apart. The energy he created as he absorbed life from the earth reflected off his silver breastplate and caused his white-blond hair to dance around his shoulders. His violet eyes were bright in the glow of the golden light as he wielded his extraordinary, lethal ability.

Raphael turned his attention to the remaining two erinyes. They turned and tried to fly away, but the lifeforce Raphael wielded erupted from his palms and shredded them before they could get away.

"That ability is amazing," Aisling said.

"It is," I agreed. "But with so many of our own on the ground, he won't be able to use it much against the craetons on the ground."

"But he can take out more of those things."

"That was the last of the erinyes," I said.

"How do you know?" Aisling asked.

"Because I was there when they broke out of Hell; I know how many of them remained."

She opened her mouth to reply, but a gobalinus plowed into her leg and knocked her off balance. She pulled out a knife and plunged it into the creature's temple. When she lifted the kicking, screaming creature away from her, I cut off its head.

"I hate those things," she said as she kicked its body away.

More lower-level demons broke through the front line, and the drakóns swept over the land to unleash more fire. One of them was fully engulfed in blue flames as it remained low. The other had extinguished its fire and was soaring higher. When it turned to the side to come back toward us, I spotted River on its back.

The drakón plunged and turned sideways until its wing nearly skimmed the ground. Lower-level demons and enemy troops scattered to get out of its way before it barreled them over, but it still took out a good number of them.

I drove my sword through another demon as I watched the drakón rise higher into the sky again. Considering there was no flesh to pierce on the drakón, I didn't know if it was possible to kill them, but if the craetons saw River on its back, they would do everything in their power to destroy the beast. The second drakón blasted another wave of fire that tore up the ground as it swept toward the woods.

The flames burst high into the air before dying back as they consumed what little fuel there was to keep them burning. When they died back, I was able to see the fresh wave of craetons pouring from the woods in a never-ending parade of malicious intent.

Where were all these things coming from? We'd cleared so much of the Wilds; of course, there was still so much more to cover, but to keep this many enemy troops hidden would have been a near impossible feat.

Except, it was entirely possible as they were here and coming at us. I kept one eye on Aisling as we continued to hack and carve our way through the demons climbing over the dead bodies to get at us. When she stumbled and almost went down, I lunged to the side and pulled her out of the way of a demon flinging itself at her.

I was so focused on destroying the demon that I didn't see the other one coming at me until Aisling buried her sword under its chin. She screamed as she planted her foot in its chest and tore it away from her sword; Corson severed its head.

The drakón River rode first swept low over our heads before settling in the center of the crowd. When demons rushed toward it, its head curled up like a cobra. In one strike, it consumed most of the demons. The others turned to flee, but it used its tail to swipe them off their feet.

Kobal's followers, the palitons, surged forward to destroy our enemy while they were down. The drakón rose into the air, and blue fire erupted over its body as it turned and flew back over the land.

"Kobal must be over there," Corson said. "Let's go!"

"Come on." I grasped Aisling's arm and started pulling her toward the drakón.

The stench of death permeated the air, as did human waste and blood. The heat of so many together and the bursts of fire made the once cool night feel like it was a part of Hell. After becoming a demon, I could tolerate extreme heat and barely break a sweat, but none of this was tolerable.

We carved our way through more of our enemies as screams mixed in with whimpers and pleas for mercy. I'd never hated our enemies more than I did then. They could have broken free of Hell and lived in peace. Some of the other demons had chosen to do this and remained in the Wilds; they stayed out of it all and lived their lives.

The craetons didn't have to do any of this, but for some of those locked behind the seals, thousands of years of hatred against Kobal's ancestors had left them unable to move on. The fallen angels wanted to destroy everything in their way.

They were twisted monstrosities of what they'd once been, and they thrived on their madness and hatred against the humans, angels, and demons. With Lucifer dead, they'd taken to following Astaroth, who was said to be more vicious, and surrounded by this massacre, I agreed with the assessment.

We broke free of the battle to find River standing before Kobal. Bale, Caim, Lix, and a group of skelleins stood by her side. The skellein Lix wore a pink tie with cartoonish unicorns and donuts on it. After the jinn destroyed a lot of his skellein friends, Lix became more reserved, but as time passed, he started wearing ridiculous things again and smiling more often.

Now, though he had no eyes in the empty sockets of his skull, I sensed Lix's displeasure in the set of his jaw. Most of the skelleins were about four and a half feet tall, but Lix was slightly taller. While in Hell, the skeletal creatures hadn't bothered to differentiate themselves from each other, but on Earth, they'd all taken to wearing clothes that emphasized their sex and personalities.

In the glow of the fire, Bale's red hair was the color of blood, and the reddish hue to her skin was more pronounced. Her lime green eyes were cold when they met mine; ruthless determination filled her face. Bale and Corson were Kobal's two most trusted advisors, and they would fight to the death to make sure Kobal and River survived.

Púca also gathered around River. Some of the shape-changing demons had chosen to protect her after their seal fell. They couldn't speak, but they could take on the form of animals or humans.

Most of them had chosen the shape of dogs as they slunk through the fighters, taking out the legs and throats of their enemies before feasting on their blood. They formed a wall around us to keep the enemies out. No one knew the púca's original form, and I'd prefer not to know as the silent creatures were disturbing while they desiccated their victims.

"It's the horsemen and fallen angels!" River shouted. "I spotted Death in the trees with one of the angels, but before we could get close to them, he vanished into the woods."

"Have the drakón torch the woods," Kobal said to River.

"Does anyone live out there?" Wren demanded.

"No," Kobal stated.

"Are you sure?" River asked.

"Yes, but if there *were* people out there, they're dead. The angels and horsemen aren't going to leave anyone alive. Torch the woods."

River nodded before lifting an arm into the air. She waved her hand until one of the drakón spotted her and banked back toward us. I kept my hand on Aisling's arm, and we all fell back when one of the drakón pulled up to hover overhead.

Dirt and debris kicked up from the ground to pelt my face and body. When Aisling lifted her arm and bowed her head to shield herself, I wrapped my arm around her head to protect her from the wind and rubble. Cradling her against me, I surveyed the battle as more fell and the bodies piled on top of each other.

One way or another, I would get her through this.

The drakón settled on the ground, and its blue flames went out when River stepped close and rested her hand against its skeletal head. If I wasn't watching it with my own two eyes, I would have believed it impossible, but the thing was more like a cat as it lowered its head and turned into her touch.

I'd known they were protective of her, but I hadn't realized how close their bond had become while we were traveling the Wilds. Bale glanced at me while River talked with the creature. She'd learned a lot more of the demonic language over the past year, and the drakón was listening to her. When she finished, she patted its cheek and kissed it before stepping away.

My eyebrows were in my hairline, and when it turned its head toward her, I swore the thing smiled.

"My God," Aisling breathed.

The drakón unfolded its wings and, with a flap that kicked up more debris, rose gracefully into the air. Its encompassing blue flames burst over it as it swept toward the woods. I didn't get the chance to watch its destruction as higher and lower-level demons broke through the wall of púca and rushed toward us.

CHAPTER NINE

Aisling

Before the demons could reach us, a wave of fire erupted from Kobal's palm and blasted into the front of their line. From out of the shadows, a hellhound pounced onto the back of another and tore its head off. It gulped down the head. With the size of the creature, I doubted the hound considered it anything more than a small snack.

When River rested her hand on Kobal's arm, a burst of golden white light flowed from her palm and took out three more of the demons. While I was stationed at the wall in Virginia, the king and queen came to visit once, but I only caught a brief glimpse of them on their tour of the wall.

Since I arrived here, I'd seen more of them, but I'd never seen them unleash their abilities, and I didn't know how anyone could turn those skeletal dragons into a pile of mushy goo. And somehow Hawk, a man who seemed more human than demon in some ways, was involved with them.

Then it hit me why his name sounded so familiar. He was their friend and one of the leaders of the mission to clear the Wilds of the demons who escaped the gateway. I'd heard a little about him and the others from the troops stationed here.

Another lower-level demon charged at me. Needing a break from swinging the heavy sword, I dropped the tip to the ground, pulled out my gun, aimed at its chest, and fired. The impact of the bullet striking its heart lifted the creature and flung it backward. I shot at the bastards who rose up to replace the thing until my gun emptied.

I holstered the gun and lifted the sword. Grim determination settled over me as I prepared to slaughter anyone who came near us. I'd killed demons before but never in this number and never in this endless wave as still more of them emerged from the woods. I would *not* give in to the hopelessness trying to rise inside me.

I would take out as many of these monsters as possible, and if I was lost in the process, then so be it.

A horde of demons broke through the dogs and raced toward us with a bone-chilling battle cry. They were ugly and bloodthirsty, but they didn't have much in the way of brains as they charged heedlessly forward.

Hawk seized the first demon and tossed it aside as a black missile dove out of the sky. I almost screamed at Hawk to duck, but at the last second, the bird switched course and sank its talons into the flesh of a demon. The raven transformed into an angel with black wings who snapped the demon's neck before tearing it off.

Caim.

I'd heard about the fallen angel who turned against Lucifer to join Kobal and River. I knew he could transform into a bird, but I'd never seen it before. I swallowed to get saliva back in my throat as I realized my heart was galloping in my chest. I'd assumed he was going for Hawk and... and it *terrified* me.

I steadied the tremor in my hands as I swung my sword at the next demon. It leaned back to avoid the arc of the blade and launched a punch at me. Unable to recover my balance from missing him, I couldn't dodge it.

Another hand shot out between us and seized the fist. It pushed the demon's hand back and bashed it into the creature's face. I gaped as Hawk stepped in front of me and severed the demon's head from its shoulders. He glanced at me over his shoulder, but before I could thank him, or hug him, or...

I had no idea what I wanted to do to him, and I didn't have time to figure it out as more came at us.

Caim transformed back into a raven and flew away as another demon swiped at me. Ducking, I dodged the beefy hand that would have knocked my head from my shoulders and thrust my sword up through its chin. I jerked the blade down, placed my foot in its chest, and shoved it back to face the next one coming at me.

Hawk caught the creature I pushed away and finished it off as River's golden light pierced into three more of them. We never got a breather as they climbed over each other and the bodies to come at us.

Blood splattered my face and coated my clothes until they stuck to my skin. Despite all my years of training, the countless drills I'd run, and the hours I spent wielding weapons, my arms and legs grew tired as the night progressed toward day.

The beat of wings drew my attention to a creature with the body of a lion and the head of a human, or maybe it was a demon head. It opened its mouth as it dove toward me. As it neared, I saw the three rows of its piranha-like teeth as I moved my sword in front of me.

I had no idea what good a sword would do against this monstrosity, but I had nothing else. I focused on its orange eyes while its body plunged toward me. A woman cried out and staggered back when a demon shoved her back and in front of me.

The creature's scorpion tail plunged into the woman's chest

and burst out the other side. I recoiled when warm blood splattered my face. It took everything I had not to start screaming and hacking at the tail with my sword, but I'd only succeed in carving the woman up if I did so. But when the creature plucked her off the ground and into the air, I realized she might have been better off if I killed her.

"Are you okay?" Hawk demanded as he grabbed my arm and spun me toward him.

Was I okay? Not at all. But I had to be okay because there was no other choice. "I'm fine."

I tried to wipe the woman's blood from my face, but I doubted it accomplished anything as the blood of so many others coated my hands. The beat of wings drew my attention to the sky as more of those things soared overhead.

"What are those things?" I demanded.

"They're manticores," Hawk said. "And I hate them."

I could understand why as another one of them dove into the crowd and speared three palitons with its lethal tail. Still in raven form, Caim landed on the manticore's back and ripped its head off with his beak. Raphael took out three more of them while River destroyed another one as it plummeted toward a group of humans.

Though their wings continued to beat above me, I focused on the demons coming at me. I couldn't watch the skies and the ground successfully, and I had a better chance of killing the demons on the ground than the ones in the air. Still, I found myself flinching and bracing myself every time I felt a shift in the air current.

We struggled endlessly on, somehow gaining ground against the demons as the drakón's fire lit the night sky. I didn't know more demons were still coming from the woods; I could only see the glow of the burning trees from here.

As we worked to gain ground, I couldn't help admiring Hawk's fighting style while he carved his way through the enemy. He was powerful, fast, and extremely well-trained with an excellent technique. Whereas I felt about ready to collapse, he didn't tire as he sliced the head from one demon before taking out the legs of another.

No matter how many of them came at us, he stayed by my side as the sky lightened toward dawn. I barely recognized him beneath the layer of dirt and blood covering him, and I knew I didn't look any better. In the distance, the smoke from the burning forest was so thick it blocked out the rising sun.

Normally, the morning was my favorite time of the day. Often, I'd slip out of my tent at dawn and walk to the edge of the hill to sit and watch the sunrise. The sweet songs of the birds would float around me as they woke to greet the day. It was such a peaceful time, and it was *my* time.

And now, instead of the birds' songs, the screams of the fallen greeted the sun. The gunfire had stopped; the drakón couldn't rain fire on their enemies without annihilating their allies too. They soared overhead, chasing the manticores while protectively circling their queen.

Our progress across the field slowed as the bodies littering the ground made moving more difficult. I stumbled and almost toppled onto a pile of dead, but Hawk caught my elbow and pulled me back. Unable to stop myself, I leaned against him as I steadied my wobbling legs beneath me.

River hit the last manticore with a blast of energy that sent it spiraling down. A pack of demons pounced on it and tore it apart. I wiped a strand of straggling hair from my face as Hawk took out another demon, but their numbers were dwindling.

I felt numb as I gazed around the blood-drenched, body-covered field. I couldn't quite process that many of these bodies were people and demons I'd talked with, laughed with, and worked with yesterday. We'd always known there was a chance of an attack, but I'd never imagined one of this magnitude, and after years of living at the wall, I'd stopped believing it could happen.

And now... well, I didn't know anything about now. I was too exhausted to process what happened, never mind what would come after. I took out the knees of a demon and wiped away the sweat trickling into my eyes, except it wasn't sweat. I closed my eyes and tore my attention away from the blood on the back of my hand. I didn't think it was mine, but I couldn't know for sure.

Nausea twisted in my stomach; I was trained to fight, I'd killed before, but this level of carnage was something I'd never expected to see.

This was... this was... Hell.

When the sun rose beyond the smoke, its rays did little to dry the blood soaking the land. With the sun came the increasing stench of death, and when I glanced toward the sky, shock gripped me as I spotted the pristine blue above us.

How could it be so horrific down here yet so beautiful above us? The incongruity of it caused my eyes to burn. I must be more exhausted than I thought if I was trying not to cry over the blue sky. And then I realized I wasn't struggling against tears because the sky was blue; it was because I was still here to see it when so many others weren't.

I held my sword high, but no more demons came at us. My arms ached from fighting, but I couldn't bring myself to lower the weapon as I searched the field for more enemies. The last of the demons fell at the hands of the king.

Scattered throughout the battlefield were the exhausted humans and demons from our side. They looked as shell-shocked as I felt as they took in the carnage surrounding us. I lowered my sword and rested the tip of it on the ground.

"We won," I whispered.

But at what cost?

I turned to Hawk when he rested his hand on my arm. I didn't know him, but I was struck with the inexplicable urge to throw my arms around him and hug him. It was so intense I had to grip my sword in both hands to keep from making a fool of myself with him.

But it didn't matter as Hawk drew me against his chest, and though I tried to resist it, my fingers twisted into his shirt. I ignored the blood coating him as beneath its coppery scent, I detected the sweeter aroma of something that reminded me of the brownies my mom used to make.

When I recalled sitting in the kitchen and watching while she melted the chocolate for the brownies, I realized Hawk reminded me of chocolate melting in a pan. He made me recall the days before the gateway opened when life was so simple and I was safe in my small world.

I was safe with him too. It was dangerous to think such things about a demon when he would move on, but in his arms, I didn't care.

"Come on," he said.

Reluctant to release him, my fingers uncurled from his back before I stepped away. He kept his hand on my arm while we carefully made our way across the field toward the king and queen.

I tried not to take in the remains littering the ground, but it was impossible not to notice the bodies when we had to step on them as we went. The hounds released a mournful howl while they prowled through the dead.

At first, I assumed they were scavenging for food, but then they pulled the remains of a hound from beneath some of the bodies. On the other side of the field, three more hounds removed the body of another one of their brethren.

Those annoying tears were back as the mournful cries tugged at my heart. They howled again, and one of them nudged a body in a way that let me know it had lost its mate. One of the drakóns still circled overhead, but the other had landed to sit protectively behind the queen.

From the other side of the king and queen, I saw someone else push through a group of demons as he walked toward the couple. It took me a minute to recognize Vargas beneath the blood coating him as the three of us arrived to stand near the king and queen at the same time. Once his leg was strong enough, Vargas started training with my team two weeks ago. I didn't know him very well, but I saw recognition in his eyes when he nodded at me.

"Where's Erin?" Hawk asked, and I heard the distress in his voice.

"She's at the hall with the children," Vargas answered, and Hawk gave him a questioning look but didn't comment.

Turning toward the woods, I closed my eyes and rubbed at them as exhaustion pulled at me. I opened my eyes, and my vision blurred until I blinked it clear. I blinked again when a cloud emerged from the smoke. I thought exhaustion was causing me to hallucinate, but the cloud drew closer with every passing second.

"Oh shit," someone said. "The angels."

And then I recognized them as they swooped toward us with their wings spread wide while they soared low over the carnage. Survivors screamed and threw themselves to the ground, but some weren't fast enough to evade the angels who tore off their heads or lifted them off the ground before flinging them away.

I was so focused on the angels that I didn't realize the ground was vibrating until it shook my legs. Tearing my gaze away from the forty or so angels clogging the sky, I focused on the small section of woods that wasn't on fire yet.

"Motherfuckers," the king snarled.

I hadn't believed it possible, but my exhaustion vanished. Adrenaline flooded my system as the nine remaining horsemen of the apocalypse barreled toward us, and behind them emerged a new wave of demons.

This wave was far smaller than before, but we were battered, beaten, and nearly broken. These bastards had waited until our troops were decimated before descending on us.

I hated and admired them for their cruel calculations.

My arms trembled as I lifted the sword, but I locked my muscles into place to keep it steady as I prepared for the next fight.

CHAPTER TEN

Hawk

Using its hind legs, the drakón behind River launched itself straight off the ground and into the air as one of the angels dropped a screaming woman. The woman would have hit River, but the drakón snatched her out of the sky and flung her away before closing its powerful jaws around the angel.

The second drakón turned in the air and raced toward the horseman as fire burst from its mouth. The flames streaked across the land, torching the bodies of the fallen as it closed in on the horsemen. Three angels crashed into the side of the drakón's head, knocking it off course.

More angels descended on both drakóns until they were bashing against the sides of the creatures. The angels had to be getting burned by the drakóns, but they moved so fast the fire didn't catch on them. The drakóns were so busy trying to fend off the angels that the horsemen and their troops closed the rest of the distance without a problem.

"If the horsemen get too close..."

Vargas didn't finish his sentence. We all knew what would happen if the horsemen got too close. They wouldn't have to fight us; Wrath and War would have us killing each other before we could do anything to stop them.

I seized Aisling's elbow as a snarl rumbled up my throat. Her warm, deep brown eyes shimmered with fear when they met mine, but the determined expression on her face remained resolute.

"Achó!" Kobal roared and pointed at the horsemen before sending a blast of fire at a couple of demons who were bearing down on him and River.

I'd been around demons long enough to recognize the word attack. The hounds howled as they bounded across the dead and raced toward the horsemen. Raphael took to the sky as Caim transformed from his raven form and streaked after him. A wave of golden light erupted from Raphael's hand and hit two of the angels. They shrieked as their bodies exploded.

One of the drakóns turned and flew straight at the other one. A hush descended as for a second, every eye latched onto the two powerful beasts and the angels swarming like gnats around them. I was sure they were going to crash into each other, but then the drakón released a wave of fire and torched some of the angels harassing its mate.

When the flame receded, only the ashes of the angels remained as they spiraled to the earth. The remaining angels tried to scatter, but the drakón swallowed them while the other, free of its gnats, dove at the angels trying to flee the first drakón.

The hounds broke free of the bodies littering the field and rushed toward the horsemen. Lust turned her horse and raced back toward the woods. One of the hounds seized the leg of an extremely thin horseman and ripped him off his underweight mount. The horseman wailed, and his hands flailed as the hounds pounced.

Apparently, the hounds weren't affected by the power of the

horsemen as black blood sprayed and they tore the man to pieces. The horseman's horse burst into ashes when the hounds succeeded in destroying its rider.

Another horseman screamed as the hounds snapped at his heels. When he tried to turn his overweight horse to flee, the hounds latched onto its thick legs and brought the animal down. I didn't see what happened after as more lower-level demons reached us.

I cut off the head of one before taking out the next. Beside me, Aisling moved with elegant grace as she battled our enemies. I saw her exhaustion in the circles under her eyes and the paleness of her face, but she still fought like the battle was just beginning.

On the other side, Vargas swung a battle ax into the head of another demon. I had no idea why Erin was with the women and children; she was one of our best fighters, but I was glad she wasn't here. Even with as good a soldier as she was, if she'd been here, she might not have survived.

I lunged forward and sank my sword into another demon before pulling the blade free. I lifted my sword to deliver the killing blow when Aisling screamed, "Hawk, watch out!"

I was so focused on the demon that I didn't see the streak of black coming at me until the angel was only feet in front of me. I swung the sword down to deter the bastard, but all I succeeded in doing was driving the hilt into his spine as he smashed into my chest.

Lifted off my feet, I flew ten feet through the air before landing on a mound of bodies. The impact bruised my chest bone, and my lungs protested when I tried to breathe. Bracing my hands on the dead, I pushed myself up but didn't get far before the angel hit me again.

Black eyes filled my vision as fingers hooked into my shirt and yanked me up. His arm was pulled back in a blow that would knock my head off my shoulders. Before he hit me, I swung my head forward and rammed my forehead into his nose. Blood burst over me when the angel's nose shattered, and he released a gurgled shout as the hand meant to hit me grasped his nose instead.

Rage filled the bastard's eyes as his face contorted. I swung a fist into his chin, but the bastard barely flinched before gripping my head. I clawed at his hands as I thrashed to break free of his grasp before he tore my head off. My efforts were useless against him as his eyes shone with bloodthirsty gloo.

A sword swung out and buried itself in the side of the angel's neck before getting stuck. Aisling planted her foot against the angel's ribs and worked to free the sword as his hands grasped at the blade.

Blood spilled free, but he didn't release the sword as he pulled it free of his body and shoved it at her. The movement caused Aisling to stumble back a few steps; she regained her balance and lifted the sword. The angel's head bobbed as he turned toward her, but I gripped his bat-like wing and jerked him back when he lunged at her.

With a fury-filled scream, Aisling swung the sword down again. The angel's head rolled away before stopping with his black eyes turned toward us and his mouth parted. Aisling lowered her sword and wiped at the blood and dirt streaking her face as she gazed at the angel's wings. They pointed into the air before they released their rigid position and slumped to the ground.

"Are you okay?" Aisling asked me.

"Yes."

I pushed myself to my feet in time to see the remaining horsemen retreating into the small section of woods that still wasn't on fire. As the last horseman vanished into the trees, the flames rolled over to consume what remained of the woods. Even if we got a group together to follow them right now, we wouldn't be able to get through the fire. But I *would* hunt them down if it was the last thing I did.

It was time to end this.

Unable to stop myself from touching her, I rested my hand on Aisling's arm. She stiffened for a second before relaxing into my touch. Her exhaustion beat against me, but she stood proudly amid the rubble as she lifted her sword again.

Some of the craetons tried to follow the horsemen as they raced toward the woods, but the hounds took many of them down, and the fire pushed back the others. They ran parallel to the flames until they found an opening and vanished into the smoldering forest.

In the sky, the drakón still battled the angels, but only a dozen of the black-winged bastards remained as Raphael, Caim, and the drakón worked their way through what remained of them. An angel I recognized as Astaroth, thanks to his bloodred hair, rose into the sky as another version of him flew low over the land. Caim once said the angel who had risen to take Lucifer's place could astral project, and I realized he'd split himself in two to avoid death.

The drakón closed its jaws over one of the angels while the other streaked toward the billowing smoke. Before it could vanish into the smoke, the other drakón plunged out of the sky and crashed into an angel, knocking him aside.

Two more versions of him materialized. One of them flew toward the woods while the other raced toward the angel the drakón hit. Before the two angels could get close to each other, Caim swooped down and grabbed the shoulders of one. He lifted it high into the air as Raphael unleashed a bolt of power straight into Astaroth's chest.

Astaroth screamed as his body bowed and his wings unfurled behind him. His legs kicked in the air as if he were trying to run, but there was nowhere for him to go as the golden light illuminated him from the inside out before erupting from his mouth.

And then he exploded into ashes that poured over the land as the angel in Caim's hands vanished. Silence descended over the battlefield as everyone watched the ashes float through the air to settle on the dead. Caim and Raphael were the only angels who remained in the sky.

"The fallen angels have fallen," I murmured.

"Could some of them have gotten away or never come out of the woods?" Aisling asked.

"They could have," I said. "But if any of them do remain, it's not many."

Gazing at the bodies littering the field, I tried to count the wings I saw amid them, but it was too difficult, and there was no way to know how many angels the drakón ate. Raphael and Caim landed on the field. They were so different from each other; one so fair and the other so dark, one a golden child and the other a fallen sinner, but they stood shoulder to shoulder as they gazed at the carnage surrounding them.

No matter how different they were, sorrow etched both their faces. Brothers and sisters, I recalled when Caim touched the wing of one of the angels. Raphael may deny they were his brothers and sisters, but he rested his hand against another fallen angel's wing before pulling it away.

He said something, and Caim looked to him. Caim opened his mouth to respond before closing it, shaking his head, and looking toward the fallen angel again. Raphael reached for Caim before stopping so that his hand hovered between them. Then, he rested his hand on Caim's shoulder, squeezed it, and walked away.

Caim remained where he was before lowering his hand and turning to survey the dead. Then he followed Raphael across the field and toward the wall. He didn't look at any of the other fallen angels, but I suspected he was aware of the location of each of them.

This time when I draped my arm around Aisling's shoulders,

she didn't stiffen but leaned into me as we stood staring at the carnage surrounding us. It had been the longest and worst night of my life, but many of our enemies didn't survive.

And soon we would hunt down what remained of the rest of them.

CHAPTER ELEVEN

Hawk

Kobal knelt to lift the edge of the green cloak draped around the shoulders of what remained of the horseman. "I'm guessing Envy."

Rising from his crouched position, he strode over to the overweight horseman. Corson, Bale, Lix, Caim, Raphael, River, Vargas, Aisling, and I followed him. Kobal nudged one of the horseman's thick legs with his boot.

"Gluttony," he said. Moving on, he stopped beside the one who was so thin his cheekbones stood out against his pale skin. "Famine."

The horsemen had once numbered eleven but were now down to six as we'd already taken out Greed and Sloth. Contrary to popular belief, there were eleven horsemen and not four, but years ago, humans separated the seven deadly sins and the four horsemen. However, they were all horsemen.

Lifting my head, I gazed at the dwindling fire and the burnt-out remnants of trees rising from the smoke. With little left to feed it, the fire was burning itself out, but a golden glow still burned deep in the woods and smoke coiled into the air.

"We have to track them," Corson said. "Before they can recuperate and devise another plan of attack."

"Yes," Kobal said.

Kobal gazed at the carnage before studying the hundred or so survivors picking their way through the field. They pulled survivors from beneath the dead and gestured for the nearby medical personnel to bring over cots. Kobal had given orders to try to separate our dead the best they could, and when they finished, he planned to have the drakón torch whatever remained.

They'd removed two surviving enemies from the dead too. Kobal didn't think the survivors would talk, but he planned to speak with them before destroying them. Most of the survivors were demons, but a few humans managed to make it out alive. More soldiers guarded the wall, but I guessed we'd lost nearly two-thirds of our fighters in the battle.

The hounds released a low, mournful howl. It took all I had not to wince as the melancholy sound carried across the field. "Were the dead hounds mated?" River asked.

"They both were," Kobal said.

River glanced at the hounds before resting her hand on Kobal's arm. He laced his fingers through hers and drew her closer. If both the hounds were mated, then that meant two more of them would die today. The hounds mated for life, and when one mate died, the other one did too. I didn't know how that death would come, but I suspected they wouldn't be here at sunset.

"With the fire, you can't track the horsemen now. Get some rest and come to the hall in twelve hours," Kobal said.

No one spoke as he lifted River and carried her across the field toward the hounds. The beasts parted as he set River down before kneeling beside the two hounds. The hounds sat on either side of him and rested their heads against his thighs while he rubbed their heads.

Aisling

I climbed out of the shower and stumbled out of the room before collapsing onto the bed ten feet away from the door. It had taken almost a half an hour of scrubbing my skin before the water stopped running red with blood. By then, there was no hot water left, but I'd grown accustomed to taking cold showers.

I should've left this place, but I didn't have the energy to lift my head off the pillow, never mind trudge back up the hill to return to my tent. And there was a chance my tent wasn't standing anymore. I had no idea whose house Hawk brought me to, and I didn't care.

I didn't care that I had no clothes to wear; I'd grown accustomed to being naked around others. In Virginia, when I first started living with the demons, I'd refused to shower naked in front of other demons like they did. Instead, I would return to my old house in town and visit with my friend Sandy before taking a shower in my old room.

After a couple of months, I realized, if I was going to embrace what I was now, then I had to accept everything about their culture. The first couple of times I showered naked in front of them, I spent the entire time with my cheeks burning and shielding my breasts.

Eventually, I realized no one was paying attention to me and relaxed enough to stop blushing. I would still hang out with Sandy a couple of times a week, but I stopped keeping my shower supplies at her house.

The scent of soap wafted to me seconds before the mattress sank. I cracked open an eye and discovered Hawk sitting on the edge of the bed with his gaze focused on the wall. His wet hair stood on end, his shoulders were still damp, and only a towel covered his waist. For some reason, I almost rested my hand on his leg.

Don't be so human.

But you are *a human, or at least you're still part human.*

When I first learned I was becoming an immortal demon, I didn't exactly shout for joy. No, there were some definite "pity me" moments. I also spent a whole lot of time inspecting myself for horns and a tail, but thankfully, I never sprouted either.

I'd felt so lost in a world that was so regimented and certain the day before. I was one of many who volunteered to become a soldier and live at the wall where I learned the truth about demons coming to Earth. Every day I woke up knowing I would eat, train, be on guard duty, and sleep.

At the time, I was sort of dating a guy. He was super cute, one of the funniest people I'd ever met, but not that great in bed. The fact he made me laugh so hard I almost piss myself made up for him rarely getting me to the finish line.

Then, one day, I woke up and everything changed. I'd always seen the souls of others, but I'd never set my sheets on fire before. I didn't even know how I activated it before flames were consuming my bed and Sandy was running in with a fire extinguisher. I stood, gawking at the mattress as Sandy doused it with white foam.

"What happened?" she demanded when the fire was out.

"I... I don't know," I stammered as I gazed from the fire extinguisher dangling from her hand to the bed and back again.

Sandy rested her hand on my shoulder. "It's okay."

But I didn't know if it was okay or not as I lifted my hands to gaze at my palms.

"The fire came from you?" she asked.

"Yes."

She set the extinguisher on the ground and grasped my hands. "You have to tell someone."

I felt the blood rush from my head at the idea and rested my hand on the wall to keep from falling over. What would they do? Would this make me more of a freak? I could conceal the soul thing, and I did from most people, but how did I hide becoming an overnight flamethrower?

As much as I preferred to live in a world of denial, Sandy was right. However, I did manage to limp through that day in the land of denial. Having to sleep on the couch that night helped break through the barrier, but melting the coffee pot the next day solidified the knowledge I had to do something.

Before I could set the house on fire and accidentally kill Sandy or someone else, I requested a meeting with the commanding officer of our base. When he heard what I had to say, he brought in the demon leader. That was when I learned demons once walked the earth, and some found their Chosen with humans and had children with them.

Unable to return to Hell without their Chosen, those demons often chose to stay and perish on Earth. When the fallen angels entered Hell, demons were barred from walking the earth and all gateways out of Hell remained closed until the humans blew one open.

It was such an insane thing to think about, but one of those demons, from over six thousand years ago, created the line that would one day give birth to me.

The news had thrown my orderly world into a tailspin. I spent the next week in a fog as I tried not to set things on fire while settling into the knowledge of who I was now. Zanta was assigned to help me through the transition and to teach me about demon things. That was when I learned fire was the beginning of my changes. I was also faster, required less sleep, food, and water, and didn't go to the bathroom as often.

During week two, and after I set the couch on fire, I decided to move in with the demons who had taken up residence in a large paddock behind what used to be a farmhouse. Sandy asked me to stay, but anxiety over what I might accidentally do next propelled me from the house. Once in my tent, I decided it was time to embrace what I was or spend an eternity wallowing in uncertainty.

It took a while, and three tents, before I learned to control my fire. During that time, many of the demons were patient with me, but my sort of boyfriend also found someone new, and who could blame him?

He hadn't signed on for the "immortal demon who could sometimes burn things" aspect of a relationship. And what kind of relationship could it possibly be when he was growing older and I was going to look like a twenty-three-year-old forever?

Once I stopped feeling sorry for myself and grieving the things I'd lost, I decided to embrace the things I'd gained. I still stumbled along the way, and there were times when I contemplated running away and burying my head in the sand, but over time, I adjusted to the demon way of life.

But, no matter how well I fit in with the demons now, I was also part human and was raised as a human. I still had all the emotions that came with my humanity, but having feelings for a demon was an excellent way to get my heart broken.

Still, I couldn't stop myself from resting my hand on Hawk's thigh. His flesh was warm beneath my palm, and despite my exhaustion, I found myself reacting to him.

"Whose house is this?" I asked.

"Mine," he said as he turned to look at me. There was a strange look in his beautiful eyes as they ran over me; it was almost one of awe. "Or it was mine anyway. I used to live here with Vargas and some other guys. Now, Vargas and Erin live here, and I crash here whenever I'm in town."

"I'll go—"

"No," he interrupted harshly, but when he spoke again, his tone was calmer. "Please stay."

I tried not to let it, but excitement flooded my veins as my pulse raced.

Damn it, do not *get attached to a demon.*

Suddenly, I became aware of my nudity in a way I hadn't been in over a year. Scooting away from him, I slipped under the blanket and sighed when I sank further into the fluffy mattress. It was *so* much more comfortable than my small cot. I could sleep for a week in this bed.

I stared at the wall as my thoughts turned to Zanta and Sandy. They'd both been transferred to this area of the wall when I relocated. I hadn't seen Zanta since she yelled for me on her way to the battle, but I hadn't seen all the survivors. I tried to recall Sandy's schedule. Was she on guard duty on the wall last night or was she at home and therefore more likely to have been on the field?

A lump clogged my throat. Sandy was my roommate, and the first friend I made when I first arrived at the wall. We were from different towns and didn't know each other, but we volunteered on the same day and were assigned together. At sixteen, Sandy volunteered as soon as she could, but I'd waited until I was eighteen.

Still, we'd become friends, and even after I moved in with the demons, we spent most of our days together and were nearly inseparable. After learning what I was, she hadn't feared me or shunned me as some of the other humans did. She was the best friend I ever had, and I couldn't leave her body with the dead on the field.

And Zanta had been my lifeline during the most confusing and challenging time of my life. She'd guided me as she taught me how to control my newfound capabilities. She never judged me, never forced me to do anything I wasn't ready for, and never treated me like my half-human status made me lesser like some of the other demons did.

They both had to be alive, but I knew the odds of that weren't good.

As if sensing my distress, Hawk enclosed his arms around me

and settled against my back. I shouldn't allow myself to take comfort in his strong embrace, but I was too tired to resist him. Tomorrow I would worry about protecting my heart, but today I would accept this small bit of comfort in a far from comforting world.

CHAPTER TWELVE

Aisling

The smell of cooking bacon woke me sometime later. Opening my eyes, I blinked as I tried to figure out where I was and what was happening? Was I home? Was that my mom in the kitchen?

For a minute, I found myself back to a time when I woke every morning to my mom humming in the kitchen while the tantalizing scent of food filled the air. I never used an alarm clock; my stomach always woke me.

A big fan of breakfast, my mom almost always had it ready by the time my dad and I made it downstairs. We'd sit together in the breakfast nook and eat whatever delicious concoction she made for us. We often talked for a bit before my mom read the paper while my dad did the crossword, and I propped open a book.

Then the war happened and so much changed. My mom still cooked for us, but instead of racing my dad downstairs for the best piece of bacon, we were often coming through the door after spending the morning hunting.

Before our laughter would follow us into the kitchen as we both arrived breathless and pushing against each other. After, no laughter followed us through the door. It was difficult to laugh when half the world was gone, though we tried.

We'd still sit together in the nook and read, but for a few years, there were no newspapers and crosswords. When a paper returned, it was put out by one of our neighbors and consisted of our small town's local news. It arrived on our doorstep once a month; we usually knew everything by then, but we read every sentence in that short paper.

But even with the bacon cooking and my confusion over my whereabouts, I knew I wasn't home. The wall across from me was white and not the warm peach of my room. I stared at the wall as my memories clicked into place. I wasn't home; I was at the wall and beyond the windows of this home was an endless sea of death.

I closed my eyes as I tried to shut out the screams of the dying and the stench of blood and smoke. Instead, I focused on the large, strong man enveloping me. If the rigid evidence of his erection in my back was any indication, he could use some release. And I was desperate to forget, if only for a little while, the events of yesterday.

Rolling over, I rested my hands on his chest and pushed him onto the bed before taking him into me. For a brief time, I forgot all about the dead as I became centered on Hawk, our bodies, and the way he could make me come apart.

Spent, I collapsed on top of him while I struggled to catch my breath. Those odd little fangs were back in my mouth, and I prodded them with my tongue as a forgotten conversation with Zanta drifted through my mind. I was at the wall in Virginia right after the king and queen arrived. The demons were whispering something about a Chosen, and I asked Zanta what that meant.

"See the marks on their necks?" Zanta asked.

"Yes." It was impossible not to notice them.

"When a demon finds their Chosen, they mate for life. Those bites make it clear to everyone they belong to each other."

I poked at my fangs again as I tried to figure out why they were there, what was happening, and who this man beside me was.

"Hawk?"

"Hmm?" he murmured as he ran his fingers through my hair.

"I have fangs."

"I'm aware," he said with a chuckle. "I recall enjoying the feel of them sinking into me."

"I've never had fangs before. I mean, I'm still relatively new to this whole demon thing, but I think I would have noticed fangs."

He stopped playing with my hair and propped his head on his hand to gaze down at me. "What do you mean, you're still new to this demon thing?"

"I mean, I've only been a demon, or I should say immortal, for two years. I've been part demon my whole life; I just didn't know it until I stopped aging and started accidentally setting things on fire."

"And no one in your family knew about it until the gateway opened."

"Exactly. It comes from my mom's side. She stopped aging too but didn't acknowledge it until I told her what was happening to me. Afterward, the military moved my parents to the wall for their protection. I didn't think anyone would attack her, but I wasn't taking any chances."

Everyone was now aware of what really happened with the war, but for years, the government kept it a secret. The collapse of the seals and the escape of the Hell creatures blew that secret wide open.

"I don't blame you," he said. "What kind of demon are you?"

"I've been told I'm part fire demon. I can create small balls of fire, and it doesn't burn me," I said. "My fire isn't strong enough to do any real damage to an enemy, but I have been known to torch a bed."

"They can be treacherous."

The smile he gave me did weird things to my belly, and I tried to ignore the butterflies kicking around in there as my gaze fell to his lips. I jerked my eyes away and focused on the wall over his shoulder. When he ran his fingers over my cheek, it took all I had not to jump on him again, but we were supposed to be discussing something here.

"I can also see souls!" I blurted to distract my traitorous body.

His fingers stilled on my neck, right over the last place he bit me, before it fell away. "You can what?"

I could think a little more clearly now that he wasn't touching me, but I was acutely aware of his body only inches away from mine.

"All my life, I've been able to see a person's soul," I said. "Looking at them, I can tell you if they're good or bad. Those with twisted souls are... well, they're hideous inside, and I can see it. Of course, it doesn't work for demons because they have no soul, but I've always known when to stay away from certain people."

His brow furrowed as his gaze ran over my face. "That's... fascinating."

"And strange, but it's pretty cool too. Though, I don't think it's an ability I have because I'm part demon. Since demons don't have souls, there's no reason for any demon to possess such an ability. I think it's an entirely human ability. My dad swore my grandma was an empath, and she told him *her* mom could see the future; I never met either of them, but I believe I inherited something from them."

"Are you sure you're part demon?" he asked. "Maybe you're something else."

"What else would I be?"

"Angel."

I frowned before shaking my head. "Angels can't produce fire."

"The offspring of the fallen angels can; look at River. And seeing a person's soul sounds more angelic than demonic to me, but we can ask Raphael or Caim."

"I sure don't act like an angel," I muttered.

He ran his hand down my side. "Which is great for me."

When I smiled at him, his eyes latched onto my tiny fangs. We had things to discuss, but I couldn't resist running my tongue over my lips. Just as I knew they would, his eyes followed my tongue.

"The demon I spoke with said they're discovering other human and demon mixes and they're all revealing themselves differently. Some remain mostly human but are immortal while others have developed demon parts such as horns and tails."

"Interesting," he said.

"I can see *your* soul," I said.

I rested my hand on his chest over the place where his beautiful soul was strongest. The way he made me feel terrified me; I'd never had my heart broken and didn't want to start now. But at least the warmth of his soul let me know he was a good man. Whatever hurt he inflicted on others wasn't intentional. I doubted that would matter if I continued to get closer to him and was left behind.

I removed my hand from his chest and rested it on the bed. I would *not* move it again.

"I don't understand how I can see your soul if you're a demon," I said.

"I was once human."

The revelation made me do a double take. "You're like me?"

"No. Last year, when we were traveling to the gateway in the hopes of River being able to close it, we were attacked by canagh demons. They took Erin and me to their nest. I believed that was the end for us, but River and Vargas followed us. During the ensuing fight, River killed Lilitu, the queen of that group of canaghs. However, when River hit Lilitu with her lifeforce, she accidentally threw the queen into me. Lilitu sliced me open as she fell on me and her blood mixed with mine while I was dying. I didn't realize what was happening to me at the time, but I survived the transformation into a demon."

"Wow," I breathed. "I didn't know a human could become a demon in such a way."

"It is possible, but not all survive it. Corson's Chosen, Wren, became a demon the same way."

Forgetting my resolve to keep my hand on the bed, I rested it on his chest and tapped my fingers against him while I studied his soul. "That explains the soul then; a human who transforms must not lose it. I mean, your soul wouldn't get pushed out of your body, would it?"

"Obviously not."

"Fascinating."

When he smiled at me, my heart did a strange flip. My gaze fell to his lips again, and before I knew what I intended, I leaned forward to kiss him. Before our lips could meet, he turned his head away, and like he was my Great-Aunt Dee, I found myself kissing his cheek.

Mortification burned through me, but somehow, I managed a smile as I removed my hand from his chest and ran it through my hair. I focused on the wall again as I tried not to bolt from the bed and this house. If I did, he would know how embarrassed I was, though I was pretty sure my red cheeks gave me away.

Idiot! You stupid idiot!

Usually, I wasn't so hard on myself, but I *knew* better. One thing I'd learned about demons since I started sleeping with them was they didn't like to kiss. I was fine with it as I was trying to learn their ways and settling into the "don't get attached" mindset they had toward sex, but for one dumb second, I'd forgotten and slipped back into my human ways.

Hawk grasped my chin and turned my head toward him. I tried to jerk my chin from his grasp, but he held onto me as his indigo eyes burned into mine. I restrained myself from punching him in the face.

"It's not you; it's me," he said.

My mouth almost came unhinged. I'd *never* expected to hear *that* line!

What the actual fuck? I wanted to hit him. No, I would kick him in the nuts. No, I was going to walk out of this house and never see him again. He'd pulled the most tired, cowardly line of all time on me; he wasn't worth the punch in the face or the castration I itched to deliver.

"It *really* is me, Aisling," he said, as if he could read my mind. But if he could, he would be protecting his nuts, and he wasn't. "I can't kiss anyone because the kiss of a canagh demon enslaves their lover."

I couldn't figure out if he was lying or not, but the stark look in his eyes tugged at my heart, and I found myself relaxing.

"It's true," he murmured.

When his eyes fell to my mouth and he ran his finger over my lips, the hunger in his gaze stole my breath. Maybe he was lying, but he couldn't fake the yearning he exuded.

"Before I knew what I was becoming and what my kiss could do to another, I accidentally enslaved a woman."

An unexpected bolt of jealousy tore through me, and my nails dug into my palms as I tried to control it. The last time I was jealous of anyone was Mary Lou Driscoll in second grade. The only thing on my Christmas list that year was a golden retriever puppy, but when I ran downstairs Christmas morning, there was no puppy beneath my tree.

There was one under Mary Lou's though.

When she came to school with pictures of her adorable puppy, I just *knew* Santa got the wrong address. Mary Lou was a brat; she lived three doors down from us, and when our parents got together, she would break my toys, pull my hair, and boss me around. My parents said to ignore her, but it was impossible to ignore someone who kept trying to stick your Barbie in your Easy-Bake Oven.

She knew Barbie wasn't edible.

Santa *must* have made a mistake. Mary Lou didn't deserve a puppy, but *I* did. When I went home and told my parents about Santa's mix-up, I demanded they write and tell him. And when they finished letting Santa know about his mistake, they had to take me to Mary Lou's house so I could get *my* present.

Unable to calm me and unable to convince me that I couldn't take Mary Lou's puppy, my parents finally told me there was no Santa. They hadn't given me a puppy because they couldn't afford one right now. I didn't know if I was more devastated over the news of Santa, or that there hadn't been a mix-up and Mary Lou didn't have *my* dog.

Now, looking back, I realized I'd been acting like a bigger brat than Mary Lou, but she really was a bitch. The war hadn't changed that about her. I hadn't seen her in years, but the last time I ran into her was right before I came to the wall. At the time, she was sticking her tongue down the throat of my best friend's boyfriend. It was the first time I slapped her before kicking him in the shin, and it felt *amazing.*

Mary Lou always wanted what everyone else had or desired; hence, why she asked her parents for a golden retriever. She knew how much I wanted that puppy. And Mary Lou always got what she wanted.

I didn't know what became of her after I left home. I hoped she found some happiness in this messed-up world because I now realized how unhappy she was. She'd seemed to have it all, but something inside her was missing.

Pulling myself from the past, I focused on Hawk again. "What happened to the woman you enslaved?"

"She died but not before she went... well, a little over the top. She started to stalk me." Anguish filled his eyes before he closed them. "Sarah had no control over herself and no concern for her life. I considered her a freak until I learned I was the one who made her like that. Then I felt sorry for her and hated myself. What happened between us was the kiss of death for the woman she'd been before me."

I couldn't stop myself from running my hands over his chest to soothe him. "I'm sorry."

He shrugged, but I sensed his lingering tension when his head turned toward me. "I won't make that mistake again. So, when I say it's not you, it's me, I am telling the truth." He cupped my cheek in his hand as he stared at my mouth. "Because I would very much like to know what your mouth tastes like."

How this man could have me contemplating maiming him one minute and longing to snuggle into his arms the next was a mystery to me, but he did it with ease. He might drive me crazy before he walked out of my life, but I couldn't deny the ride to Insanityville tempted me.

I hesitated before replying, "Okay."

Not being able to kiss him was disappointing, but no matter how good he made me feel, I preferred not to spend eternity chasing Hawk around like some lovesick schoolgirl. Death was a far preferable option.

"So, back to these fangs." I pointed at my mouth as I recalled what started this whole conversation. "Why do I suddenly have them?"

"I'd assumed you knew, but if you weren't raised as a demon, you wouldn't," he murmured more to himself than to me. "You have fangs now because you are *my* Chosen, and we have claimed each other as such."

The ground lurched out from under me.

CHAPTER THIRTEEN

Hawk

I'd never expected my Chosen to look like she was going to throw up after bonding with me, but that was exactly how Aisling looked. Her face paled, and her hand went to her mouth as she stared at me. In the shadows of the room, her eyes were nearly black, but the moonlight seeping around the curtains illuminated the pretty, paler flecks of brown in them.

She was beautiful, and she was mine, despite that she still looked ready to vomit. I cupped her cheek and ran my thumb across the delicate curve of her jaw before brushing my thumb over her lips. I would give almost anything to taste her and learn the stroke of her tongue, but I could never risk doing to Aisling what I did to Sarah.

I moved my thumb away.

"But... but how is that possible?" she whispered.

"That's the way demons work."

"So, I guess that rules out the possibility of me being an angel instead of a demon?"

I pondered this for a minute. "Probably, but I still think it's worth asking one of the angels about your ability to see souls."

She didn't blink as she continued to stare at me. "Are you saying we're supposed to be bound together for eternity now?"

"Yes."

"I'm only twenty-five."

"I'm only twenty-six."

"I wasn't looking to settle down. I was just looking for a... a..."

"Good fuck?"

I twisted the sheets in my hands at the idea of her with another man, but of course, there were other men. She wasn't a virgin that first night. She lived with the demons, and she *was* a demon, which meant there were probably a fair number of men before me.

I wanted to kill *every* one of them, and I would if one of them dared to touch her again. Taking calming breaths, I gritted my teeth against my overwhelming impulse to have their blood staining my hands as I tore them to pieces. Enough blood spilled yesterday, but I'd never felt this possessive of anyone before.

"That's exactly what I was looking for," she said, though I detected a hint of hurt and annoyance in her clipped tone. Then her eyes narrowed on me. "I certainly wasn't trying to trap a man."

I almost laughed, but there was nothing funny about this. "And I wasn't trying to trap a woman. I was also looking for a good time."

She smiled halfheartedly. "It was a good time."

"Yes, it was."

The best time I'd ever had with a woman, and my hunger was still more satisfied with her than with anyone else before her. Even after the battle, and the fact I hadn't taken as much from her as I did with some of my other partners, I was still more sated than ever before. A Chosen made a demon stronger and, in my case, she also nourished me more.

She was also an end to my lonely existence—a lifeline in a world I was drowning in before. But I suspected Aisling, and every other woman, did not want to hear they were bound to a man who was relieved to have them.

It would probably result in her punching me in the face. I hadn't missed the fury that blazed through her when I told her that it wasn't her, it was me when it came to kissing. I couldn't believe those words had come from my mouth; I'd always scoffed at the guys who uttered that cliché saying, but the words popped out before I could stop them.

"Maybe we can meet up again in a year or something," she said.

My hands tore into the sheets. "You want other men?"

"I didn't say that, but I'm not ready to settle down. It's not part of my plan right now."

"And what is your plan?" I grated, which only caused her eyes to narrow more.

"To survive the next day and then the next and the next."

"And you can't do that with a Chosen?"

"Look, my life has been tossed upside down numerous times; I'm not ready for another curveball right now. Maybe we can discuss this again after we've had time to think about it more. We can meet up again in six months."

"No."

She looked like I'd poked her in the eye. "No?"

"No. Maybe this isn't what either of us wanted, but it's done."

I *had* wanted to find my Chosen, but she didn't need to know that either. And what was I going to say to her? I wanted this, but I didn't know it was *you* I wanted. Another thing all women were eager to hear from the man they would spend eternity with. I didn't have much experience in sweet talk, but I knew when to keep my mouth shut.

This was not the way I expected finding my Chosen to go, but then I don't know what I'd expected. Had I thought it would be easy? No, I'd seen enough of my friends find their Chosen to know it wouldn't be easy.

As a demon, I did expect her to be more open to this, but she'd been human for more of her life than not. She'd probably expected to meet someone, date for a while, get engaged, and then get married.

"I know you weren't expecting to have sex and have your life tied to another, and neither was I, but we can't change it," I said.

Her nostrils flared as she leaned closer to me. Despite the rage she radiated, I found myself entranced by her when red flickered through her eyes. I suspected that red was another new development of her newfound demonhood. I probably should have been concerned I'd pushed her too far, she had de-nutted a demon after all, but I couldn't tear my gaze away from hers.

"I don't care who you are; you don't own or control me. If I decide it's going to change, then it will change," she said.

"The Chosen bond unites us for the rest of our lives."

"That doesn't mean we have to shack up and start playing house together. You can go on about your life, and I can go on with mine if *I* choose to."

My teeth grated together as I tried to navigate this minefield. I wanted to bend her to my will, but that was impossible. If I attempted to order her around, she'd only pull further away. My Chosen was a stubborn, infuriating woman, but I couldn't help admiring her. She was a fighter, and scared, and if I pushed her too far, we'd fight each other for the rest of our days.

I hadn't known her long, but she'd made it clear she knew what she wanted. She wasn't a woman who wavered; she was a woman who set her sights on something and got it. If she decided to spend six months without me, she would do it no matter how unhappy it made us.

"Neither of us expected this to happen, but now we have to learn to live with it," I said. "And constantly fighting each other will make for an eternity of misery."

Her eyes remained narrowed on me, and those cute little fangs were still on display, but her body relaxed, and the red vanished from her eyes. However, I sensed she'd hit me if I said the wrong thing. The only problem was, I didn't know the right thing to say.

"We may not have expected this, but we should make the most of it," I said.

"And what does that mean?"

What did that mean? Unable to resist, I rested my hand against her cheek and ran my thumb over her lips while I pondered her question. And then I said the words that probably no other canagh demon had ever uttered.

"It means we get to know each other better... outside of the bedroom."

She quirked an eyebrow, but I saw a tiny smile tugging at the corners of her lips. "And what if we discover we hate each other?"

The possibility of an eternity with a woman I despised made my stomach clench. What if the two demons in the Chosen relationship hated each other? I'd never considered the possibility before; I'd only ever seen them in love. However, it could be possible they started out hating each other, or that centuries of telling the same demon to pick up their socks made them ready to kill.

I would rather spend the rest of my life alone than with someone I loathed and who hated me in return. Unfortunately, I didn't have that option.

"That's something we'll deal with if it happens," I said. "But so far, I like what I know about you."

She rolled her eyes. "You only know what it's like to fuck me."

I leaned closer to whisper in her ear. "And I've more than liked every second of it."

Grasping her hand, I enclosed it on my hardening cock. For the first time since becoming a canagh demon, I wasn't ravenous, but I still couldn't get enough of her. She melted against me before pulling away.

"No," she said as she released my shaft. "You said we should get to know each other better *outside* of the bedroom, and we're going to do that. No more touching."

I bit back my groan of disappointment and leaned back, but I kept my hand on her hip until she lifted it and rested it on the bed. She patted it before she removed her hand. I could almost taste her desire as her nipples tightened, and I imagined bending my head to kiss her flesh.

Seeming to sense my thoughts, she flung back the blankets and scooted down the mattress to the end of the bed. Rolling onto my back, I propped myself against the headboard as she jumped up. I admired the sway of her hips and firm ass as she strode over to the closet.

CHAPTER FOURTEEN

Hawk

She pulled open the closet doors to reveal a couple of my shirts and pants within; she removed a shirt and slipped it on. The bottom brushed her knees and exposed the curve of her breasts as she buttoned it. She had no idea seeing her in my shirt only made her more alluring, and I wasn't going to tell her as I folded my hands behind my head.

"I also know you're a fighter," I said. "At any time, you could have given up in that battle."

"And died."

"But you didn't."

She lifted her head from the buttons and in the dim glow of the moon, I saw the anguish on her face. "So many others did."

I almost climbed off the bed and went to her, but I stopped myself. We were getting to know each other, and she'd said no touching. "I know. But we damaged them more than they damaged us yesterday, and we *are* going to finish them."

"I hope so." She walked over and sat in the chair in the corner, putting some distance between us.

Smart woman.

I watched as she settled onto the chair with elegant grace. She pulled the shirt down when it rode up her thigh to expose the curve of her ass. I tongued my fangs when they throbbed with the need to sink into her flesh, but I didn't move.

"Why don't you tell me about yourself," she said.

"What would you like to know?"

"What's your last name?"

"Hawkson."

She pursed her mouth as she crossed her legs. I admired the muscles in her calf while she kicked her leg in the air. "So that's why they call you Hawk."

"Yes."

"Then what's your first name?"

I glanced at the ceiling; my first name wasn't something I shared regularly, and few knew it, but I couldn't keep it from her. "Sue."

"*Sue?*"

"Yes. My mom was a big Johnny Cash fan."

She gawked at me before chuckling. "She named you after the song 'A Boy Named Sue'?"

"You know the song?"

"One of my daddy's favorites."

The hint of her southern accent was thicker when she said this.

"Then you know the story in the song," I said.

"The boy's father leaves him, but before he goes, he names him Sue in the hopes it will make him tougher. Your dad left?"

"He died in a plane crash before I was born."

"I'm sorry."

I shrugged. "It would have been nice to know him, but that was never an option, and I accepted it a long time ago. My mom told me stories about him, and he was a good man. Dax, my stepfather, was my dad. I was two when they started dating, and he always treated me like his son, even after my sisters were born."

"*Was* your dad?"

"He died of cancer when I was fourteen."

"I'm sorry."

This time, I couldn't shrug it off. I hadn't known my real dad, but my stepfather's death devastated us all.

"It was a… difficult time." Those words couldn't begin to explain how shitty that time in our lives was. "The war occurred two years before he died. Until then, we never had to struggle for anything. Dax was a doctor; we had a big house, and he'd planned well enough that his life insurance and savings would keep us going after his death."

"But money didn't matter after the war."

"Exactly. When you go from having luxury cars, a boat, and designer clothes to nothing, it's a bit of a shock. We still had our house; it's not like the banks were around to take those back anymore, but trying to keep it protected from looters or those trying to upgrade their housing was difficult. We abandoned it a few weeks after the war."

"Where did you go?"

"All our family was in Connecticut, and after the war, the bridges to Cape Cod were shut down, so we had no way of getting to them. We lived in our car until we moved into a small, abandoned ranch house that I discovered. We were fortunate in the beginning because people would trade food for Dax's services, but he got sick a year later and was gone by the next year."

"What did you do afterward?" Aisling asked.

"In those first months, I spent a lot of time begging for food in the streets and bringing home whatever scraps I could. My mom had learned a lot from Dax and tried to keep his practice going, but she wasn't as good at it, and people didn't trust her as much, but we still got some food that way. Neither of us wanted my sisters on the street, so we tried to keep them out of it, but they weren't stupid, and by then they were far from naïve."

"What did they do?" Aisling asked.

"They would sneak out to beg for food too, but when I found out, I told my mom. It was the first time I ever saw her lose her temper and hit one of us. I'm not sure who cried more, my mom or my sister. That was when I knew something had to change, but I wasn't sure what to do. By then, I'd stopped being a cute kid people felt sorry for; I'd grown five inches and become a nuisance.

"Because I was taller, I tried to volunteer for the wall at fifteen, but one of my old teachers ratted me out. After that, I started stealing. It's not something I'm proud of, but I didn't know what else to do. I refused to let something happen to one of my sisters because they were on the streets, and I couldn't stand the broken look in my mom's eyes anymore. She'd always been young and radiant, but she aged ten years in a matter of months."

Aisling pulled her feet onto the chair and wrapped her arm around her legs while she studied me. "They never caught you?"

"No, thankfully." If someone did catch me, they might have killed me instead of turning me over to the Guards for punishment. "After I turned sixteen, I volunteered for the wall and made sure they never had to beg for anything again." The government took care of the families of volunteers.

"My mom cried so hard she soaked my shirt, but we knew I had to go," I continued. "I used to write to them every day, and when the trucks came back from their yearly volunteer trip to my town, I'd have hundreds of letters from her and my sisters. I only read a few every day so they would last all year."

"You used to write them?" she asked.

Unable to hold her gaze, I stared at the curtains covering the windows as anger and sorrow churned in my chest. "Lucifer killed them after he fled Hell."

Her hand flew to her mouth as she gasped. "I'm... I'm so sorry."

Only a little over a year had passed since Lucifer slaughtered my family; the grief of their loss still twisted like a knife in my chest. Even with the dangers of the Wilds to distract me, I'd spent a great deal of time grieving the loss of the family I volunteered to save.

I signed my life away to make sure they survived, and in a fit of rage, Lucifer destroyed them, everyone in my town, River's town, and another town bordering ours. I hadn't met River until we were both at the wall, but we'd grown up only miles away from each other.

"Hawk..."

Her words trailed off when I looked at her, and she started to rise, but I held up my hand to halt her. "Don't come to me because you feel sorry for me. You'll come to me because you're ready for me and everything that comes with us, but not before then."

She opened her mouth to protest but then closed it again and settled onto the chair. Her eyes gleamed in the darkness as she studied me before asking, "How many sisters did you have?"

"Three and they were pretty awesome."

She smiled as she propped her elbow on the arm of the chair and rested her head on her hand. "What were their names?"

It took me a minute to answer around the lump in my throat. "The oldest was Jen. She had hair the same color as mine and clear blue eyes. She was so serious about everything and had this analytical way of looking at everything. As she got older, she would spend hours reading books and absorbing knowledge that she *had* to share with everyone."

I couldn't help but smile as I recalled her following me around with her nose in a book while she told me about the different rock formations. I'd found it endlessly annoying and would often shut a door in front of her just to have her walk into it because she was still staring at her book.

"You're a jerk!" she'd yell at me and then proceed to keep

reading until I put on my headphones and cranked up the music to drowned her out.

Then, the war came, and our lives turned upside down. Jen stopped reading books to focus all her energy on making sure her younger sisters were taken care of while everyone else worked to bring in food.

"Sherry was my middle sister," I said. "She was... she was like *no* one I've ever met before. I've never known anyone who loved life as much as her. *Everything* delighted her, and she had this beautiful laugh. When she laughed, people stopped what they were doing to look at her, and they would smile or laugh too because it was impossible not to laugh with Sherry. She had this beautiful blonde hair and blue eyes that never stopped twinkling. My mom used to swear she smiled in her sleep, and I believed her.

"And the youngest was Judy. She was painfully shy but the sweetest of the three. She'd bring me a book to read her, curl up in my lap, and stick her thumb in her mouth. When she fell asleep, I'd sit there for hours waiting for her to wake up again because I couldn't bring myself to disturb her."

If I let myself think about it, I could still feel her silken brown hair against my chin as her brown eyes stared at me. Her tiny body had been so warm, and she was so trusting.

"I loved all my sisters, but Judy had a special place in my heart. She was almost two when my stepdad died, and she looked at me like a father figure. I found her body first, and what Lucifer did to her..."

I looked at the wall as the memory caused my eyes to burn; I feared I might choke on the lump in my throat. I volunteered to keep my family safe, and I'd failed them. If I hadn't volunteered, if I'd been there...

If I'd been there, I'd be dead too. I never could have stopped all the fallen angels and demons who descended on them. I would have died for them, and they still would have died too. And if I hadn't volunteered, one or all of us might have starved to death, or I could have been caught stealing and been killed.

I'd done the right thing when I volunteered, but I'd always regret not being there for them at the end.

I never heard Aisling move, but the heat of her palm branded my arm when she rested it against my skin.

"I'm... I'm—" And because she couldn't find any other words, she repeated what she'd already said twice to me. "—sorry."

I hated her pity, but I couldn't deny her touch. I grasped her hand and held it as she stared at me with tears in her eyes.

"Don't cry for me, Aisling, and don't feel sorry for me," I said as I wiped away the tear sliding down her cheek. "So many lost a lot when the gateway opened. I had more time with my family than a lot of other people got to experience with theirs."

"It's still not right."

"We wouldn't be here if everything in the world went right." I squeezed her hand again before releasing it and smiling at her to soften my next words. "No more touching."

She gave me a sad smile before taking her hand away. She muttered, "Stupid rule," as she walked away, and I almost laughed but didn't bother to remind her she'd been the one to set it.

Settling back into the chair, she drew her legs up against her chest again. When she looked away from me, I saw her wipe away another tear.

"Is there anything else you'd like to know about me, Aisling?"

"I'm sure there's a lot more to learn about you, Hawk, but I think that's enough for now."

"So it's my turn to ask the questions?"

"It's your turn."

CHAPTER FIFTEEN

Aisling

"Where are you from?" Hawk asked.

"Virginia."

"How old were you when you volunteered?"

I suspected his rapid-fire questions were a way to distract him from the bad memories I dredged up with my questions. I wanted to kick myself in the ass for the sadness in his eyes. It took all I had not to rest my hand over my heart and sob for the family he lost.

"Eighteen," I said. "I was going to volunteer at sixteen, but my mom begged me to wait until I was eighteen, so I did. We weren't bad off after the war. I mean, things weren't great by any means, but my dad was a hunter and fisherman, and we lived in a pretty rural area, so we got by on game and fish.

"I'd only gone hunting with a bow a few times before then as my mom didn't think I was old enough to handle a rifle. We used to fight over it, not because I was in a rush to go in the woods and kill things, but because I was eager to learn how to use a gun. She didn't argue about it after the war, and though I was finally getting a chance to learn how to shoot, I wasn't excited about it anymore."

"Why were you so eager to leave home if things weren't bad there?"

"Because before the war, *all* I wanted was to travel the world. I planned to join the Marines and serve my country while going to different places. I never wanted kids, so I planned to be career military, and when I retired, I was going to travel to all the places I didn't see while serving."

"You don't want kids?"

"No. Don't get me wrong, I like them, but they were never part of my plan. However..." I tried to think how to explain it to him. "I think before the gateway opened, not wanting kids was more about being young and only thinking about freedom. The last thing I wanted was a child tying me down, but I might have changed my mind. And now it's about... well, look at this world. This is no place for children."

"Maybe not right now," he said, "but we're going to make it a world for them, and if the human world is going to continue, then children are necessary."

"Rebuilding the population isn't a reason to have children."

"Then what is?"

I bit my lip as I pondered this. "I guess there are many reasons, but for me, it would be love and having enough trust in someone to believe they would always be there for our children and me."

"Those are good reasons."

And there were a lot more reasons not to have children, something I'd have to be more aware of now that I'd found my Chosen. Sex and life were a lot simpler when the guy I was with couldn't get me pregnant. I rested my chin on my knee and studied Hawk. I bet he'd make a fantastic dad, but if finding my Chosen hadn't been in my plans, then having children wasn't even on my radar, especially after yesterday.

I suppressed a shudder as images of the battle and blood-soaked field played through my mind. If the craetons succeeded in getting past us, the children of this world wouldn't exist. Closing my eyes, I swallowed the lump in my throat. I may not want kids of my own, but I'd kill over and over again to keep them from ever having to witness something like what happened yesterday.

"So, you volunteered so you could travel to the wall?" Hawk asked.

I focused on him to keep from being lost in the screams of yesterday. As I stared into his indigo eyes, the sounds of steel clashing against steel and the flashes of blood dimmed until I could breathe normally again.

"This place isn't exactly the Great Wall or the pyramids, but it's not my hometown either. And I've done some traveling since coming to the wall, not much, but Massachusetts isn't Virginia. Not to mention, I've met creatures from Hell and become one of them, so things are a lot different than they once were."

"I see."

"I volunteered to go into the Wilds," I said. "I'm one of the troops who is supposed to be returning with you."

Who knew what would happen now that there were a lot fewer troops to guard the wall.

"The Wilds are dangerous," he said.

"So is the wall."

"Not like the Wilds. There are things out there that no one has seen in thousands of years."

"And I'm going to fight them. After yesterday, I don't think there are any Hell creatures left that could surprise me."

He glanced away from me to stare at the window to my right. "Believe me, there are. I've been to Hell, I've seen a lot of what it had to offer, and I'm still amazed by what we encounter in the Wilds. You're safer here."

His words intrigued me far too much for me to acknowledge the last part of his sentence. "You've been in Hell?"

"I went in with River."

They were friends, but it was still weird to hear him use the queen's name in such a casual way. "What was it like?"

"It's what you'd imagine Hell to be like—hot, gruesome, full of monsters and spirits, but there was also something beautiful about it."

"So it was like Earth, except we have seasons."

A small smile quirked the corners of his mouth, but sadness shone in his beautiful eyes. "I guess so. There was a forest in Hell with these trees that came alive; it was so terrifying and magical. Those trees are some of the deadliest things I've ever seen, but they were also gentle and protective of the nymphs and River. They're amazing, and some of them made it to Earth. Have you seen the calamut trees yet?"

"I don't think so."

"You would know."

I should hear about deadly trees and want to stay far away, but I found myself intrigued. Before I could ask him anything more, a board squeaked in the hall before a knock sounded on the door.

"It's time to get up, Hawk. We have to meet Kobal in an hour," Vargas said.

Aisling

Erin sat at the table with a plate of toast in front of her and a glass of orange juice. I'd seen the woman a few times in town, but she hadn't joined us when Vargas started training again. I had seen her working with the queen and the queen's brothers before Vargas returned to training, but it had been a good month or so since I last saw her.

She smiled at us when we entered the kitchen, and I couldn't help but admire how radiant her soul was. Erin pushed back her chair and rose to hug Hawk. I focused on the toast as I ignored the twinge of jealousy their embrace caused. They were just friends, but I didn't like anyone touching him. I almost groaned when I realized how much the Chosen bond was messing with my head, but I stopped myself.

My stomach rumbled when Vargas tossed some more bacon on the stove and it sizzled. I could go days without food if I fed on wraiths, but the scents in this kitchen were close to making me drool as I recalled how good food tasted.

I stared at Vargas's soul as he flipped the bacon. It wasn't as vibrant as Erin's, but it was strong and had a streak of red like Hawk's. Their souls were a good combination; whereas Erin's came across as warm and open, Vargas's was more reserved, but they tempered each other nicely.

"I'm glad you're okay after yesterday." Erin kept hold of Hawk's arms as she pulled away to examine him. "That was a vicious battle."

"You saw?" he asked.

"I may have snuck out to watch some of it from the wall," she said, and Vargas grunted in disapproval.

When Erin released him and stepped away, I spotted the ball of golden light in her belly and barely managed to stop myself from exclaiming *aw*! The baby's soul flashed brighter with every beat of its tiny heart. Erin's stomach had a slight roundness to it that I wouldn't have noticed if not for the soul inside her. With as radiant as Erin's soul was, she could have been pregnant the last time I saw her too, but her glow covered the baby.

This was why she'd been in the hall with the children and why she wasn't training with us. I understood why Hawk was so confused by her not being a part of the battle; he didn't know about the baby yet.

"At least more of the horsemen are dead," Erin said as she sat at the table again and lifted a piece of toast.

"And most of their troops *have* to be dead," Vargas said as he removed the bacon from the stove.

"I don't know," Hawk said. "I don't even know where they all came from as we've cleared a fair amount of the Wilds. And for them to have attacked us with so many at the wall, they had to have been hiding somewhere."

"But where?" Vargas asked.

"In the Abyss," Erin said.

"No, Amalia and the jinn still have control over the Abyss," Hawk said.

"What is the Abyss?" I asked.

"It's a separate plane ruled by the jinn," Hawk answered. "But we took it back from the horsemen and the jinn who sided with them."

"There are still some jinn fighting for the other side," Vargas said. "Maybe they've taken it back from Amalia and Magnus."

"No," Hawk said. "They'd send word if they lost control, and it's only been a couple of weeks since we last saw them. There is no way the horsemen gathered and moved that many troops into the Abyss in such a short time. They've been amassing those demons all year and hiding them somewhere."

"But where?" I asked.

Hawk ran his fingers through his hair and tugged at the ends of it. "I don't know."

"Maybe they've discovered another plane, like the Abyss," Erin suggested.

"Or maybe there's something else out there entirely," I said.

"Whatever it is, we have to find it, and them, before they can recover enough to come at us again," Hawk said.

"I didn't see any jinn yesterday," Vargas told them.

"Neither did I," Hawk said.

The crackle of the bacon was the only sound in the kitchen. I shifted as I tried to think of where the horsemen and angels could have been hiding, but I didn't know the Wilds, and I certainly didn't know anything about different planes.

"They must have believed they were strong enough to move against us," Hawk said as he pulled out a chair and looked to me.

I stared at him for too long before figuring out he was holding the chair for me. "Oh, thank you," I said as I sat.

"Would you like anything?" Vargas asked us.

"No," Hawk said.

"I wouldn't mind some toast, bacon, and coffee," I said.

Erin coughed as she choked on her toast, and Vargas turned to stare at me. Erin sipped her orange juice before speaking. "I'm sorry, I thought you were a demon."

"I am, but I was once a human, and sometimes I still eat."

"Interesting," Erin murmured as she studied me.

"I can get it," I said as I started to rise.

Vargas waved me down. "I've got it."

I started to protest, but he was already pouring coffee into a mug for me.

"How do you take it?" he asked.

"Just a little milk," I said.

"So are you like Hawk?" Erin asked.

"No." I took the warm mug Vargas handed me and blew on it before taking a sip. "I didn't know, until recently, that I have a demon ancestor. The opening of the gateway activated their DNA. Then, one day, I stopped aging and started setting things on fire."

"That must have been a surprise," Vargas said.

"A tiny one," I said with a smile.

"Are you returning to the Wilds with us?" Hawk asked the couple.

Erin and Vargas exchanged a look as he placed a plate of toast before me. I pulled the butter dish over and kept my eyes focused on it as I spread some on the toast. It wasn't my place to tell Hawk about the baby, but it felt weird knowing something about his close friends that he didn't.

"No," Erin finally said. "We planned to see this battle through until the end, but" —her hand fell to her belly, and she grinned at Hawk— "we're going to have a baby."

The tick of a clock in another room resonated through the house as Hawk stared at her before laughing loudly and rising. Before Erin could react, he picked her up and crushed her against him. When he set her back on her feet, she looked like she might throw up, but Hawk didn't notice as he turned and embraced Vargas. They slapped each other on the back as Hawk congratulated him.

"Congratulations," I said.

"Thank you; it's still early, and we're a little afraid..." Her voice trailed off as she rested her hand on her belly. "We're fourteen weeks, so we're past the twelve-week mark; things should be okay— no, they *will* be okay."

Her apprehension was evident in her voice and face as she rubbed her stomach. I opened my mouth to tell her the baby was a strong, vital piece of life within her, but stopped myself. It might reassure her, but I doubted anyone wanted to hear a stranger tell them how glowing their fetus was. Instead, I nibbled at my toast and tried to go unnoticed while they discussed their plans for the baby and this house.

"Congratulations to you too," Erin said.

"I'm sorry, what?" I asked when I realized she was speaking to me.

She waved a hand at her neck before gesturing toward mine, and I realized she was pointing at the bites Hawk left on me.

"We've been around enough demons to recognize the mark of a Chosen. Congratulations."

"Oh... ah..." I looked to Hawk for help, but he smiled smugly at me. Determined to wipe that smile off his face, I grinned at him as I said, "We're not so sure about that yet."

CHAPTER SIXTEEN

Aisling

Hawk's smile vanished while Erin and Vargas exchanged a confused look. Now, it was my turn to smile smugly as I took another bite of toast. I wore Hawk's brand for all the world to see, but that didn't mean we'd resolved this.

Hawk crossed his arms over his chest. "Aisling feels we may have rushed things."

I couldn't stop myself from snorting; that was the understatement of the year. "We're getting to know each other better before we decide our future."

"That's... ah... always a good thing," Vargas said.

"Hawk can make you want to stab him, but he's a good man," Erin said.

I couldn't argue with that.

A knock sounded on the front door, but before anyone could move to answer it, the creak of it opening sounded from the other room. Something clicked against the hardwood floors, and I put my toast down. What was that?

My hand fell to the side of Hawk's far too big pants and

gripped the handle of my knife as a voice called from the other room, "It's just me, humans and ex-human. I've come for a visit with my favorite girl. If you're ill-prepared, then tell me to go."

Erin smiled before she called out, "We're in the kitchen, Lix."

They all relaxed, but I remained tensed to kill until one of the creepy skelleins stepped into the kitchen. He wore a checkered tie with a picture of Porky Pig on it. A red fedora, tilted slightly to the side, was perched on his head. The outfit was absurd, but I'd seen far worse on some of them.

His jawbones pulled into a grin, and his feet clicked against the floor as he walked toward Erin. "There's my favorite riddle genius!" he cried as he opened his arms to her.

"Lix," Erin said, and the radiant smile on her face was one of love and friendship as she rose to embrace him. "I'm so glad you're okay."

"It takes far more than a demon army to take me out," he said. "My beautiful unicorn tie didn't fare so well, but that's no skin off these bones."

I couldn't help chuckling as Vargas rose from the table and gestured for Lix to take his seat. Lix removed his fedora as he settled at the table and removed a flask from the pouch tied around his waist. I'd seen some of the other skelleins in camp, but I'd never been this close to one or seen them drink.

Lix took a long swallow before recapping his flask and returning it to his pouch. My hands gripped the table as I resisted looking under it to see if the liquid was pouring all over the floor.

"Isn't it a little early for drinking?" Erin asked.

"It's never too early for fun, my dear. And after yesterday..." He retrieved his flask and drank some more. "There are only four skelleins left, including me."

"Oh, Lix." Erin rested her hand over his.

The skeletal creature sat with his head bowed before he smiled and patted her hand with his other one. "Some of us are still on the other side of the world. We'll see them again."

"Of course you will," Erin said.

I couldn't stop myself from marveling over the closeness of their relationship. Out of all the demons I'd met, the skelleins unnerved me most. Those eye sockets may be empty, but they bored straight into me, and how could they possibly retain liquid when they were nothing but bones?

When Lix's empty eye sockets swung toward me, I felt them examining every inch of me as Lix took another shot of alcohol. Then he turned back to Erin. "How are you both doing? We haven't had much time to catch up."

"We're good," Erin said and took Vargas's hand when he rested it on her shoulder. "Or at least we were. Yesterday..."

Tears filled Erin's eyes, and she wiped them hastily away. The reminder of yesterday caused my stomach to turn, and I set my remaining toast on the plate.

"Yesterday was bad," Lix agreed. "But many of our enemies were destroyed."

"And we do have some good news," Erin said.

I stared at the wall while she told him about the baby, and they exchanged more hugs. I barely listened to their words as I tried to decide my next step. I had to find out how Sandy and Zanta were; as much as I dreaded the answer, I had to know it.

"I needed this good news!" Lix said as he sat again and slapped a hand on the table. "We must celebrate!"

"*After* the baby is born, we can celebrate. When we know everything is going to be okay." Erin rested her hand protectively over her belly. "But not until then."

"It's a very healthy baby," I said.

I didn't realize I'd spoken the words out loud until all their eyes swung toward me. My mouth went dry, and I gulped down my coffee. I'd intended to keep my mouth shut, but sometimes the damn thing had a mind of its own.

"Sorry." I wiped my mouth with the back of my hand. "I, uh…"

I'd been trying not to look at Hawk, but now my gaze darted to him. When he clasped the hand I was digging into my knee, I was annoyed by how much his touch soothed me. I wasn't ready to have my life hinge on the existence of someone else, but I couldn't deny the connection between us.

"How do you know that?" Erin asked.

Instead of shoving Hawk's hand away, my fingers entwined with his while I spoke. "Ever since I was a child, I could see a person's soul. Unlike everyone else in this world, I know who to stay away from by looking at them. The baby inside you has a strong heart and a beautiful soul."

Tears filled Erin's eyes as her hand flattened over her belly. "Really?"

"Yes."

"How… interesting," Lix murmured as he took another drink.

"Is your ability to do that because of your demon ancestry?" Vargas asked me.

"Demons can't see souls," Lix said. "We don't have souls to see, so there's no need for such a talent. That's a human trait, and it's a fascinating one."

I shifted uncomfortably when they all looked at me again.

"Did you have any abilities manifest after becoming a demon?" Vargas asked.

I removed my hand from Hawk's and rested it on the table, palm up. I stared at it until orange sparks danced across my fingertips and a small flame sputtered to life in my palm. I jerked back when the fire went from being a couple of inches high to nearly a foot tall. It didn't burn me, but it had never been so high before.

I recalled Zanta telling me that demons who found and bonded with their Chosen became stronger. Excitement and apprehension coiled in my stomach as I stared at the fire. If I wanted to walk away from Hawk, it might already be too late. But did I want to walk away?

I'd ask myself that question after I got to know him better, but I couldn't answer it now. I did know I wanted the freedom to walk away if I chose to do so, and it scared me that I might not have the choice.

"This is why my team calls me Ash," I said as I pulled myself from my troublesome thoughts. "Well, this and it's a common nickname for my name. The ability to produce fire started after I stopped aging, and it's how I learned I was a demon."

Closing my hand, I smothered the flame and lifted my coffee cup. "It's an interesting world we live in now."

"It is," Hawk murmured and sat back.

"My baby really has a beautiful soul?" Erin's question came out as more of a whisper, and I realized she was scared to ask it not because she didn't know me, but because she was anxious about her child.

"Yes," I said and prayed nothing happened to the baby. This conversation would only make things worse if something awful occurred.

"Like its mother," Vargas said and squeezed Erin's shoulders.

She beamed at him with so much love it stole my breath; I hoped to have that kind of love one day. I glanced at Hawk from the corner of my eye. We were bound together by some quirky demon DNA, but could I love him?

He was a genuinely good man; he had the soul of a warrior, fought like a champion, and he could make my eyes roll back in my head and my body come apart like no other man, but love? I'd have to wait and see.

I hadn't planned to settle down for years, especially since I was immortal now, but I also hadn't planned on the country being torn apart and having to live with demons. Life was a series of compromises.

And at least Hawk wasn't an asshole. Many of the demons weren't bad, but some were complete assholes; I could have been stuck with one of them, or worse, a craeton. Maybe one day we could learn to love each other. I couldn't imagine spending an eternity with a man who didn't love me and who I didn't love.

"So, my dear," Lix said to Erin. "I have a riddle for you."

Erin's smile grew. "I've missed your riddles."

"And I've missed trying to stump you."

"Lix has been trying to stump Erin for over a year," Hawk said to me. "The skelleins once guarded the gateway to Hell, and for us to gain access to it, we had to pass their test."

"What was the test?" I asked.

"We had to answer three riddles. They allowed us to nominate Erin to answer for me, River, and Vargas. She was our champion and saved our asses. Since then, she has yet to get one wrong."

"You'll jinx me," Erin said.

Hawk snorted. "Hardly."

"What would have happened if you got a riddle wrong?" I asked.

"Now, nothing would happen," Erin said. "But if I got one of the original three wrong, they were going to take a pound of flesh from each of us."

I gulped.

"Those were the good old days," Lix said with a sigh.

I had no idea how to respond. He sounded so forlorn about not being able to strip the flesh from others. He continued to creep me out, but the others didn't mind that he would have skinned them.

"If we'd been demons, they would have waited for us to regenerate the flesh before asking us another riddle," Hawk said. "But as humans, we would have died."

"That's, ah..." *Gross, horrific, cruel!* I couldn't utter any of those words as I liked my flesh exactly where it was. "Terrifying."

"It was," Erin admitted.

"Now we play for fun," Lix said. "Are you ready?" he asked Erin.

"I am," Erin said.

"With pointed fangs, it sits in wait. With piercing force it doles out fate. Over bloodless victims proclaiming its might, eternally joining in a single bite. What is it?"

I pondered this as Erin sat back and crossed her legs at her ankles. Hawk gestured at my coffee mug; when I nodded, he picked it up, rose, and went to fill it. Watching the graceful movements of his body as he poured me another cup, I realized I could enjoy having him in my life.

I smiled when he returned and set the mug in front of me. "Thank you."

I almost jumped out of my chair when he kissed the top of my head before settling beside me; there was something so natural and right in the gesture. My skin prickled as my body reacted to his nearness. Even if we ended up discovering we were opposites who barely tolerated each other, we could never deny the attraction between us. It amazed me the others couldn't feel or sense it as my skin prickled and goose bumps broke out on my arms.

My attention was drawn back to Erin as she murmured the words to the riddle. Recalling the question, I tried to sort through the words, but a knock on the front door distracted me. Before anyone could rise to answer it, the door opened, and a voice shouted inside.

"Five minutes!"

A click sounded when the door closed again. "Corson," Hawk said at my confused look.

I leapt to my feet. "I've got to get dressed."

There was no way I could go to a meeting with the king and

queen while dressed in Hawk's clothes. I'd stopped caring about what others thought about my sex life a while ago, but I could *not* go before my leaders dressed in Hawk's clothes.

"It was good talking to you and thank you for breakfast," I said to Vargas and Erin. "Let me know the answer to that riddle when you get the chance."

"It's a stapler," Erin said.

"So it is," Lix said with a laugh.

CHAPTER SEVENTEEN

Aisling

Hawk and I slipped into the hall and nearly walked into a wall of bodies. I'd changed as fast as I could, but we were still a few minutes late. Demons and humans packed the hall as the king stood on the dais at the far end. The queen held her son in her arms while she surveyed the crowd with a look that promised death to anyone who came near her child.

At her feet, her youngest brother sat with a book in his hand. With his blond hair, blue eyes, and chubby little body, Bailey looked about three and a half or four years old. Her other brother, Gage, stood by her side. His lips were clamped into a firm line, his sandy blond hair was brushed back, and his brown eyes surveyed the crowd. No older than fifteen, he looked more serious than men twice his age.

Colonel Ulrich MacIntyre also stood on the dais and to the right of the queen. The colonel oversaw the humans at this section of the wall. His graying brown hair was trimmed short, and the lines on his face appeared deeper than the last time I saw him as he stood with his shoulders back.

"I've called for more troops to join us here, and they should arrive tonight or tomorrow, but we can't wait that long to go after the horsemen," the king said.

My gaze ran over the walls and the intricate symbols etched into them. In the grand scheme of things, I was relatively new to this demon world, but the power thrumming through this building radiated through every fiber of my being and made my skin tingle.

I didn't know if that power was supposed to be mine for the taking or if it would smash me to pieces, but I was tempted to see what my flame would be like in here. With the tension emanating from the bodies around me, someone might take my small fire as a threat and lop off my head.

"We'll be sending troops after the horsemen tonight," the king continued.

Hawk shifted beside me, and I stifled a small bolt of panic. He would go back into the Wilds after those *things*. I was supposed to go too, but after yesterday, the plan would change. They couldn't afford to send a bunch of troops to hunt the horsemen; even with new ones arriving, they needed as many people and demons here as they could get. They were vulnerable, and if the horsemen returned with more craetons, they might not be able to fend them off again.

Would they still send me into the Wilds?

Excitement pulsed through my veins at the possibility. I didn't have a death wish, but I was determined to help bring down the monsters who ruthlessly slaughtered so many yesterday.

Rising onto my toes, I searched for Sandy and Zanta in the crowd, but I didn't see them. I rubbed at my chest as I reminded myself that didn't mean they were dead. Humans and demons were still combing the field for our dead and injured. Sandy and Zanta could be there, guarding the wall, or in the clinic.

I'd look for them when we finished here.

The king pointed to someone in the crowd and waved them

forward. The crowd parted to reveal Corson and Bale striding toward the dais. When the queen's son let out a small squeak, one of the skelleins in a pretty blue dress emerged from the shadows behind the stage. The queen shook her head and held her son closer as the colonel and king walked to stand beside her.

Corson and Bale climbed onto the stage; their boots thudded across the wood as they strode over to join the couple before turning to face the crowd. Hawk clasped my hand and started to wind his way through the crowd toward the dais. He didn't acknowledge the disgruntled grunts of those he elbowed out of his way.

We were almost to the dais when he stopped beside a demon who was at least eight feet tall with hands that could engulf my head. Each of his three eyes was a different color—the right was green, the left orange, and the one in the center of his forehead was aqua blue.

Despite the additional eye, he was handsome with his broad cheekbones. I'd seen him around town, generally with the queen, but I'd never been this close to him before, and my neck hurt from looking up at him.

"Calah," Hawk greeted. "Lopan."

The giant nodded a greeting while the small creature at his side grunted. Lopan was another one I'd seen around town, often near the queen, but I'd never been close to the odd-looking man with brown hair that hung in ringlets to his shoulders and deep-set chestnut eyes. The ridiculous red outfit he wore had a green belt and hat. The pink toenails on his bare, hairy feet were neatly trimmed.

He flashed a mouthful of razor-sharp teeth at me when I leaned over to peer into the black pot he carried with him. I spotted the yellow liquid within before he moved it to his other hand and glowered at me over the tip of his bulbous nose. I smiled at him in the hopes he'd relax a little, but his scowl only deepened.

Note to self: don't look at his pot or smile at him.

A few feet away and closer to the stairs, I spotted Erin and Vargas talking with another demon.

"We have agreed," the king said, drawing all our attention to him. "That, for now, it's best to send only a small group after the horsemen. It could be they are trying to lead us into a trap, or they really could be fleeing. Either way, it's best to have fewer people who can move faster in their pursuit.

"When backup arrives here, we will send more into the woods after them. Corson and Bale will lead this mission, and they will take Wren, Lix, Hawk, Caim, and Raphael with them. The rest of you will remain here to help the others in the field and to guard the wall."

My heart plunged into my toes. Hawk would leave, and I would remain here. Unexpected longing speared my heart along with an anger that burned like acid up my esophagus. I couldn't let him go out there without me, and I couldn't be the one left here, desperate to hear any word about the mission.

And as much as I hated to admit it, I would be desperate. The not knowing would drive me *nuts*! I wasn't exactly thrilled to discover myself bound to a man I barely knew, but I was far less excited about the idea of him out there without me. I could protect him better than anyone else.

"Come on," Hawk said.

He led me toward the stage as Erin and Vargas climbed the steps and walked toward the royal couple. I didn't look at the crowd as we climbed the steps, but I felt their eyes boring into me with every step we took across the stage.

"Are we going to get Magnus, Shax, and Amalia for this?" Hawk asked as we stopped in front of the others.

"There's not enough time," Corson said. "We're leaving as soon as we're ready."

"I'd like to go," I said, and Hawk's hand tightened on mine. "I was supposed to leave for the Wilds on this trip."

I was amazed my voice didn't tremble when I spoke. I'd never been this close to the king and queen before, but I could feel their power as the king's unnerving black eyes studied me. Then his gaze fell to the marks on my neck, and when he looked at the ones on Hawk's flesh, his eyebrows rose.

He didn't look at Hawk as he spoke. "If you survived the battle yesterday, then you stand a chance of surviving the Wilds."

Uh... thanks? But this time I managed to keep my mouth shut as I didn't think my thanks would go over well.

Then, I noticed Corson staring at Hawk, whose face was unreadable, before Hawk gave a brisk nod. I glowered at Hawk when I realized Corson would have allowed him to turn down my offer and he'd *considered* it. Hawk's eyes were unapologetic when they met mine. I tried to tug my hand free of his, but he held on.

Son of a bitch. I ground my teeth together until I was sure they were going to be stubs, but I didn't try to pull my hand free again. I wouldn't make a scene, but I wanted to kick him.

"You can find two more demons to go with you," the king said. "But no humans, they'll only slow you down."

"I'd like to go," Gage offered.

"Absolutely not," the queen said.

"But I'm immortal too, and I've been training," he protested.

"You're not immortal yet; you're still growing, and you are *not* going."

He glared at her, and she glared back until the king rested his hand on Gage's shoulder. "One day, you can go, but not until you stop aging."

Gage stopped glowering at his sister to look at the king. "Okay, but one day?"

"One day," the king promised and squeezed his shoulder.

The queen turned her glare on the king; she was a good foot shorter than him and easily a hundred pounds lighter, but she showed no fear of the man *created* by the fires of Hell. Not for the first time, I noticed the purity and strength of her soul. Whereas most good humans had a white soul with some other colors mixed in, hers was a brilliant gold color streaked with shades of violet and blue. I'd never seen anything like it before, and I doubted I ever would again.

Gage and Bailey possessed some similarities to her soul, but theirs were whiter with gold encasing the edges. Flecks of violet and blue danced through the white. These were the souls of those descended from the angels.

"Where did the horsemen and angels come from?" Erin asked.

"That's an excellent question," Corson said, "and one we can't answer."

"We haven't cleared all of the Wilds," Wren said, "and there is still enough land for them to hide an army, but there's no way they moved an army of that size across the secured land without someone noticing them."

"And if they killed off all witnesses?" Vargas asked.

"Do you think they could find and kill *all* witnesses?" Wren inquired.

"I didn't think they could do what they did yesterday," Vargas replied.

"I don't see them being capable of hiding that many troops in the Wilds," Erin said.

"They might not have hidden all those troops in one place," the king said. "Each horseman could have had a group of troops sequestered in different places until they were ready to move. A smaller number of craetons sequestered somewhere would have been more difficult to detect, but it would have increased their chances of someone stumbling across them."

"So we have no idea how they managed to keep so many hidden for so long," Hawk said.

"No," the king admitted. "I think they've found somewhere to hide. Which means your mission is going to be more difficult than before."

I took a deep breath as I surveyed the crowd below us. They'd decimated our numbers at the wall. We'd also destroyed their army, but so few of us were going to hunt down some of the worst creatures to ever exist. I rubbed the trickle of sweat away from my nape before anyone else could see it. They couldn't know that a part of me was contemplating crawling into my bed, pulling the covers over my head, and pretending the monsters couldn't see me like I had as a child.

"Should we also bring Lopan and Calah with us?" Hawk asked.

"They probably won't leave River," the king said. "But you can ask them."

"I'll ask," Lix said and strolled across the dais toward the stairs.

"Where are Caim and Raphael?" Hawk asked.

"Caim is following the horsemen from a discreet distance; he's leaving signs behind in case the rest of you have trouble tracking them. Raphael left to bring word to Shax about what happened," the king said. "He'll meet you after."

"How will he find us?"

"He'll probably have to come back to the wall and follow your trail from there. Shax and the others will probably be little help to you; it will take them too much time to find you."

Hawk glanced at me; if he suggested I stay behind, I'd kick him. I didn't care if it caused a scene or not.

"What happened to the telepathic demon with Magnus?" Hawk asked, and I breathed a sigh of relief when he turned his attention away from me. I gave a subtle tug on my hand, and this time, he released me.

"I haven't heard from him in a week; I assume he's dead," the king said.

"Shit," Corson said. "I hope the others are okay."

"I'm sure they're fine," the king said. "You know telepathic demons don't last in the Wilds."

Hawk chuckled, but they all shifted nervously, and I sensed their unease over this development. "Raphael must have been pissed to learn he was the messenger again," Hawk said.

"He said something about not being a carrier pigeon and hating Earth before he left. I felt bad for him." The king's smile said he felt the exact opposite as Wren, Corson, and Bale laughed.

"We keep losing telepathic demons in the Wilds," Hawk said to me. "And Raphael has become our go-between when it happens."

"He *hates* it," Wren said, and they all laughed again.

The click of Lix's feet on the stairs drew my attention back to him, Lopan, and Calah. "What is in Lopan's black pot?" I asked.

"It's a caultin," Gage said. "He can use it to conjure things."

"He's a leporcháin," the queen said. "His kind is where our legends of leprechauns originated."

"Fascinating," I murmured.

Lix returned to the stage without the two demons and rejoined us.

"They said they would come with us, but they'd prefer to stay, especially after what happened yesterday," Lix said.

"I know of a demon who could be an asset, if she survived," I said. Zanta also volunteered to go into the Wilds this time, and I hoped that, if she was alive, she would still want to leave the wall.

"Take two hours," the king said. "If you don't find anyone else, you'll have to go without them. Don't forget, you'll have some hounds with you too, and they're immune to the horseman's abilities."

CHAPTER EIGHTEEN

Hawk

I followed Aisling as she wound her way expertly through the streets of the town. Clothes and whatever weapons she couldn't strap to herself weighed down her backpack. The bun she'd pulled her hair into emphasized the contours of her high cheekbones and doe eyes. The set of her jaw was one of determination as she made a right onto another tree-lined street.

Before the war, this town was like any other town in suburbia. Kids rode their bikes in the streets, parents barbecued, and neighbors talked over their fences. Flags lined the streets on the Fourth of July, and people waved when they passed each other.

After the war, they evacuated the survivors and erected the wall dividing this town from the rest of the surviving areas. The government turned the once quaint town into a military base and assigned the houses to those who guarded the wall.

Over the years, the sidewalks cracked, the streets became riddled with potholes, porches sagged, and the paint started chipping from the once pristine homes. It wasn't that the soldiers didn't have pride in their homes and town; they didn't have the time or resources to care for things like they once did.

Leaves crunched beneath our feet as they floated down from trees that had turned the color of a sunset. I knew, from past years, most of those leaves would pile in corners where they would remain until the wind took them away or someone finally cleared them out in the spring.

Stars lit the sky as the quarter moon hung over the wall. The flashing red lights of the wall illuminated the soldiers patrolling the top of it. Some of the backup troops had arrived and were already helping to separate the dead and secure the town.

Aisling made a left toward the medical clinic that was a part of the town before the military took over. After packing her clothes for our upcoming journey, she spoke with a couple of demons and learned her friend, Zanta, hadn't survived the battle. She'd taken the news with a brisk nod and a thank-you, but I saw the sheen of tears in her eyes when she turned away.

I'd reached for her, but she dodged my hand, gave me a scathing look, and walked away. I knew that look had nothing to do with the loss of her friend and everything to do with the fact she was aware I'd debated not allowing her to join us on this journey.

"I don't want you going with us," I said.

"No shit," she retorted. "I didn't miss your exchange with Corson. I'm not your little woman. You don't get to decide what *I* do with *my* life. If I decide to go into the Wilds, then I'm going."

I grabbed her wrist to pull her to a stop as I turned her to face me. She looked like she was considering hitting me when she lifted her chin.

"If I believed you weren't capable of handling the Wilds, then *no* you would not go. Incompetence only gets you killed out there," I told her.

"I am *not* incompetent, and it's not your decision—"

"Yes, it is. I've been in the Wilds; I know the monsters and horror out there, and I know who can't handle it. Corson and Bale may be Kobal's seconds-in-command, but I'm also one of the leaders, and I help decide who watches our backs. You are my Chosen, and I would prefer you here, where it's safer—"

"Did you miss what happened yesterday? It's *not* safer here."

"But it is, or at least it is for now. You have more numbers here, and while there's a chance the horsemen could come back, it's unlikely. We slaughtered their troops, and they're on the run. I don't want to separate from you, but if I believed you couldn't handle the Wilds, I would leave you here. However, you're a good fighter, and I think you can handle it."

I also preferred her with me, where I could protect her. I didn't think they'd attack the wall again, but there were other dangers out there, and I had to know she was safe.

Red flickered through her eyes. "I *can* handle it."

With that, she tugged her wrist free and started down the street again. I went to stop her but decided it was best to leave her alone. I had a feeling pushing Aisling would only end up with her digging her heels further in and becoming more stubborn. Her anger would ebb eventually—I hoped.

We turned a corner, and the clinic came into view. There were so many tents set up outside the building that they blocked the street. Cots full of the wounded packed the tents; their moans drowned out the beeping equipment and shouts of the medical staff. They didn't bring any of the injured demons here; they were on the hill in what remained of the tents while their bodies repaired themselves.

"What are we doing here?" I asked.

"I'm looking for a friend," she said as she ducked into the first tent.

A pen scratched against a clipboard as the nurse within marked something down while a man slept soundly. The nurse glanced up and stopped writing to stare disapprovingly at us. "You can't be in here."

"I'm trying to find my friend, Sandy Mayhew," Aisling said.

The nurse's irritated expression faded, and she stepped away from the bed to point at the doors of the clinic. "The list of injured is posted on the door."

"Thank you."

Aisling hurried out of the tent; she walked three steps before breaking into a run and racing for the door. I paused for a minute to watch her. She hadn't seemed frantic, but I sensed her desperation when she dropped her backpack on the ground. She'd lost one friend today, I didn't want her to lose another, but I had a bad feeling about this.

I trudged over to stand beside her as she ran her finger down the list of names. "This can't be everyone," she muttered when she got to the end. "They have to be missing some of them."

"Aisling—"

She spun toward me. "There's only fifty names on the list. There has to be *more*."

I rested my hand on her shoulder, and though her face remained pinched with annoyance, her tensed muscles relaxed a little.

"The craetons don't leave survivors behind," I said.

"But some people might not be able to give their names yet."

I couldn't give her false hope, but I couldn't destroy it either. "True. Let's go find out if there are more."

Opening the door, I waited for her to put her backpack on and followed her inside. The stench of blood, death, and excrement assailed me as doctors and nurses rushed back and forth. With the rooms filled, more of the injured packed the hallway, and the sounds of their agony reverberated off the walls.

Aisling inspected their faces as she walked, but then she stopped so suddenly I nearly walked into her. Paler than the sheets draped over those around us, her lips compressed as she gazed at the wounded. "Their souls," she whispered.

I frowned at her. "What about them?"

She grasped the straps of her backpack and pulled them forward as she whispered. "Some of them are so weak."

"What does that mean?"

"I don't know."

But the look in her eyes said she was staring at death in a way I could never see it. Unable to resist, I rested my hand on her shoulder and drew her closer. She resisted for a minute, and then she placed her head on my chest and wrapped her arms around me. I inhaled her sweet scent as I rubbed her back to ease her sorrow. Then, she bowed her head and stepped away.

"Why don't you go back outside," I suggested. "And I'll ask about your friend."

"No. I can handle this."

I suspected her determination to see this through was because of my hesitance to bring her into the Wilds. "This isn't the same as the Wilds."

She didn't look at me as she turned away and marched up to the front desk. The harried-looking woman behind it didn't look at her.

"Excuse me," Aisling said. "I'm..."

The woman walked away before Aisling could say anything more. "I deserved that," Aisling muttered as she turned to survey the stretchers. "I'm going to check the rooms. They'll probably hate me for it, but I have to know what happened to Sandy."

I gritted my teeth against pulling her away from this place; I doubted her friend was here, but she would fight me tooth and nail if I tried to get her to leave. I followed her around the desk and down the rest of the hallway as she checked the patients in the hall before moving on to the rooms.

She entered every room but came away paler than before.

Finally, she walked out of the building and stood by the doors as she surveyed the tents in the street. "Do you know where they took the dead?" she asked me.

"They're still on the field."

Her gaze went to where the smell of smoke still wafted on the night breeze. The houses blocked the fire, if any of it still burned. "How much time do we have before we have to go?"

I glanced at my watch. "An hour."

Aisling

I tried not to breathe in the stench of death as we made our way through the bodies laid out on the field. It took all I had not to put my hand over my nose or run out of here vomiting, but I *refused* to let Hawk see me do either. If I couldn't handle this, he might think I couldn't handle the Wilds and leave me behind.

I'd be irate if he left me, but I hated to admit I would understand. I was at the wall because I was a soldier, and soldiers took orders. I listened to commands because it was for the greater good of the entire world. If he decided I couldn't handle this, and therefore couldn't handle the Wilds, he would make sure I was ordered to remain. And after being pissed at myself, him, and the world, I would get over it and continue to protect every innocent on the other side of the wall.

"Do you want a mask?" Hawk asked when we passed a station of supplies the workers had established in the middle of the dead. Along with containers of water, the table included masks, gloves, and soap.

"No."

"You know, being able to handle bad smells isn't a requirement in the Wilds."

He stopped to lift a mask from the table and put it on. When he lifted another and dangled it from his finger in front of me, I took it and slipped it on. It didn't block out the smell, but it helped ease it as I searched the faces of the dead for Sandy.

In a short time, they'd managed to separate a lot of our dead from those of the craetons and laid them out in rows that reminded me of a cornfield. Except in this cornfield, no green leaves would sprout from the ground as life bloomed and there was no sign of the green grass once stretching for acres across the land. I didn't think it would ever come back.

I had no idea why I was doing this; there was nothing I could do for Sandy, but I *had* to see her if I could. I just didn't know where to start. The bodies stretched out in at least twenty-five rows, and there were easily fifty people and demons per row.

Beyond these neat rows of the dead, the field remained cluttered with more dead. The bounce and sway of flashlights lit the night as people and demons picked their way through the bodies in search of more palitons. They would be out here for days, if not weeks.

I was starting down the tenth row when a woman with blonde hair caught my attention. My heart thundered as I rushed to her and knelt at her side. Biting my lip, I tried to keep my hand from trembling as I brushed the hair off her face.

Please. I pleaded as the last of her hair fell away, but through the blood and grime covering the woman, I saw she wasn't Sandy.

"Ash?"

The sound of my name caused me to turn as two women made their way down the hill with a body between them. I blinked at the woman who spoke as I tried to sort the familiarity of her voice with the blood, dirt, and mask covering her face. Her reddish-brown hair hung in a limp ponytail against her neck as bloodshot, blue eyes blinked at me from over the top of her mask.

It took me a minute to realize her hair wasn't naturally reddish-brown; blood and grime covered it. The woman lowered the legs of the body and stepped toward me.

"Sandy," I breathed. Before I knew it, I was running to her, and we were hugging in the middle of one of the rows. "I thought you were dead!"

She sniffled. "I kept expecting to uncover your body."

I repressed the sob lodged in my throat and ignored the stench of death clinging to her as I hugged her tighter. I didn't know how much time passed before my grip on her finally eased and I stepped away. She pulled off the mask to reveal a circular section of cleaner skin around her mouth. I removed mine too.

"How did you survive?" she asked.

"I'm just that good," I said, and she laughed. "What about you?"

"I was on the wall when the attack occurred. We shot a few of those flying assholes, but we were mostly out of the fight."

"Good."

"Were you on the field?"

"Yes."

She squeezed my arm as she let out a loud breath. "That must have been awful, Ash."

"It was," I admitted.

A subtle shifting behind me drew my attention to Hawk. I couldn't stop myself from beaming at him as I stepped aside to let him see Sandy better. "This is my friend, Sandy."

He extended his hand toward her. "I'm Hawk."

Sandy smiled as she shook his hand; I ignored the questioning look she sent me. "I'm going into the Wilds with Hawk and some others to hunt for the horsemen," I told her.

Sandy released Hawk's hand. "Ash..." Her voice trailed off, and she pulled off a glove to wipe at her eyes. "I know it was your plan before all this, but are you sure you still want to go?"

"Yes. They have to die."

Sandy snorted as she surveyed the dead. "I can't argue with that."

"Have you been here since last night?"

"Yes."

"You must be exhausted."

"I missed most of the battle; this is the least I can do."

"Sandy—"

"I'll only be here for a few more hours, and then I'll head home."

"Are you all alone there?" I asked.

"Yeah, I found my new roommate an hour ago, but I'll be fine. I should get back to work; these bodies won't move themselves. At least I hope they won't."

I forced myself not to step away from the bodies closest to me. "I don't know when I'll be back, but when I return, I'll find you," I promised.

"Just make sure you return."

I closed my eyes when we hugged again and tried not to think about the possibility this might be the last time I saw her. Tears burned my eyes, but before I could shed them, I stepped away from her. She smiled at me before slipping her glove and mask on; she waved goodbye to Hawk and returned to the woman who was still standing by the body Sandy had released when she saw me.

Some of my happiness faded as we made our way back through the bodies. The horsemen had to pay for what they'd done.

I walked with Hawk back into the town and to his house. We didn't speak as he packed a backpack full of supplies before we returned to meet with Corson, Wren, Lix, and Bale. There were no other demons with them, but they'd all gathered supplies too. Since this was a demon mission, there were a lot fewer supplies than would have been required if humans were joining us.

I'd packed a couple of bottles of water and granola bars that would keep me going; plus, I could always hunt if I got hungry.

"Ready?" Corson asked.

"Always," Hawk replied.

The king, queen, Erin, and Vargas came out to join us and escorted us to the road we'd have to take to bypass the still smoldering ruins of the forest. They broke away and waved goodbye as we continued with six hellhounds. It was going to be a long journey.

CHAPTER NINETEEN

Hawk

After a week of traveling on foot, riding the hounds, and briefly using a couple of vehicles we found parked in a garage, we were closing in on Caim and the horsemen. We were also deeper into the Wilds than I'd ever been before and exhausted. Demons required less sleep than humans, but only sleeping an hour or two at a time was not enough.

Riding the hellhounds was also a miserable experience, but it was the fastest way to travel. Unfortunately, the beasts pounded up and down hills and through the woods with no concern for whoever was on their backs. They could often go around some of the obstacles they hit, but I think they took joy in running us into low-hanging branches and knocking us off.

They wanted us on their backs as much as we wanted to be there. We could have taken some of the horses from the wall, but they couldn't cover as much land as fast as the hounds could. The horses required more rest and a steady food and water supply that we couldn't guarantee for them.

So we were stuck riding the hounds, and they expressed their dislike in every way possible, but the beasts were relentless in their pursuit of the horsemen.

During the week, we caught and fed on some wraiths we discovered at an old cemetery, but another hunger festered inside me. However, Aisling was still determined we get to know each other better, and so we were.

We rarely took breaks, but when we did, we asked each other random questions. I knew her birthday was March fourteenth, she was a Pisces, her favorite color was green, she hated blueberries, loved Pearl Jam, and her favorite book was *Of Mice and Men*. In return, she knew my birthday was September first, which made me a Virgo. She also knew my favorite color was red, I hated popcorn, loved hard rock, despised disco, and there were too many good books to have a favorite.

"Favorite place in the world?" Aisling asked as she slid her leg over the back of a hellhound. She winced as she stretched her back while walking in a circle and shaking out her legs.

I climbed off my hound and restrained a wince when my legs protested the movement. I felt saddle sore despite the fact there were no saddles on the beasts. When Aisling ambled closer to me, I rested my hand on her elbow and leaned over to whisper in her ear, "Does inside you count?"

A blush crept up her cheeks before she laughed. "No, it doesn't."

Being this close to her without being able to have her was a torture fit for the depths of Hell.

"Favorite place," she prodded.

"Before the war, my stepdad built me a treehouse in our backyard. I'd spend hours in it reading, playing with friends, and making sure my sisters stayed out. That fort was my second home. Your favorite place?"

A wistful look came over her face as she brushed back a strand of loose hair and tucked it behind her ear. Longing to be her fingers,

I followed every move she made like a starving man gazing at a banquet.

"Home," she murmured. "Something I never thought I'd say. Traveling *everywhere* was always my dream, but I would give anything to wake up to the smell of my mom cooking breakfast again."

Unable to resist, I rested my hand against her nape and pulled her close to kiss her temple. "If you'll let me, I'll give you a home one day."

Her fingers encircled my wrist as she leaned into me. Being this close to her was both torture and bliss. She pricked my hunger and drove the canagh part of me crazy, but strangely, she also calmed me.

The funny thing was, no matter how badly I desired her, this getting to know her aspect was fun. The more I learned about her, the more I liked her. We had our differences—she disliked horror movies, never liked sports, and was sacrilegious in her belief that disco music was good—but they were differences we laughed about as we argued over them.

I found myself growing to like her more with every passing day, and when she smiled, I found myself smiling with her. She didn't laugh often, but when she did, it was a clear, beautiful sound that made me smile.

"This is fresh."

Wren's words drew my attention away from Aisling and back toward the reason why we stopped. Wren stood before an arrow carved into the trunk of a pine tree. The arrow pointed east through the forest.

Over the years, the Wilders developed a universal language. They kept it simple so each group would understand what another group was trying to tell them. During our time in the Wilds, we'd all learned to use and read the language. Caim hadn't dated this marking, probably because he didn't have time, but a date wasn't necessary as fresh sap leaked from the tree.

"We should proceed on foot." Bale shot a look at the hounds. "It won't do us any good to be run into a tree while trying to sneak up on the horsemen."

I swear the hounds grinned at her as their tongues lolled from their mouths. They could tear a horseman to shreds, but they looked as innocent as a puppy.

"Come on," Corson said. "Hopefully we find Caim soon."

He took Wren's hand, and they started into the woods together; Bale and Lix followed. When I held my hand out to Aisling, she didn't hesitate before taking it. When she moved closer, I caught the scent of the woods we'd traveled through and something sweeter beneath the aroma.

I couldn't quite place the fragrance, but a memory of my home in Falmouth came to mind. My sisters and I stood by some bushes as I picked berries from them so they wouldn't poke themselves on the thorns. The red berries were round in our hands and squirted juice in our mouths when we bit on them.

Raspberries, I recalled with a smile. Aisling smelled like raspberries.

Releasing her hand, I pushed a branch out of her way. She ducked the next limb and sidestepped a log while she glided through the trees. Sunlight danced across the ground as it filtered in and out of the trees surrounding us, and a steep hill rose before us.

I didn't know what state we were in, but we were on the outskirts of a mountain chain. The leaves on the trees had all turned burnt orange, red, and yellow. A lot of them had fallen, but some floated on the air as the wind swept them from the boughs.

If we continued to chase the horsemen into the mountains, we would run into a problem when the weather turned, but if we were closing in on Caim, that meant the horsemen were nearby. We'd find them and get out of here before we had to worry about the cold and snow.

Aisling stopped and pulled a red leaf from her hair before inspecting it. She tilted her head back to the sky and inhaled a deep breath as she closed her eyes against the rays dancing over her beautiful face. I couldn't tear my eyes away from her serene expression.

Then she lowered her head and opened her eyes. Flames burst out of her palms, and the leaf turned to ashes, which she scattered from her fingertips. Every time we stopped for a break, she worked on her ability.

"It's getting stronger," she said to me before starting up the hill again.

"It is," I agreed.

She'd already told me it was stronger since we completed our bond, but every passing day, I saw the flame growing brighter and lasting longer. She'd never have Kobal-level abilities, but she might attain River's fire level and possibly surpass her if she kept working at it.

Last night, she'd rolled up the sleeves of her shirt and held her hands out. We all watched as the flames spread from her palms to her wrists, up her arms, and around her biceps. The fire intensified when I touched her back before she extinguished it.

The hounds prowled through the woods and spread out as they slipped into the shadows. If something tried to come up behind us, they would tear it to pieces. Corson held up a hand to halt the rest of us before he continued toward the peak of the hill.

I stepped closer to Aisling as I surveyed the woods. The six hounds sniffed the air as they moved. If something were out there, they would let us know, but something about this place didn't feel right.

I surveyed the trees as a squirrel crept to the end of a branch and looked down at the hounds. Even with the sign of animal life, something felt off about this place as leaves floated on the air.

Corson knelt at the top of the hill and leaned forward as he peered over. Wren took a couple of steps toward him when he turned to wave us forward. I knelt beside Corson and rested my hand on the ground as Aisling knelt beside me.

The hill descended into a valley awash in color from the trees. A fog hanging low over the valley blocked the bottom of it. Beyond the mist, more hills and mountains rose and fell with the earth. Some of their peaks touched the pristine, blue sky and snow covered the farthest mountain tops.

Aside from the swaying trees and the rustle of the wind moving through the leaves, nothing stirred below. I searched for any sign of Caim but didn't see him anywhere. He had to be nearby; that carving in the tree was only a few hours old.

"Where's Caim?" Bale murmured.

"He could be below or on the other side of that mountain. We won't know until we go down there," Lix said.

He was right, but I didn't want to take Aisling down there. Unfortunately, I didn't have a choice.

CHAPTER TWENTY

Aisling

Hawk stayed by my side as we moved from tree to tree to keep from falling down the steep hill. We were almost to the bottom when my feet skidded on some leaves, and I almost went down. Hawk caught my wrist before my ass could hit the ground, but I was stuck in some weird Twister move as my backpack weighed me down and my feet kept skidding on the leaves.

Hawk plucked me off the ground and set me on my feet. He grinned as he released me. "Easy there, graceful."

"Thanks," I said.

"No problem. Are you okay?"

"Yeah," I muttered as I wiped the dirt from my palms.

We were near the bottom of the hill when thin tendrils of mist coiled out toward Corson and Wren as they moved deeper into the fog. I bit my lip while I studied the thick fog covering whatever lay ahead of us. At least we were off the hill, and the going was easier through the flatter section of land.

"Maybe..." I had no idea what I was going to say. Maybe we should turn back? Maybe this was a bad idea? We could climb back out of the fog and try to walk around it, but that could take hours, and we were so close to Caim. There was no turning around, and we all knew it was a bad idea, but we had no other choice.

"Maybe?" Hawk prodded.

"Nothing," I muttered as a tendril of fog brushed against my cheek.

I almost slapped it away, but it was impossible to hit fog. Still, when another one coiled around my arm, I couldn't stop myself from trying to brush it away. It did no good, of course, and more of them drifted around me as we progressed deeper into the fog.

Beads of water formed on my skin and stuck my clothes to me as the mist caressed my skin.

Through the fog covering the ground, I caught glimpses of my boots, but the further we walked, the thicker it got until my ankles vanished and then most of my calves.

I wiped away the sweat on my nape before lowering my hand to one of the knives at my side. The day wasn't chilly, but goose bumps covered my arms, and the ice seeping into my bones caused my teeth to chatter.

The hounds slid from the trees and prowled closer to us. I wasn't exactly thrilled with the oversized furballs—I still had a bruise on my forehead from the one who ran me into a branch— but I was glad they were here. If anything was out there, they'd be the first to know, wouldn't they?

Dogs and other animals sensed things before humans, but these were Hell creatures. Their definition of dangerous was probably a *lot* different than mine.

"Have you ever encountered anything like this before?" Corson asked Wren.

"I've encountered fog before," she said. "And I've been in thicker fog, especially in mountainous areas, but something doesn't feel right about this."

"No, it doesn't," Bale agreed.

When the mist rose to my knees, I almost grasped Hawk's arm, but I restrained myself. I wasn't a scared little damsel in distress. I was a trained killer, and this was *fog*. But the fog was so thick that it was impossible to see more than five feet ahead of me. It also distorted and muffled all sound. When Hawk stepped on a branch, it sounded as if it were coming from my left and farther away, but it was coming from a few feet directly behind me.

With the fog distorting our senses, we would be more vulnerable in this place. And then, one of the hounds growled.

Corson stopped, and his earring spun in his ear as he turned his head toward the hound. The hair on the hound's back rose as it stared at something to my left. I pulled my gun free.

"Shit," Wren muttered.

When the hound growled again, the others prowled closer to it, and Corson turned to Wren. "Stay here."

When he walked away from her, she grabbed for him, but he'd already moved beyond her reach. She started after him as Corson approached the hound. Then, through the swirling fog, figures emerged.

I raised my gun and gripped it in both hands while holding it before me; I'd prefer my enemies didn't know I had the weapon until I put a bullet in them.

"Hello," a beautiful, melodic voice called.

Corson didn't relax, and the hackles on the hounds rose as the fog parted to reveal one of the most gorgeous women I'd ever seen. Her golden-blonde hair swayed against her hips as it spilled in thick waves down her back. Her blue eyes were so vivid they pierced through the mist gliding across her perfect features.

Her body would stop most men and women in their tracks, and she emphasized it with form-fitting pants and a shirt that looked about to bust open over her breasts. A smile curved her lips as she stopped walking and jutted out a hip.

Despite her beauty, what lay beneath her surface was something so hideous it caused bile to rise in my throat.

Her soul wasn't a light anymore; it had twisted itself into a malformed beast with two glowing, yellow eyes. Its head kind of resembled a Doberman, but it was far more revolting than that beautiful dog. The flesh of the dog thing's muzzle had been stripped away to reveal all its pointed teeth, and it surveyed us with the calculation of something seeking to devour us.

I'd seen many corrupted souls over the years, but only one came close to this level of hideousness. That soul belonged to a man who went to church every Sunday, played against my dad's softball team, worked at the factory, and was always seen laughing and slapping his friends on their backs. He hung out at the local bar, volunteered at the food pantry, and was an all-around great guy... who terrified me.

I was only three when I first encountered him at a bake sale for our church. He wasn't a parishioner there, but his wife made some cookies for the sale anyway. My mom said I screamed so loud and cried so much when I met him, they had to take me home. My parents didn't understand why I was rambling about a monster living inside the man, but they kept me away from him anyway.

Thankfully, I didn't see him again until he started playing in the same softball league as my dad. I was seven, and by then, my parents and I knew I was different. When I saw him this time, I could articulate there was something wrong with him instead of screaming about a monster. I could tell they wanted to believe me, but by all accounts, he was a great guy who was a pillar of the community.

Three years later, the police led him away in handcuffs for doing things to his daughters that no child should have to endure. Then the FBI went in, raided his house, and pulled out boxes of pictures and videos. The community was stunned; it couldn't be true, he was such a great guy, but the life sentence with no chance of parole calmed the chatter.

And now, I was staring at a woman who had me on the verge of screaming *monster* all over again. My finger twitched on my gun and slid toward the trigger. I was better off putting a bullet in her head right now, but before I could pull the trigger, six more figures emerged from the mist. None of them were as corrupted as she was, but maliciousness tinted every one of their souls.

They're humans, but as I thought it the fog shifted around us until the whirling, disorienting pattern caused me to sway. I closed my eyes but quickly opened them again. I didn't dare take my attention off the woman who was smiling at Hawk in a way that made me want to rip her mongrel soul out of her body.

CHAPTER TWENTY-ONE

Hawk

I stepped closer to Aisling when more people emerged from the fog, but my gaze returned to the woman at the front of the group. She oozed sex as her eyes ran over me, and she smiled before licking her lips. I didn't smile back.

Usually, a woman like her would have excited me, especially since I was hungry, but the idea of touching her repulsed me. Something was not right here; I had to get Aisling away from this woman and this place.

"Who are you?" Lix demanded as he pulled his sword from his back.

"I'm Amber," she said. If she was surprised to find herself talking to a walking skeleton, she kept it hidden. But, if she lived in the Wilds, nothing probably surprised her anymore. "And you are?"

"A Guardian of the Gates."

I'd never heard Lix give this response to someone. It was true; before humans tore a hole into Hell and blew it open, the skelleins had guarded the gateways to Hell with the hounds and the varcolac demon. The first step to passing through the gates was to have the balls to approach the skelleins; the second was to answer their riddle.

"I see," Amber murmured before she looked questioningly at the rest of us. No one offered their name. "And what are you doing in our valley?"

Aisling shifted beside me, and her lips compressed into a flat line. I'd never seen the hardness in her eyes before. Her finger rested against the trigger of her gun, and something about her demeanor said she was close to firing it.

"What are *you* doing in this valley?" Wren countered. "I didn't see any sign of Wilders in the area."

"Wilders?" Amber's voice dripped disdain. "We're not Wilders."

"Then, what are you?" Bale asked.

"Just a simple group of people looking to survive the apocalypse. Obviously"—she waved a hand at Lix—"you are something more, but we came to offer you help."

"She's lying," Aisling whispered so low her words didn't travel past us. "She's hideous."

Amber was far from hideous, but Aisling saw more than I could of the woman. I rested my hand briefly on her arm and felt the tension in the honed muscles beneath my palm. Aisling's eyes flickered toward me before locking on the woman again.

"We don't need any help," Bale said and whistled for the hounds. "Let's go."

The hounds slunk out of the mist and prowled closer to Bale. All of them kept their heads low and their attention on Amber's group as they surrounded us. Aisling hesitated before falling into step behind Lix as Bale led the way through the fog.

"Are you sure that's the right way?" Amber called after us. "The mist can be disorienting."

Bale didn't reply, and Aisling didn't put her gun away after we left the humans standing in the mist.

"What do you think she meant by that?" Wren asked.

When we were on the hill, the fog hadn't seemed that thick, but standing in the middle of it was like standing in the middle of a moving room. The walls followed us everywhere we went.

"She's evil and repulsive," Aisling said.

"I don't think she's up to any good," Lix said, "but she wasn't repulsive."

"Yes, she is." When Aisling stopped walking, so did the rest of us. Her hand trembled as she rested it against her chest. "On the outside, she's perfect, but *inside* she has one of the most corrupted souls I've ever seen, and those people with her were also malformed."

"What do you mean?" Corson asked.

"I can see souls. Not born demons, of course, because you don't have one, but I can see the souls of humans and demons who have human DNA in them like Hawk and Wren. I've always possessed the ability, and I've run into some pretty shitty humans in my life-time, but *that* woman is one of the worst. Whatever she's done, it's turned her into a monster, or maybe she was born one. I don't know, but she's evil."

"No one is born evil, and there is no such thing as good and evil. There are shades of gray in all things," Bale said. "The angels aren't all good, and demons aren't all bad."

"Fine," Aisling said impatiently. "She wasn't born evil, but her piss-poor life choices have turned her into a monster. You don't understand how rare *that* is. I've seen the corrupted souls of people who have hurt others and who are cruel and manipulative, but until today, I've only encountered one other soul so corrupted it was a *beast* inside a person. And *all* the people with her were corrupted, but none as bad as her."

Panic tinged Aisling's voice, and she glanced nervously behind us when she stopped speaking. I gripped her elbow and drew her closer.

"They're watching us," she whispered.

And I knew she was right as I could feel eyes boring into us as the mist rolled around us like a living, breathing thing. I didn't know how, but I suspected Amber or one of her friends was controlling the fog.

"We should have killed them all," Aisling said.

Corson's eyebrows shot up before he nodded approvingly. He gave me a thumbs-up that Aisling couldn't see and flashed a grin. I shook my head at him. Demons often didn't understand the more emotional side of humans, but they did understand destroying their enemies, and apparently, Corson approved of Aisling's words.

I stroked Aisling's arm as I tried to ease some of the strain from her. I'd seen her ruthlessness during the battle, and she may kill when necessary, but she wasn't cruel. She wanted them dead because she'd seen something that terrified her.

"We have to get out of this valley," Wren said. "We only saw seven of them, but there could be more."

Aisling shuddered at Wren's words, and I bent to kiss the top of her head. "It will be okay," I promised.

Corson rested his hand on the small of Wren's back as Bale started into the fog again. I released her elbow but stayed next to Aisling as the mist thickened until I could barely see Corson and Wren before us.

The scrape of metal against leather rebounded off the mist as Bale pulled the sword she wore on her back free of its sheath. I saw her do it, and she was no more than two feet away from me, but I couldn't tell if the sound came from beside me or a hundred feet away.

From the corner of my eye, I saw something darker slip through the fog. As soon as I turned toward it, it vanished. I slid the blade hanging from my side free and gripped it in both hands as something darted through the fog. Laughter trailed behind it.

"Son of a bitch," Corson muttered.

I could barely see him anymore, and I had no idea where the hounds were. I stepped closer to Aisling; I'd tear every last one of these assholes apart if they hurt one hair on her head. I never should have brought her with us. She would have been safer at the wall. It would have pissed her off if I left her behind, but better her anger than her death.

"It's *her*," Aisling whispered. "She's having them do this."

"She's not controlling the fog," Bale said.

"And how do you know she's not?" Lix asked.

No one had a reply for that as we had no idea what Amber could do. The laughter increased until the maniacal sound rebounded all around us. The almost mechanical sound of the laughter reminded me of those toy monkeys that laughed as they crashed their cymbals together. I kept waiting for the bang of those instruments, but there was only the endless laughter.

"I'm not playing with these fuckers," Corson spat.

When something flashed past me, I lunged out with my blade. A gasp came from the fog, and when I pulled my knife back, blood dripped from it. The laughter ceased as suddenly as it started. In the ensuing hush, I sensed an increased hostility emanating from the fog when it thickened around us and pulsed in a way that reminded me of a throbbing vein.

"Maybe she *is* controlling the fog," Aisling said.

If I'd learned one thing since arriving at the wall, it was that anything was possible. Aisling had seen Amber's soul, so she was at least part human or had been human, but she could be something more too.

"Keep going," Lix said.

"Going where?" Bale asked.

"Straight."

Straight into a trap? Bale didn't ask the question, but I knew we were all thinking about it when no one moved.

A low growl came from my right, and a startled cry died away. One of the hounds had found its dinner.

"Follow me," Lix said.

He took the lead and started into the fog as something else flashed by us. Aisling spun and aimed her gun at the fog but didn't fire.

"Shit," she muttered before returning her gun to her holster and removing a trench knife. "I don't want to accidentally shoot a hound or let the horsemen know we're coming."

I nodded as something else darted out of the fog. I yanked Aisling back as a knife arced toward her. I didn't have time to do anything more than drop my arm in front of her. The blade cut through my skin and muscle before the tip embedded against my bone.

The man's mouth parted as shock over stabbing me registered on his face. When his eyes went to Aisling and I saw the malicious gleam in them, a snarl tore from me. I grasped the back of the man's head and threw him to the ground. He'd been sent here to kill her, and I had no doubt the others would come for her too.

It seemed Amber disliked Aisling as much as Aisling disliked her. My blood pounded in my ears as I restrained myself from plunging into the fog and breaking her neck, but I couldn't leave Aisling unprotected, and I had to get her out of this fog.

I planted my foot on the small of the man's back and gripped the knife handle. Black blood spilled from my arm when I ripped the blade free. Human or not, he was going to die for attacking Aisling, but before I could drive the knife through his back, two more figures charged out of the fog. The noises they emitted reminded me of a cross between a hissing snake and a pissed-off squirrel.

They're insane.

That much was evident in the twisted glimmer in their eyes and the chatter of their jaws as they raced for Aisling. Corson's talons arced through the air and carved through the midsection of the first one like a Thanksgiving turkey.

I plunged the knife into the chest of the second one. When I yanked it free, red blood spread across the man's chest as his hands clawed at his shirt. I shoved him into the fog before bending to slice the throat of the first one who went after Aisling.

When I rose, Aisling grasped my arm and dragged it toward her so she could inspect the wound. "Are you okay?" she demanded.

"I'm fine." The bleeding had already stopped, and my skin itched as it worked to close over the healing muscle.

"Your blood—"

"Canaghs have black blood," I said as I gently pulled her hand away from my arm. "It's already healing."

She opened her mouth to say something more but closed it again when an eerie chatter started from the fog. It took a minute for me to realize they were clicking their teeth together to create the noise.

"Keep moving," Corson said.

Clasping Aisling's elbow, I pulled her against my side as we started forward again. They had targeted her, and there was no way I would let one of these teeth-clattering fucks get their hands on her. They were humans; if there were no fog covering them, we could take them out without a problem, but this was their world, and they were using it to their advantage.

More shadows slid through the fog, but they didn't try to attack us again. Most of the hounds stayed close to us, but some of them vanished into the mist before reappearing again. The clattering of the teeth didn't ease until it abruptly silenced.

Aisling stepped closer as the fog shut out all sounds of the world beyond it. Behind me, a hound emerged from the mist while in front of us two materialized. They fell into step beside Corson and Bale and directed them toward the right.

The mist lifted so suddenly that I recoiled from the sudden

influx of light and squinted against the sun. I kept Aisling moving forward as I turned toward the fog. A tendril brushed against my cheek, and I thought the chattering resumed, but it was difficult to tell as, outside the mist, a rush of sound returned. The singing of the birds and the squirrels jumping from tree to tree grated against my previously dulled eardrums.

I watched to make sure no one followed us from the fog; I didn't see anyone, but I could still feel their eyes following our every movement. I didn't have to see them to know they weren't happy about our escaping them.

"What *was* that?" Wren asked.

"Just another part of Hell on Earth," Lix said as he uncapped his flask and gulped some down.

"But they were human, or they had souls..." Aisling's brow furrowed as she pondered this. "I guess you could call them souls anyway, but they could have been like me or Wren and Hawk."

Lix recapped his flask and returned it to where it hung on his waist. "And they've discovered a way to trap and kill others."

"But could one of them create the fog?" Wren asked. "It's definitely *not* natural."

"Yes, and it was probably Amber who created it," Corson said. "Humans have abilities, such as Aisling's talent for seeing souls, and many demons and angels have different talents. Some demons can control the elements. Besides, anything is possible now that Hell has come to Earth."

CHAPTER TWENTY-TWO

Aisling

Caim was leaning against a tree when we arrived at the top of the next mountain. He had his black wings folded behind him and his arms over his chest as he smiled grimly before waving a hand at the valley below us. "Aren't *they* a bunch of assholes?"

I cast a nervous glance into the valley below us. The wall of fog shimmered in the sun, but nothing followed us, and it wasn't expanding. Still, I didn't like being this close to it or the vile people inside it. I wouldn't relax until we were miles away from Amber and her crew.

"You could have warned us," Corson said.

"I didn't get the chance. I got a little lost in the fog, as did the horsemen. I landed to try to get a better view, and that was when I met Amber and her bunch of merry fucking nutsos. You were already in the fog by the time I came out. Instead of getting lost in there again, I figured you were at least smart enough to find your way out and, my goodness, so you have!" Caim exclaimed; Corson glared at him.

"Where are the horsemen?" Bale asked.

"Where indeed," Caim murmured. "They went into the fog, and I went in after them. I'm the only one I saw come out. Personally, I think those assholes down there are working with them. I've searched the mountain for the past hour, but I can't find any sign of them."

"You *lost* them?" Corson accused.

Caim blinked at him before replying very slowly. "They went into the fog. I went in after them. They disappeared. I. Can't. Find. Them."

Corson scowled at him, but Caim pretended not to notice the furious glint in his eyes or the blood dripping from his talons as he yawned and scratched the ear of one of the hounds.

"Now, what do we do?" Wren asked as she rested her hand on Corson's arm. He visibly relaxed beneath her touch, but his anger still simmered beneath the surface.

Caim glanced at the sky. "I'll keep searching for them, but..."

"But?" Hawk prodded when Caim stopped speaking.

"But I don't think I'm going to have much luck," Caim finished.

I glanced back at the mist. "Do you think they're still in the fog?"

"I don't know," Caim said, "but I don't think so. If the horsemen are working with them, then it was to distract me, which they succeeded at doing. They would have used that distraction to get as far from me as possible."

"If they were still in the fog, the hounds would know," Corson said. "It probably distorted their senses too, but they would have detected the horsemen. I think Caim's right; I think they used it as an opportunity to lose him."

"Then we have to find them again," Bale said. "Let's go."

Aisling

When night descended, Bale and Corson called a stop to our journey, which was beginning to feel pointless. Before there had been a goal, but now it felt aimless. Caim had spent a lot of time in the sky and covered a lot of land, but he discovered no sign of the horsemen.

I didn't know what we would do if we couldn't find them; we couldn't go back to the wall without destroying them, but we couldn't keep wandering the Wilds with no idea where we were going. That wouldn't accomplish anything and seemed like an excellent way to end up dead.

I took off my pack before releasing it and resting my back against a rock as a giant raven descended with a flutter of wings. Caim transformed from his raven form and sauntered over to a cluster of trees. He slid down one of the trees to sit with his wings spread out like he was cooling them.

Bale pulled out her sword and settled it across her drawn-up knees as she gazed into the forest with a look promising death to anyone who attacked us. Lix walked a few feet away from Bale and removed his flask as he settled against a tree. The hounds lay within the shadows of the forest.

"I wanted to ask you something," I said to Caim as Hawk settled beside me.

His rainbow eyes shone with amusement as he smiled. "I always love a good question. Ask away."

"I can see people's souls. I can tell if they're good or bad by looking at them. Those people in the fog are some of the worst I've ever seen; we should have killed them."

He rubbed his chin. "Interesting."

"It's something I've been able to do since birth, but I never knew why. When I became a demon, I assumed that's why I had the ability, and it was just something I could always do; unlike my ability to create fire."

"You can wield fire?" he asked.

"Yes, but I couldn't do it until I became immortal."

"I see. So what is your question?"

"Hawk said he didn't think my ability to see souls was a demon power because demons have no souls, so it would be useless for them."

"I agree with him," Caim said.

"But he wondered if I was part angel too and *that's* where the power originated?"

I refused to look at the others as I asked this question, but I could feel their eyes boring into me while they hung on every word.

Caim closed his wings. "Angels don't have souls either, so the ability would be useless for us too. We were forged in the image of man, but we weren't infused with souls. You were born with a gift— one meant to keep you safe from those who would harm you. Some humans are blessed that way."

"I can handle being blessed," I said.

He chuckled as he closed his eyes. Corson took Wren's hand and started toward the woods with her. "We'll be back in a little while," he said to Bale who nodded.

I removed the small blanket in my pack and draped it over myself. Hawk's arm brushed mine when I pulled it over him too. A bolt of need pierced through my exhaustion and struck straight into my soul as I leaned against him.

A tingling started in my newly awakened fangs, and before I knew what I was doing, I slid my hand into his beneath the blanket. My heart pounded as I rested my head on his shoulder. I was supposed to keep my distance until I got to know him better, but I wanted to strip off his clothes and forget the awful events of this day in his arms.

"Rest," he murmured as he ran a hand over my hair and kissed my forehead.

I didn't think there was any way I could rest after losing the horsemen and with being this close to him, but the stars danced in the sky when I opened my eyes again. Corson and Wren sat across from us; Wren had her head in his lap while she slept. Bale had also fallen asleep while sitting against the tree.

Lifting my head from Hawk's shoulder, I surveyed the others before turning to him. Bright in the moonlight, his eyes shone as I traced my fingers over his cheek and jaw. I bit my lip when I recalled the way he felt inside me.

Even as I recalled the blissful feel of him, I noted the lines around his eyes and clamped mouth. Those lines hadn't been there before, and neither had the stress in his rigid body.

"Want to go for a walk?" I asked.

I didn't know if it was safe for us to leave here, but he unfolded himself from the ground before holding his hand out to me. I took his hand and allowed him to pull me to my feet. I suppressed a shiver when the blanket fell away and the chilly air caressed my skin. When Hawk slid his arm around my waist and pulled me close, I forgot about the cold air as he enveloped me.

CHAPTER TWENTY-THREE

Aisling

"We'll be back, and we're not going far," he said to Corson.

Corson nodded, and a couple of the hounds lifted their heads, but everyone else remained asleep as we walked into the forest. The moonlight barely penetrated through the trees but becoming a demon enhanced my vision, and I could see well enough to avoid walking into a tree or rock.

"Are you okay?" I asked him.

"Yes," he said and nuzzled my hair.

When his warm breath tickled my neck, my thoughts went in a million different directions, but I refused to let him distract me. "You seem... stressed."

He leaned back to look at me. "It's not exactly fun times right now."

"I know, but I want to make sure you're okay."

"Don't worry about me." He turned his attention back to the trees. "Tell me something about yourself, Aisling."

I wasn't expecting the shift in topic. "Like what?"

"Tell me something no one else knows."

"Something no one else knows," I murmured as I puzzled this. "I had a dog named Duke when I was a kid. He was a yellow lab, and I got him for Christmas." He arrived a year after the Mary Lou fiasco. Although he wasn't a puppy, he was the best gift I ever received.

"They adopted him from the local shelter, and he was sitting under the Christmas tree with a big red bow. We were always together, but after the gateway opened, he *refused* to leave my side. *Everywhere* I went, Duke went with me, even to school. Eventually, my teachers gave up trying to chase him out of the building and would let him sit outside the classroom door. I didn't know it at the time, but he must have sensed what happened with the gateway and was trying to protect me."

"Sounds like he was a good dog."

"He was a *great* dog."

"What happened to him?"

"Old age and bad hips; when I was seventeen, we had to put him down. I was so heartbroken." I rested my hand over my heart as a familiar ache built in my chest. "Now, here's the part no one else knows; I *still* cry over him."

Hawk's arm tightened around me. "I never had an animal like that."

I didn't think I ever would again. "Tell me something about yourself."

"I'm as intelligent as I am good looking."

I gave him a sharp look, but when I saw the twinkle in his eyes, I laughed. "Then you must not be too bright."

"Ouch," he said and rested his hand over his heart. "That was a mortal wound."

I was still laughing when we reached the bank of a small stream. I stared at the water as it flowed over rocks and meandered through the trees before vanishing around a bend. It was small enough that I could take a big step over it.

"I thought I was in love once," he said. "I've never told anyone that; not even the girl I was sure I loved."

I ignored the jab his words inflicted on my heart. "You thought?"

"I've realized it was an infatuation, but I would have done anything for her. However, I think most teenage boys will do almost anything for the first girl who lets them go all the way."

"Who was she?"

"Cindy Wallis. We went to school together and hooked up one night at a party. I was fifteen, she was sixteen, and I believed we would get married and have babies." He laughed as he ran a hand through his hair.

"*Fifteen?*" Thanks to the war, I wasn't much of a child by then, but I was still more concerned with books than boys and sex.

"What can I say? I've always been irresistible."

His tone was teasing, but I sensed something more beneath his words.

"I was still reading Nancy Drew," I said.

He didn't speak as he stared at the water with his head bowed. I tried to picture him at fifteen. He would have been handsome but probably a little awkward as he went through growth spurts, facial hair, and maybe some acne. Girls still would have tripped over themselves to get at him, and he'd said he looked older than his age.

"If I'd known how much sex would come to rule my life, I would have waited a lot longer," he said.

I rested my head on the thick muscles of his arms. Seeking to ease the strain he radiated, I wrapped my arms around his waist and hugged him.

"What happened with the girl?" I asked.

"She wasn't thinking about marriage and was planning to give my best friend a test drive. They hooked up a week later. The two of us got into a fistfight over her, but when Cindy moved on to her next victim, we stole some of his dad's homemade vodka and got drunk together. That girl was a man-eater," he said with a laugh.

"What happened to Cindy Wallis?"

When the smile left his face, I knew I'd asked the wrong thing. "She was slaughtered with the rest of my town."

I inwardly winced when I tore that wound open again.

"Come on," he said.

He released me but took my hand as he stepped over the stream. Keeping hold of his hand, he helped me cross the creek, and we walked deeper into the woods.

"Where are we going?" I asked.

"Not far; we have to stay close to the others."

"Okay." I enjoyed being with him too much to care about how far we walked. "The animals are quieter in the Wilds than I expected."

"They aren't as active out here; there are too many predators here for squirrels and birds to be as free as they are on the other side of the wall. In the areas we've cleared, the animal populations have become more active again."

"This area hasn't been cleared?"

"No. I've never been this deep into the Wilds, and neither has Wren. When we have time to do a thorough sweep of this area, those fog people will be at the top of the list."

"Good. I can still see that *thing* staring at me from inside her."

Hawk released my hand to drape his arm around my shoulders and pull me closer. When his breath tickled my cheek, longing seeped through my body. We were supposed to get to know each other better, but over this past week, I'd learned a lot about him.

He'd told me about the losses he endured, and I'd witnessed his loyalty to his friends and the way he joked with them when a hound dumped one of them. I'd experienced the warmth of his body against mine at night, yet he never made a move on me.

He had to know I'd cave like a house of cards if he stroked me in the right way. He had to sense my desire as strongly as I sensed his. Yet, every morning, he rolled away from me. Hawk was a study in patience and restraint while being this close to him was causing mine to unravel. Everything I learned about him, and the closer we got, the more I liked my Chosen.

It should have come as a relief, but it also scared me. It might have been easier if we hated each other; then I wouldn't have to worry about my heart. I wasn't in love with him, but I could see it happening one day, and it scared me. Life was far too precarious in this world, and what if he never loved me back?

What a miserable, lonely life that would be.

He stopped to tilt his head back. I followed his gaze to the clear night sky and the thousands of stars dancing overhead. Despite his casual demeanor, I'd never seen him look so tense as lines etched the corners of his mouth and eyes.

"When I was a kid, I always wished on the first star I saw," I said.

"What did you wish for?"

"A good grade, a dog, to go to a concert—you know, kid stuff. Then the war happened, and I stopped wishing."

"Why?"

"Because I wasn't a kid anymore."

When his head tipped down, my breath caught at the beauty of his indigo eyes. He was so damn handsome, and he was mine. My gaze fell to the marks on his neck. It had been over a week since I left them, and they were fading from his sun-bronzed skin.

My fangs lengthened as I was struck by the overwhelming *compulsion* to mark him again. Those marks couldn't fade from him. Like a rabid animal, something clawed at my chest until I was sure it would tear my ribs apart, and I realized it was the demon screaming to be set free to claim its Chosen again.

And I so badly wanted to give in to it.

CHAPTER TWENTY-FOUR

Hawk

As the scent of Aisling's increasing desire drifted to me, I somehow managed to keep myself restrained from tearing her clothes off and taking her on the forest floor. I was starving, but I would wait for her to be ready.

I could usually go longer between sexual encounters, but resisting Aisling was weakening my restraint with every passing day. Waking up next to her every morning only reminded me of what I was missing, but I'd forced myself to stay away from her.

She'd asked for time to get to know me better, and I would give it to her. I *would* keep myself under control.

It would probably be better if I didn't sleep next to her every night and experience the warmth of her ass nestled against my groin, but I couldn't stand the idea of sleeping without her. She was *my* Chosen; I wouldn't part from her, and if I couldn't have her sexually, I could at least hold her.

Unable to stop myself, I grasped a piece of her hair; the silken strands of it slid through my fingers and fell against her cheek. I followed her hair to trace the curve of her cheek while her doe eyes followed my every move. The accelerated beat of her heart thumped in my ears as her raspberry scent intensified.

When she licked her lips, my already aching cock flooded with blood, and I nearly groaned when it strained against my zipper. I tried to pull my hand away from her, but I couldn't stop touching her as I ran my thumb over those gorgeous lips. With my thumb, I pulled her plump, lower lip down a little. I *needed* to taste her, but I would never risk enslaving her.

Instead, I bent to kiss her nose, her cheek, and then her other cheek. Her eyelashes brushed my cheek when her eyes fluttered closed, and I placed two kisses against them too. Her hands clenched in my shirt as she swayed toward me. I pulled away when she turned her head toward me and her lips nearly grazed mine.

Her shoulders slumped, but she didn't turn away when I kissed her cheek again. Clasping her chin, I lifted her head until her eyes met mine. I drank in the beauty of her while I traced her lips.

"Don't move," I commanded.

Lowering my head, I stopped when our lips were only centimeters apart. She remained still as I inhaled her sweet breath and relished the warmth of her exhalations. I had no doubt she'd taste better than I was imagining, yet I didn't move to kiss her.

Her hands constricted on my shirt, and a soft mewl issued from her. I thought she was going to turn away, but she pulled open the buttons and rested her palms against my chest. Pushing her hands up, she undid my shirt until it hung free around my shoulders.

And then she bent her head and kissed me. My breath hissed in as the heat of her mouth burned into my skin. Her tongue left a trail down the center of my chest, and her fingers ran over me as she made her way lower. She knelt in front of me and tugged my pants open.

My hands went to her shoulders to pull her away, but they froze there. She didn't know what she was playing with as hunger burned through my veins. If this continued, I would be too far gone to stop, but I couldn't get the words out of my mouth.

"I never got to return the favor," she said as she gripped my erection.

I couldn't tear my gaze away from her when she bent to flick her tongue against my head before sucking the tip into her mouth. I ran my fingers through her hair as I resisted thrusting my hips forward and sinking further into her. Holding her still, I braced my legs apart as she took me deeper into her mouth while working me with her hand.

"Fuck," I groaned when she ran her tongue along the thick vein in the side of my shaft.

Her fangs grazed my flesh, but instead of being unpleasant, my spine prickled at the sensation. I couldn't tear my gaze away from her as the familiar sensation of semen rising returned. The pressure built until I could barely contain it.

"Aisling." I gripped her shoulder to pull her away, but she grasped my ass, and her fingers bit into my flesh. "Aisling, I'm going to come."

Instead of pulling away, she guided my hips until they were rocking into her mouth. She removed one hand from my ass and gripped my dick. That touch was my undoing, and I bit back a shout of pleasure as I came.

Aisling drank me down before releasing me and leaning back on her knees. Then, she rose with fluid grace and gave me a wicked smile as she stepped closer. "I hope you're not done."

"I'm far from done," I assured her. I needed to be inside her, feasting on her, claiming her and everything she offered.

"Good."

When I gripped the bottom of her shirt, she lifted her hands, and I tugged it over her head. I let it fall to the ground as I stepped back to savor the splendor of her lithe body. I slid my fingers over the curve of her exposed breasts in her bra before bending to run my tongue over them.

My fangs scraped her flesh when I pushed the bra aside to expose her nipple. She gasped as her fingers threaded through my hair. "Bite me," she commanded.

I was more than willing to obey as I sank my fangs into her flesh. Her body arched against mine, and she pulled me closer as she squirmed against me. I tongued her nipple while I renewed my mark on her.

She tasted as sweet as she smelled as I crushed her against me. Her fingers threaded through my hair, and she rested her cheek on my head as we clung to each other like a drowning man to a lifeline. Releasing her, I rose to stand over her as she gazed at me with an expression of awe.

With deft hands, she pushed my shirt the rest of the way off. Her hands were unhurried as they stroked my chest, and she seemed to be memorizing every inch of me. I couldn't help doing the same as I unhooked her bra and let her breasts spill free.

She clasped my cheeks and rose onto her toes. I stiffened when I thought she might try to kiss me; instead, she did what I did to her earlier. Her lips found my cheeks, my eyelids, and my chin. When she finished, she ran her thumb over my mouth before her eyes met mine.

I was starved and half mad for her, but time slowed as she gazed at me from those wide, brown eyes. Something inside me shifted, and suddenly it was more than lust and demonic instinct fueling my need for her. She was mine to protect and cherish, and I would do so every day of our lives together.

The overwhelming impulse to kiss her gripped me, but I resisted as I undid the button on her pants. I pushed her pants down her hips and bent to tug them lower before stopping to untie her boots. I lifted one shapely calf and then the other to remove her boots and pants.

I untied my boots and kicked them off before tugging my pants the rest of the way down. When I rose over her again, she gave me a sultry smile as she draped her arms over my shoulders. I plucked her off the ground, and she wrapped her legs around my waist as she rose over me.

～

Aisling

Hawk's muscles flexed when I skimmed my hand down his chest and bent my head to kiss him. I was desperate to feel his mouth against mine, but I contented myself with touching and tasting him in this way.

His fingers found my already wet core and slipped inside me. I nipped at his chest, and my hips moved faster as his hand teased me to the brink before pulling away.

I sank my fangs into his shoulder to keep from screaming in frustration and reached between our bodies to clasp his cock. The thick, heavy length of it pulsed in my hand when I guided it inside me. A feeling of rightness stole through me as he stretched and filled me.

Releasing my bite on him, I lifted my head to meet his stark, ravenous gaze. I struggled to breathe as the need in his eyes shook me. With trembling fingers, I traced the lines at the corners of his mouth before stilling on his lips. Every part of me yearned to lean forward and kiss him, but I didn't try. He would only turn away, and I would ruin the moment.

Instead, I lifted my hips until I felt only the tip of him inside me before I sank onto him again. I moaned as tendrils of pleasure spiraled from my belly and out to my legs. I couldn't tear my eyes from his while I rode him. I'd never forget the sensation of his firm flesh against mine or the scent of the woods and earth on him. I'd never forget the way his hands stroked me with such reverence.

I felt him feeding on me as our bodies moved faster, but instead of being frightening or unpleasant, a rush of power washed over me; I was the one nourishing him. This powerful, magnificent demon only wanted me.

I smiled when his fangs sank into my neck. Adjusting his hold on me, he kept me up as his knees dropped to the earth. When he fell back, I placed my hands on his chest and rode us both to completion.

CHAPTER TWENTY-FIVE

Aisling

I leisurely stroked Hawk's chest as I lay nestled in the crook of his arm while staring at the stars. We should get up to return to the others, but we lacked the energy to move. Lifting my head, I propped it on my hand as I gazed at him.

My brow furrowed when I realized the lines around his mouth and eyes were gone and tension no longer emanated from him. I almost smacked my forehead when I realized what changed.

"You were hungry," I said. "And not just for wraiths but for sex."

He frowned at me, but I had a feeling he was feigning his confusion. "What do you mean?"

"You know what I mean. Before this, you looked exhausted and... well... older."

"You sure can sweet talk a man," he teased.

"It's not funny; why didn't you tell me you were hungry?"

"Because you asked for time to get to know each other better, and I was giving it to you."

"And how long were you going to wait to tell me?"

"I wasn't going to tell you; I was waiting until you were ready."

"And what if that was another week or months? Were you going to feed on someone else?"

A vein throbbed to life in his forehead as his jaw clenched and his skin flushed. His reaction was so volatile that I leaned away from him.

"I would *never* do that," he snarled. "Do you *really* think so little of me?"

It took me a couple of seconds to find my voice as he stared at me with a mixture of anger and hurt. I'd never felt so horrible before. "You said you need sex to survive."

"I do."

"Then what were you going to do if I asked for more time?"

"Give it to you. I've gone longer without sex, and no matter what it took, I would have abstained until you were ready."

"And starve and weaken yourself in the process? We're chasing the horsemen; you have to be as strong as possible."

"By weakening *you* in the process?"

"I don't feel weaker after being with you. Tired from being so thoroughly used and pleased by you, yes, but in a *really* good way. I can feel you feeding on me, but I don't feel weaker because of it."

When he studied me as if he were trying to discern the truth, I held his gaze and tried to make him understand I wasn't lying.

"Maybe that's because you're my Chosen," he murmured. "The Chosen bond does make demons stronger."

"Then you should have told me you needed to feed."

"No, I shouldn't have. You had to make your own choice about what this is between us, and you couldn't do that with additional pressure from me."

"I had a right to know."

"No, you didn't. You're my Chosen; you're the only woman I'll ever be with again, and I will do whatever is necessary to make sure you're safe and happy, even if it means going without."

I resisted kicking him for his stubbornness at the same time I almost threw my arms around him and hugged him. Instead of telling me he was suffering, he'd kept it to himself to make me happy.

Something inside me shifted, and this time, my reaction to him had nothing to do with my demon DNA. Instead, it had everything to do with my very familiar, human emotions; I was losing my heart to this man.

"Did you think I would have sex with you again if you told me you were hungry?" I asked.

"I suspected you would; it *is* amazing between us."

"You're pretty sure of yourself," I said.

He grinned as he rested his hand on my hip, and his fingers slid down to my thigh. His touch instantly brought my body to life. It was as if I'd spent my whole life waiting for him to come and wake me up.

"I am," he said. "I smelled your desire in the mornings, but I wanted you to come to me because you were ready and not because you felt sorry for me."

"I don't feel sorry for you."

"Hmm," he said as he ran his thumb over my bottom lip.

"Next time, you'll tell me when you have to feed," I said.

"If that's what you want."

"It is."

"And what of us? Do you still need space?"

I still wasn't thrilled about my demon DNA declaring my single life was over without any warning, but if I was going to be bound to someone for eternity, it would be Hawk. He was a good man who put my needs ahead of his, I liked him, and if I was honest with myself, I felt more for him than just like, but one step at a time.

I could easily see myself spending the rest of my life with Hawk. If we were still human when we came across each other, I would have chosen him. As a little girl, I sometimes dreamed about my future husband, but none of those imaginings compared to this man.

I wasn't in love with him yet, but it would be so easy to tumble into it with him. Still, I had to keep a part of myself distant from him. I'd never experienced a broken heart, and I wasn't about to start now. Just because I was his Chosen didn't mean he had to love me, and I couldn't imagine anything lonelier than being in love with a man who didn't love me back.

"I'm not going to let you go hungry," I said.

His eyes darkened as that vein in his forehead reappeared. I knew I'd said the wrong thing before he spoke and cursed my runaway mouth again.

"I can handle it. I'm not going to have sex with you because you feel sorry for me or think you have to feed me."

I grasped his arm when he sat up and stopped him before he rose. "That's not what I meant! I don't feel sorry for you."

I gulped when his head turned toward me. He'd never hurt me, but if I was an enemy and he looked at me like that, I would have tucked tail and run. Instead, my hand tightened on his arm.

"I'm not going to deny myself either," I said. "We can work through this together."

His fingers entwined in mine, and he lifted them to kiss my knuckles. "We should return to the others."

I glanced at the lightening sky and sighed. I wasn't ready to resume our search for the elusive horsemen, especially since I sensed a distance in Hawk. I'd said the wrong thing, and I couldn't figure out how to make it better without baring more of myself to him. I wasn't ready for that.

I let him pull me to my feet and wiped the leaves from my ass before gathering my clothes. We stopped to bathe in a river yesterday, but I stopped at the stream and knelt beside it to splash water on my arms and face. Hawk knelt beside me and scooped some water into his hands to scrub his face.

Leaning back, I studied his profile as water dripped from his chin and onto the ground. Cold dirt slid between my fingers as I resisted the impulse to touch his cheek; I pushed myself to my feet instead. I didn't know what to do about the realization I was starting to care for him more than I'd anticipated. I'd rather face the horsemen than the turbulent feelings churning inside me.

I jumped to my feet and started tugging my clothes on. The wetness of my skin made dressing more difficult, but eventually, I got my clothes settled in a way that felt okay instead of clingy and twisted.

I finished tying my boot as the distant, lonely howl of something drifted over the land. I froze and dropped my hand to the knife on my belt as another cry pierced the night. "Is that the hounds?" I asked.

"It's too far away to be them."

"Are there more hellhounds out here?"

"No. The hounds stay with Kobal unless commanded otherwise, and I know he didn't leave any of them out here."

"Then what is it?"

"It could be anything. We live in a world that belongs to Hell too. Whatever it is, it isn't close, but we have to get back."

CHAPTER TWENTY-SIX

Hawk

Aisling stayed by my side as we traversed through the mountainous passes. I didn't think we had any chance of finding the horsemen out here, but none of us were ready to give up yet.

"Do you know where we are?" Corson asked Wren.

"No. I've never been this deep into the Wilds before," she said.

A shadow blocked out the sun filtering through the sparse trees as Caim flew low overhead. He stayed out of view as he scouted ahead and behind us to make sure the horsemen hadn't somehow doubled back to come up behind us. The hounds slipped in and out of the shadows as they took turns going ahead before returning to the others.

I watched Aisling as she walked with her head bowed and a pensive look on her face. I'd love to know what she was thinking, especially after our conversation earlier. I didn't know what to make of this woman who was so eager and warm in my arms but also quick to hold herself apart from me.

Was it a fear of commitment or something more? Sometimes, I swore we were getting closer and then she'd pull back again. I knew women were a mystery, but she was a conundrum I didn't think I'd ever solve.

Then, she looked up at me and smiled in a way that lit her face and caused her eyes to sparkle in the sunlight. For a second, I couldn't breathe as the beauty of her struck me. I didn't care if I never figured her out if she smiled at me like that every day for the rest of our lives. This conundrum had wormed her way into my heart, and I wasn't going to let her go.

Caim landed ahead of us and settled his wings against his back as he strode toward us with a perplexed look on his face.

"What is it?" Corson asked.

"There's a town with people in it ahead," Caim replied.

"People are living *in* the town?" Wren asked.

I understood her disbelief; during my time in the Wilds, I'd never seen humans living in a town. The Wilders were nomads who moved because of the weather, food supply, or level of risk.

Many of the people living near the gateway were killed during the initial rush of demons fleeing Hell. A lot of the others were cleared out during the mandatory evacuations that followed the gateway's opening. The Wilders only returned to those abandoned towns to scavenge them or travel through them, but for the most part, they stayed to the woods.

"It appears that way," Caim said. "There are demons with them, and it looks like they're living in peace together."

"I've never come across Wilders and demons living in a town, but I've never been here before either," Wren said. "Things might be a lot different in these mountains. The people in town can tell us more about the area, and they might have seen the horsemen or know something about where they're hiding."

"There's also an old mine above the town. It's set into a mountain, and there are some carts outside it, but I didn't see anyone working it," Caim said.

"They probably use it as an escape route or hiding place in case something happens," Wren suggested. "They may be living in a town, but if they're anything like Wilders, they'll have more than one way out. We should talk to them."

"Should we all go in?" Aisling asked.

"We'll leave the hounds and Caim behind as backup," Corson said. "If everything's okay, they can enter after us."

"Thank you very much for allowing us to join you later," Caim muttered.

"You can stroll on in there if you'd like," Corson said. "I'm sure they'll all be eager to see a fallen angel. Maybe they'll pluck and stuff you like the rest of us have wanted to do since meeting you."

Caim unfolded his wings to reveal their six-foot wingspan. His head tilted to the side as he studied the rainbow colors shimmering through the black feather. "They're too pretty to pluck and so am I," he said before closing them again. "And I'll gut anyone who tries."

When one of the hounds walked closer to him, Caim absently rested his hand on its head. I expected the creature to move away from him, but it sat beside him and turned into his touch. I clenched my teeth to keep my jaw closed at the sight of a fallen angel and hellhound being so friendly with each other. But then, Caim could turn into a raven, so maybe it was an animal thing.

"We'll stay here," Caim said, and Corson rolled his eyes.

"Aisling—"

"I'm coming too," she said before I could finish speaking.

The humans and demons appeared to be living in harmony, but something didn't feel right. Nothing, since the gateway opened, had been simple or easy, and I preferred to keep Aisling away from the town until we knew more about it.

"I'm going," she stated before walking over to join Wren and Lix.

Corson gave me a sympathetic look that swiftly turned into a shit-eating grin as he slapped me on the shoulder. "Welcome to the 'she's going to drive me crazy' club. All new members get a T-shirt."

When he strolled away laughing, I scowled after him. I didn't know if I wanted to punch him or tie Aisling to a tree more. She had no idea what the Wilds hid; the fog people were nothing compared to some of the monsters who hunted these lands, but I'd agreed to let her come with us, and I couldn't hold her back now.

"Let's go meet some people," Lix said and drank from his flask before recapping it and heading into the trees.

We followed him through the woods until the backside of a wooden building came into view. Lix slowed his step as we crept out of the trees and crossed the thirty feet of space separating the woods from the town. From my angle, I could see people and demons walking the street.

Some of them stopped to speak to each other, but others kept their heads down as they walked. I didn't see any lower-level demons amongst them, but my view of the street was limited to fifty feet. I didn't think they'd be so relaxed if there were lower-level demons with them; unlike some demons and seal creatures who had chosen one side or the other, all lower-level demons sided with the craetons.

The wooden buildings and dusty street reminded me of an old western movie. My stepdad used to love old John Wayne and Clint Eastwood movies. We'd spent many Saturdays on the couch with a bowl of popcorn while we watched the westerns together. They were old and outdated, but I still enjoyed them and my time with Dax as none of the female members of our household had any interest in the movies.

Kneeling at the edge of the town, I felt like I'd been transported back to one of those old movies. I kept waiting for some black-hatted cowboy to turn the corner and start pushing people around, but no evildoer emerged.

The residents of the town moved about freely, but tension

emanated from them as their heads moved steadily back and forth like they were searching for something. A woman sweeping the front porch of the building across the street set her broom against the side of the building. When it slid over and crashed to the ground, the people closest to her jumped like a bomb had gone off. A man let out a startled squeak before ducking his head and practically running away.

The woman glanced around before picking up the broom and placing it against the porch railing. She practically tripped over herself as she ran down the steps and strode away.

I clasped Aisling's hand and squeezed it as I looked to Corson and Bale. "Something's not right here."

"No, it's not," Corson muttered.

"I don't think we need anything from the people here," Bale said.

"I agree," Lix said.

Drawing Aisling away from the corner of the building, we stayed to the shadows as we made our way back toward the woods. We were almost to the tree line when I smacked into something and staggered back into Aisling.

"What's the matter?" she whispered.

That was a fantastic question and one I couldn't answer as I stared at the trees only five feet away from us. I stretched my hand out, but it only made it a foot before it smacked up against an invisible barrier.

"What the fuck?" I muttered as I released Aisling's hand to press both my palms against what should be wide open space.

Corson swore when he stepped forward and his fingers brushed up against the same, unseen wall. His talons burst from the back of his hand, and when he pulled back his fist to plunge them into the barrier, they came to a stop against the wall.

I pulled Aisling closer to me as Lix and Bale moved further away in opposite directions; they kept their hands out as they followed the curve of the barrier. I pulled back my hand to slam it against the invisible wall, but lowered it. If Corson's talons couldn't slice through it, my hand wouldn't do any good. Bale and Lix were a good hundred feet away from us and still feeling along the barrier.

We were trapped here.

"The beast won't let you leave once you enter," a tiny voice said from behind us.

My hands fisted as I spun toward the voice. I was prepared to kill anyone and everyone I encountered until I saw the boy. He was about three or four years old and held a blanket against his cheek while sucking his thumb. His disheveled brown hair hung into the corners of his blue eyes.

"What did you say?" Wren asked as Bale and Lix stalked back to us.

The boy scanned all of us before he pulled his thumb from his mouth and pointed at Lix. "What is he?"

"I'm a skellein," Lix answered. "What did you say about a beast?"

"The beast doesn't let us go free," the boy whispered.

He glanced anxiously toward the mountain; over the top of the houses, the entrance to the cave was visible. Pushed back from each side of the entrance were piles of boulders and a good fifty feet separated the shadowed interior from the carts. I'd never seen a mining cave before, but the stones outside the entrance seemed out of place. I assumed those would have been cleared away, but what did I know?

When the boy turned back to us, his eyes were wide over his blanket. "The beast *eats* us."

I edged closer to Aisling; I'd destroy this whole town before I let anything happen to her. Aisling stepped out from behind me and walked over and knelt in front of the boy. I kept my eyes on the town as I followed her over to the boy.

"Where are your parents?" she asked.

The boy's eyes filled with tears, and he stuck his thumb back in his mouth. Aisling rested a hand against his cheek as another woman ran around the corner of the building and skidded to a halt when she spotted the boy.

"Oliver," she breathed and ran for the boy at the same time Wren blurted, "Nadine!"

CHAPTER TWENTY-SEVEN

Hawk

The name Nadine tickled something at the back of my memory, but I couldn't quite place it. With her brown hair, slender build, and gently lined face, she didn't look familiar, but Wren knew her. Nadine's head turned toward Wren, and she stopped her heedless rush toward the boy, and her mouth fell open. Her hazel eyes filled with tears, and a radiant smile lit her face.

With tears streaming down her face, Wren rushed forward and embraced the woman. I looked to Corson for an answer, but he was smiling at them while Bale and Lix remained focused on the mountain.

"Wren," Nadine breathed as she stepped back to wipe the tears from her eyes. Then her elation vanished. "Oh, Wren, you shouldn't be here!"

"It's already too late."

Nadine's lower lip quivered, and she rested her hand on Oliver's shoulder when he tottered over to stand beside her.

"Where's Randy?" Wren asked.

Suddenly the memory of where I heard Nadine's name clicked

into place. After the gateway opened, demons murdered Wren's parents. Randy found and raised her, and he later married a woman named Nadine. Before we started working with Wren, Randy and Nadine had split off to travel deeper into the Wilds in the hopes of mapping out more land and finding somewhere safer for everyone to live.

"He's okay, and he's here. Right now, he's helping me look for this little troublemaker," Nadine said and lifted Oliver's hand.

"Oh, thank God," Wren said and wiped the tears from her eyes.

Nadine gripped Wren's wrist and squeezed it. "*Why* are you here?"

"We were following the horsemen."

Nadine blinked at her. "The horsemen... of the *apocalypse?*"

"We have a lot to catch up on," Wren said, and removing Nadine's hand from her wrist, she hooked her arm through Nadine's and turned toward us. "But first I'd like you to meet Corson, Bale, Lix, Hawk, and Aisling. Everyone, this is Nadine, she helped raise me."

If Nadine was shocked to discover Wren working so closely with demons, she hid it well as she smiled at us. Before Wren approached Kobal about working together, the Wilders kept their distance and much preferred to slaughter any demon they came across.

"It's nice to meet you," Corson said and held out his hand.

Nadine didn't hesitate before taking it. "I wish it was under better circumstances." She released Corson's hand and turned to Wren. She smiled as she brushed back a strand of hair from Wren's forehead. "Randy is going to be so happy to see you, even if it is in this place."

She released Wren and lifted Oliver into her arms. The boy sucked his thumb as he studied us. Those big, soulful blue eyes had far too much wisdom in them for someone of his tender years. Without thinking, I rested my hand on his back as I smiled at him.

He smiled back and laid his head on Nadine's shoulder while I lowered my hand.

"What is going on here?" Wren asked.

"I'll explain when we find Randy," Nadine said. "Come with me."

She started to walk away, but a voice behind us halted her.

"Hey," Caim said as he strolled toward us. "Have you—"

"Stop!" Bale commanded. "Don't take another step."

Caim froze with his foot in midair. One of the hounds emerged from the shadows and edged toward the invisible barrier.

"Partka," Corson commanded the hound.

He didn't have to tell it to stay as the hound stopped before the barrier and sniffed the edge of it. Its hackles rose, and it bared its teeth before it sat.

"What do we have here?" Caim asked as he lowered his foot and placed his hand on the hound's head. "I don't see anything."

"Neither do we," Corson said. "And you can walk freely toward us, but we can't get out of here."

"Well, isn't that just a 'fuck me' kind of day," Caim murmured.

"I guess that would be the best way to describe it," Corson said. "I wouldn't risk flying over the town either."

"I already have," Caim said. "I didn't miraculously know the town was here before I told you about it."

If Corson could have gotten through the barrier, I think he would have choked him. "I would suggest *not* flying over it again," Corson grated through his teeth. "Maybe there's no barrier over the top of the town, or maybe you got lucky and missed it."

Caim tapped his chin as he pondered this. "I *am* a lucky sort of fellow."

"We need you outside the barrier," Corson grated through his teeth.

Caim lowered his foot and saluted him. "Whatever you say, boss."

"And keep the hounds with you."

Caim glanced at the hound by his side. "I don't think they have any interest in joining you."

"Come on," Corson said and turned away from Caim.

"Is that a fallen angel?" Nadine whispered as she led us around the side of the building.

"He's more like an annoying pigeon," Corson muttered, and I laughed.

When Corson shot me a look, I shrugged as I clasped Aisling's elbow. "He had a point, and he's *our* annoying pigeon."

"Did he lead you here on purpose?" Nadine asked.

If she'd asked that question a year ago, I would have said probably, but I knew better now. Caim was a little crazy, a whole lot annoying sometimes, but he was on our side.

"No," Corson said. "He didn't know we wouldn't be able to leave this town once we entered. I want to choke him most of the time, but he's a loyal asshole."

"Just not loyal to Lucifer," Aisling said.

"He wouldn't be loyal to us either if we decided to destroy the world," I said. "He's loyal to life, people, and the continuation of the world. He didn't fall far enough to rid himself of that allegiance."

Aisling

I grasped the mug of water Lix set on the table in front of me. "There's no alcohol in this place," he muttered as he took the chair across from me.

"Are you going to survive not having it?" Corson asked.

"I'm not sure any of us are going to survive this," Lix replied.

I wasn't much of a drinker, but I suddenly wished the potent mjéod was filling my mug instead of water. Glancing around the barroom, I wasn't surprised to find it full of demons and humans. Even without alcohol, a bar was a social place, and people and demons wanted to be where other people and demons were.

Most of them drew closer to us as their curiosity attracted them to the newcomers. The sympathetic looks on their faces set my teeth on edge. I had no idea what was going on here, but they all acted like we were as good as dead. Even the ones who sat on the barstools thirty feet away were turned with their backs to the bar so they could give us sympathetic looks.

Studying the humans, I didn't see anything threatening about them, and their souls were what I was used to seeing. They had good, strong souls, but fear made people do crazy things and there was a *lot* of fear in this town.

The middle of the room was filled with tables and chairs while booths lined the outer wood-paneled wall. The bar was on the wall furthest to the left, but no bottles lined the shelves, and nothing remained of the glass in the mirror frame hanging behind the shelves. The windows at the front of the building were dirty, but the sun's rays illuminated the room as there was no electricity.

Antlers made up the lamps hanging overhead; spiders had turned them into their jungle gym. The layer of dust on the lamps was so thick it was impossible to tell if there was once any color to them. Square and rectangle patches of darker wood revealed where pictures once hung, but those pictures were all gone.

Randy sat to my right with Nadine and Wren beside him. Brushed back from his handsome face, Randy's sandy blond hair was graying at the temples. His warm brown eyes were full of love as he spoke with Wren. The warmth and strength of his soul made me smile while Nadine's gave me a sense of comfort.

The three of them were eagerly catching each other up on the details of their lives. Wren had revealed she was a demon now and Corson's Chosen, she told them about something called the Abyss, the horsemen, the fallen angels, and the battle at the wall. Everyone in the room hung on her every word.

The most shock Randy and Nadine revealed was over her and Corson; they kept glancing between the two of them as if they couldn't believe it. Wren tapped her fingers on the table, shifted in her seat, and pulled at the collar of her shirt as she revealed this detail.

Corson clasped one of her hands and held it on the table, but it did little to calm her. The glimmer in his orange eyes said he would kill Randy if he hurt Wren.

"I had no choice but to go to the demons," Wren blurted. "I needed their help to protect us after the seals fell."

Randy rested his hand on top of the one drumming against the table. "I would have done the same. Things have changed a lot since we last saw each other."

Some of the tension eased from Wren's shoulders, and when her head bowed, Corson rubbed her neck.

"You did the right thing, Wren," Randy assured her and squeezed her hand before releasing it.

She smiled at him and relaxed further into Corson's touch. "Did you make it all the way across the Wilds?" she asked Randy.

"We did," Randy said as he grasped Nadine's hand.

"And?" Wren prompted.

The sad look on his face said what he'd discovered there before he spoke. "And we mapped out more of the land and know where batches of demons have clustered, but we didn't discover anywhere safer for the Wilders to live. We made it to the wall in California before deciding it was time to return home. That was when we got trapped here."

"How long have you been trapped here?" Wren asked.

"Almost a month," Nadine said.

"*What* trapped you here?" Corson asked.

"The minotaur," Randy said.

"I thought so." Lix sighed as he uncapped his flask and took a swig. When he finished, he shook the last few drops into his mouth before recapping it and setting it on the table. "It's a bad time to run out of alcohol."

I stared at the sunlight shining off the surface of the flask as I processed Randy's words.

"*The* minotaur as in the labyrinth minotaur?" Hawk asked.

"That's what it looks like," Randy said.

"That's what it *is*," one of the demons said. "I know the minotaur; I've seen its pictures on the caves in Hell, and it's here."

"The minotaur was behind seal one hundred twenty-six," Corson said, and his gaze went to the doorway. "Humans got some of its story correct, but instead of the labyrinth being created to house the minotaur, *it* created the labyrinth to trap and hunt its prey."

"Wonderful," Wren muttered.

"This town is its holding pen, and its maze is in the mountain, or at least that's what we assume. It comes down to hunt at night and takes its captives up to the mine," another demon said.

Bale sat with her back ramrod straight and her eyes on the door. "It only comes down to hunt at night?"

"Yes," Randy said.

"How often?"

"It's always different," the same demon said as he ran a hand through his blue hair. "I've been here for three months, and it's never come down at regular intervals, which is why we think its maze is in the mountain. We think it turns its prey loose to hunt through the labyrinth, and some prey takes longer than others to catch."

"I'd say that's a good assumption," Corson said. "Why don't you all group together to fight it?"

"We do," Randy said. "Every time it comes down, we try to fight it, but we haven't found a way to stop it."

"It barges in here, we fight it, sometimes someone ends up dead, and it still takes who it wants," another demon with two tusks curling like a handlebar mustache out of the side of his face said. "Sometimes, it takes multiple people and demons back to its lair. The selection is completely random too. We've seen it take people and demons who arrive that day and others who have been here for months. It doesn't care about sex or age, human or demon. It randomly decides who it's going to play with next before taking them away."

"With no pattern, its harder to anticipate its movements," Bale murmured.

"I can anticipate slicing its head off," Lix stated as he tapped the handle of his sword.

"I've come across many creatures in Hell and more of them since the seals fell," the blue-haired demon said, "but nothing like this. The thing's a ten-foot-tall, unstoppable beast."

"It has to have a weakness," Hawk insisted.

They all looked at each other, and most shook their heads while a few shrugged.

"It doesn't like fire," a man said. "But fire doesn't stop it."

"Great," Hawk muttered.

Nadine glanced at where Oliver sat in the corner tossing a ball back and forth with a demon who had two clear horns on his head. Nadine leaned over the table and cast her voice low. "It took Oliver's mother a couple of weeks ago and his father before we arrived here. We've been taking care of him, and he'll stay with us if we ever get out of this, but if that thing comes for him..."

Her voice trailed off as tears filled her eyes. Randy took her hand and lowered it into his lap. A sense of panic clawed at my chest while I watched the beautiful boy giggle and toss the ball back.

Despite everything he'd been through, joy still radiated from his glowing, white soul. There was little hope in this world, but

Oliver offered so much of it. He was the future and I didn't care what I had to do, I would make sure he survived this.

"We won't let that happen," Hawk said.

"Why didn't you put up signs or set guards to warn people away from this place?" I asked.

"We have put up signs," Tusks said. "But the beast tears them down, and there is too much land to cover to place guards all over town. There are still some signs left on the other side of town, and we were going to place more up today, but you arrived before we could."

Lucky for us.

"What about blowing up the entrance to the mountain and caging it in?" I asked.

"We tried that," Randy said. "It dug itself out again."

"*That's* why there are boulders on either side of the mine," Hawk said. "I thought it was strange."

"That's why," Randy confirmed. "We blocked the entrance two weeks ago, but we still couldn't escape the barrier and even with the entrance covered, the minotaur found a way into town and took a woman."

"So there's at least one other exit from the mountain," Bale said.

"Yes," Tusks said. "And it's outside of the barrier as we went up the mountain to search for it, but couldn't get beyond the wall."

"It's created a labyrinth within the mountain," Corson said. "And it's given its prey a chance to escape."

"How many do you think have made it out?" Bale asked.

"Probably no one, but there's a way out."

Lix pulled his sword from its sheath and set the blade on the table. "Killing the beast is another way out."

"And if fighting doesn't work?" Hawk asked.

"It doesn't," Tusks muttered.

"I'm not dying in this place," Lix said.

"Neither am I." Bale's chair skidded across the battered

wooden floor as she rose and walked over to the door. She opened it to stare at the mountain. "We're going to kill it."

The blue-haired demon snorted as another one muttered, "Good luck."

"What about Raphael?" I asked. "Maybe weapons and strength can't take it down, but his ability to wield life would."

"It would," Corson agreed. "But if we send Caim for him, what if they somehow end up missing each other?"

"But he could already be on his way." I refused to give up hope the golden angel might arrive in time to kill this thing they believed was invincible.

"He could, but I think we're going to have to deal with this on our own," Corson said.

I refused to let my trepidation and disappointment show as I switched the focus to something else. "What is the barrier?"

"Part of the minotaur's labyrinth," Bale said. "It uses its power to keep us locked into what I guess you could call its holding pen. Its weaved its magic all over this town and that mountain like a spider creating a web to trap a fly."

"And we walked right into its web," Lix said.

Hawk clasped my hand and squeezed it in his. "And we will destroy it."

CHAPTER TWENTY-EIGHT

Hawk

The wooden steps creaked as I followed Randy and Aisling up the set of dusty stairs to the top floor of the hotel. Randy had said this building offered one of the best views of the mountain.

"We don't sleep here," Randy said. "We stay in the library. It's big enough to house all of us in one room, and even if it doesn't help stop the minotaur, we all feel safer together. We leave the building when it comes down from the mountain. We used to stay in the school, but when we refused to come out, it tore the building apart so, to keep our shelter, we go outside to face it."

When Aisling glanced at me, I saw the terror in her eyes before she turned away. I briefly rested my hand over hers on the railing before she climbed further up. I ground my teeth as I watched the stiff set of her back and shoulders; she shouldn't be here, but neither should anyone else.

Somehow, I would get her out of this mess.

"Have you tried spreading out through the town and hiding from it?" Aisling asked.

"Once. It only destroyed more buildings on the other side of town until it uncovered who it was hunting. Having to look for us excited it more," Randy said.

"There has to be a way to stop it."

"There is," I said. "It just hasn't been discovered yet, but we'll find it."

At the top of the stairs, Randy turned left. I fell into step beside Aisling as he led us down a hall of closed doors. "These are all rooms," Randy said as he waved at the doors. "But the mattresses were removed from them awhile ago. Most of them are in the library now."

"How long has the minotaur been doing this?" Aisling asked.

"Probably since it escaped Hell," I said.

She bit her bottom lip. "That's a lot of victims over a year."

"Too many," Randy said as he opened the door at the end of the hall and stepped back to let us enter.

A scarred brown bureau stood against the wall on my right, and a dusty blue throw rug lay in the middle of the room. Dust caked the TV mounted to the wall across from the bed frame for a queen-sized bed. A musty smell permeated the room.

Striding across the room, I pulled back the red curtain covering the window to reveal the mountain. The entrance was about twelve feet tall and six feet wide. I didn't know if it was that big when this place was a working mine or if the minotaur made it larger.

Aisling came to stand beside me, and, unable to resist, I rested my hand on the small of her back as I drew her closer. Inhaling her sweet scent, I let it wash over and relax me as I studied the shadows of the entrance before turning my attention to the town.

Three streets away, a row of toppled buildings blocked the road, and on the next street, only part of a brick building remained standing while the rest of the bricks littered the ground. That must have been some of the buildings they tried hiding in and the school. A few streets further away from the school was another row of toppled buildings, and I suspected they'd tried to hide from the minotaur on more than one occasion.

"What did you use to blow up the entrance of the mine?" I asked Randy.

"There was a demon here who could make things vibrate enough that he brought the rocks down. The minotaur has taken him since then."

"What do you do for water and food?" I asked.

"Animals sometimes cross the barrier," Randy said. "There were a couple of crab apple trees, but the apples have gone now, so we rely on the animals. I don't think anyone has lived here long enough to be concerned by the lack of variety and nutrients. Wraiths also find their way beneath the barrier, and the demons feed on them."

"And water?" Aisling asked.

"There's a well by the library and a couple more behind some of the homes. We pull water from them and store it in the library, restaurant, and a few other places in case something happens to the wells."

"That's good," Aisling said. "Can we get closer to the mountain?"

Randy shifted beside me as he glanced uneasily at her. "You can, but it won't do you any good. There's nothing to see there either; unless you plan to enter."

"Maybe that's not such a bad idea," she said, and I felt like someone kicked me in the chest. "It's not expecting its victims to venture in there willingly. We could turn the tables on it."

"You want to go in there *willingly*?" Randy asked.

"No, but if staying in this town and fighting it isn't working, then maybe it's time to try something new."

"It would kill us all."

"Would it? Or would some of us get away before it found us?"

Randy closed his mouth as he turned his attention back to the cave. Her idea wasn't entirely insane, but I couldn't stand the thought of her entering that cave.

"Oliver has already lost so much," Randy said.

A shiver ran through Aisling, and she rubbed her arms. "We can't let it take him," she murmured so low I didn't think Randy heard her.

On the street below, Bale, Corson, Lix, and Wren strode into view with Nadine and some of the others from the restaurant. Nadine carried Oliver as they walked toward a two-story brick building spreading across three lots.

When they stopped at the bottom of the stairs, Nadine pointed toward the mountain before they climbed the steps. Over the front doors was a black sign with the word library etched with gold lettering onto it. The double glass doors opened before they reached them, and they disappeared inside.

"I think the minotaur knows who it's going to take before it comes into the town," Randy said.

"What makes you say that?" I asked.

He placed the tip of his index finger against the glass as he pointed at the town. "That toppled wood building over there."

There were so many of them that I couldn't be sure which one he meant, but I still asked, "What about it?"

"Oliver's mom stayed inside with him. It bypassed all of us to get at her. Thankfully, Nadine remained inside to help her with Ollie, and she was able to get him out, but that thing wanted *her*, and there was nothing we could do to stop it."

When Aisling shuddered, I wrapped my arm around her waist and drew her close. "I'm going to keep you safe," I vowed.

She rested her hand on my chest as she leaned against me.

"How do you know when it's coming?" I asked Randy.

"You'll learn it's impossible not to know," he said. "Come on, we should meet up with the others."

I remained where I was as I tried to process everything we

learned since entering this town. There had to be some way to kill the minotaur, but we couldn't learn its weaknesses without seeing it first, and I did *not* want it in this town and near Aisling.

However, if the people in this town were right, it didn't sound like it had any weaknesses. They couldn't be right; *everything* had a vulnerability.

∾

Hawk

Stepping into the shadowy interior of the library, I took in the mattresses spread across the floor, the rows of shelves, tables, and the front desk to my left. At least twenty people and demons were scattered throughout the room. Some of them sat on mattresses with their shoulders slumped forward and a dejected air about them, while others prowled the place like they were about to tear it apart.

The scent of old, musty books brought me back to my child-hood and the time before the war when my mom took my sisters and me to the library every week. While they did story hour, I roamed the shelves and picked out books to read.

When I finished, I'd return to sit at the edge of story hour and listen while I waited. Sometimes, I'd watch the delight on my sisters' faces as the librarian made strange faces and used silly voices. Sherry loved this the most. She'd scream and cover her face with her hands or squeal with excitement while she laughed. Her blonde hair bounced against her shoulders while her blue eyes sparkled with amusement.

An unexpected ache filled my chest, and I rubbed the place over my heart. The memory was so vivid I felt like I could touch her, but Sherry had traveled far beyond my reach.

"How many are here?" I asked Randy.

"Including your group, there's thirty-seven of us."

"Thirty-seven against one."

"It's not that easy," Randy said and smiled when Nadine walked over with Oliver in her arms.

"Nothing ever is," I said.

Oliver stuck his thumb in his mouth as he rested his head on Nadine's shoulder. The strange blend of having seen too much and innocence in his eyes reminded me so much of Judy. I couldn't save Judy, but I would save him and Aisling.

Across the room, I spotted Corson and Bale standing by the front desk as they talked to a giant demon with maroon skin and green eyes. I clasped Aisling's elbow before slipping my fingers into hers and starting toward Corson and Bale.

She fell into step beside me as we strode across the room. On our way, I spotted Wren and Lix standing near the card catalog and going through a pile of weapons stacked beside it. My step faltered as I took in the hundreds of knives, swords, guns, spears, and various other deadly instruments.

Those weapons once belonged to the demons and humans who entered this town and never left. Seeing them piled there was like seeing a mound of their bones as this was all that remained of them.

Aisling's hand went to her mouth. "Oh."

Her delicate beauty stole my breath as she looked between me and the weapons and back again. Drawing her closer, I released her hand to clasp her cheeks in my palms and lowered my forehead to rest it against hers. Her warm breath tickled my lips as she stared at me.

"We're going to be okay," I assured her.

Her hands gripped my wrists. "We are."

I kissed the tip of her nose before reluctantly releasing her and stepping away. Her hand caught mine, and she detoured from Bale and Corson to join Lix and Wren at the pile. To the left of the pile and card catalog was a row of tables with computers spread out across it. Dust covered the machines, and a few of the tables had been pushed aside to make room for the growing mound of weapons.

Wren lifted a throwing star into the air before releasing it. It clattered as it fell on top of the other weapons and tumbled down the side. "Obviously these weapons were useless for their past owners."

"Or they didn't know how to use them," Lix said as he hefted a spear and tapped the end of it against the floor. The metal tip gleamed in the light from the floor-to-ceiling windows across the room.

"Did you ever see the minotaur?" I asked Lix.

"No. It was before my time," he replied. "And I never went down to the seals to look at it."

Wren lifted a set of brass knuckles before tossing them back on the pile. "We can choose any weapon we want."

Since becoming a demon, I'd tried to rely on my natural defenses more than human weapons. Canagh demons didn't have some of the more physical defenses other demons had, like Corson's talons or Aisling's fire, but I was fast and strong, and my kiss could make someone a mindless sex slave. However, I didn't see the minotaur bending down to let me kiss it or walking under some mistletoe anytime soon.

This pile made my fingers itch for some of those weapons, and I suspected my natural defenses wouldn't do much against this beast. Then again, these weapons were useless against it too.

"Bullets don't work against it." I looked up as a man walked over to stand before Aisling, who held a rifle. "They barely slow it."

Aisling stopped inspecting the gun to study the man. "But they do slow it?"

"Most weapons are useless against it, but some have made it bleed. I can show you what works best against it."

When the man's gaze ran leisurely over her, I growled as I stepped closer to Aisling and rested my hand on the small of her back. I leveled the man with a look that made his eyes widen, and he took a staggering step back.

"You can show *me* what works best against it," I told him.

The man blinked at me as he started stuttering. "I, uh... yeah... well..." He glanced at his watch. "I forgot I have guard duty. It was nice to meet you."

The man hurried away so fast he tripped over a mattress and nearly fell on his face. He glanced back at us before righting himself and rushing down the stairs to the front doors.

"Marking your territory?" Aisling asked.

I rested my fingers against my bite on her neck. "I already have, but humans aren't as aware of it as demons."

"I am still my own person."

I stiffened as my hand fell from her neck. Wren and Lix lowered their weapons to the pile and glanced around the library before wandering away to join Bale and Corson.

"Were you interested in him?" I demanded.

"Not at all, and this has nothing to do with any nonexistent interest in another." She shoved the rifle into my chest. "I'm not a thing to be claimed."

"You've claimed me too," I reminded her.

"And if someone started flirting with you, and I got all pissy about it, what would you do?"

I smiled as I clasped her wrist and moved her arm behind her, pinning it to the small of her back. Dropping my lips to her ear, I whispered, "Anytime you want to stake your claim on me and get all pissy about it, feel free to do so. I'll enjoy it."

When she leaned back to look at me, I hated the uncertainty in her eyes.

"I'm yours, Aisling; I always will be."

Her mouth parted, and her eyes fell to my lips. Her need blasted against my skin; I'd give anything to make her happy and to taste her, but I couldn't give her this. I would *never* let what happened to Sarah happen to Aisling.

She sagged against me, and I kissed the top of her head before resting my cheek against her silken hair. "I wish I could give you everything you need," I whispered, "but I can't."

She lifted her head and kissed my chin. "I have everything I need." Then she glanced around. "Except freedom."

"We're going to get that too."

"Damn right, we are."

When she stepped away from me, I released her. I started to turn away when her voice stopped me, "I'm yours too, Hawk."

I grinned at her, but she was already admiring a wicked-looking machete. Still, I couldn't stop smiling as I walked over to Corson and Bale.

"Did you talk to Caim?" I asked them.

"Yes," Bale said. "He's going to try to find Raphael or a way to get him here sooner."

"Good," I said as I glanced around the library. "Hopefully we won't need him."

CHAPTER TWENTY-NINE

Aisling

Nestled within Hawk's arms, I listened to the muffled sounds of the others as they tossed and turned in their sleep or snored. The moonlight spilling through the floor-to-ceiling windows only ten feet away from us was the only source of illumination in the library, but it revealed most of the mattresses spread across the floor.

Trying to sleep in this place was challenging enough without having Hawk's body draped protectively around mine. The last thing I should be thinking about in this stifling building was sex, but my body pleaded with me to roll over and take him inside me. I was almost to the point where I didn't care who saw us, but while sex in a public place sounded like fun, sex with others watching did not.

Plus, there was the possibility a half-man, half-bull monster could show up and wreak havoc any second now. That was enough to tamp down my growing desire even as Hawk's fingers slid through mine and he gripped my hand.

Someone coughed in the shadows, and a sob came from somewhere to my right. I almost threw aside the blanket and bolted to my feet. I couldn't take the oppression of this place or the hopelessness of these people anymore. Instead, I burrowed closer to Hawk and tried to shut out the despair enshrouding the building.

His lips nuzzled my cheek as he cradled me against him. Locked in his arms, I didn't feel as overwhelmed or sad and melted against him. And then, I felt the faintest vibrations in the floor.

I held my breath as I waited to see if something would follow it, but I didn't sense anything else. I was starting to relax when I felt it again and, behind me, some books rattled on a shelf. Someone cried out, and the sobs became louder as the next vibration caused the metal in the pile of weapons to click.

I realized the vibrations were the steps of the minotaur when the next one caused the light fixture overhead to sway. The next step rattled the glass in the windows. Through the shadows, I saw people sitting up on their mattresses before pushing themselves to their feet. Something about the resignation encasing them caused sorrow to rise in me.

They were already so defeated. I hadn't let myself think about what would happen when the minotaur arrived, but no matter what, I would not let myself accept the inevitable fate they'd chosen.

It was time to kill a beast and get out of here.

Hawk's breath tickled my ear as he spoke. "Stay close to me."

"If you stay close to me," I whispered.

"Always."

He kissed my cheek before releasing me and rolling away. I instantly missed him against my back, but I shoved my feet into my boots and tied them while I tried to shut out the muffled sobs of those around us.

Their acceptance of their inevitable deaths irritated me, but it unnerved me too. There were some strong and powerful demons here, yet they were as convinced as the humans that the minotaur was unbeatable.

I tried not to think about that as I slung a rifle over my back before lifting a spear. I'd picked out both weapons earlier in the hopes they would keep me from having to get too close to the beast. I raised my palm before me and willed a ball of fire to life.

The flames danced across my face as I made it grow before shrinking it again. I'd practiced with it every day, and it was a lot stronger since I bonded with Hawk, but I didn't know how effective it would be against the minotaur, and I preferred not to get close enough to use it against the beast. Still, if that thing grabbed me, I'd torch its ass.

"Come on, everyone, outside," Randy said.

I glanced at Hawk when he moved closer to me and rested his hand on the small of my back. The minotaur's next step caused a book to tumble off a shelf; it hit the floor with a bang that caused me to jump.

Get your act together. You've trained for this and worse.

Then why did I feel like the virgin sacrifice climbing up the mountain to throw herself into the erupting volcano to appease the gods? The gods would be greatly disappointed if *I* was their virgin sacrifice; the volcano would probably belch me up.

We fell in at the back of the group as everyone funneled down the stairs to the swinging doors below. Nadine remained sitting on her mattress with Oliver on her lap. The boy clung to her, but no tears streaked his face as he watched everyone walking past.

And then we were going down the stairs and out the front doors to the street below. Leaves and dust covered the cracked asphalt, and the weeds poking through large patches of the road made it more green than black. I hoped no one broke an ankle on the broken street as we gathered in the middle of it.

When I turned to look at the mountain, I expected to find the minotaur already making its way down the road, but I didn't see it anywhere.

"Where is...?" My question trailed off as what I'd assumed was part of a house on the hill suddenly moved.

My throat went dry when I realized it wasn't a house, but the beast. The thing was still a quarter mile away, but each of its steps vibrated the ground with increasing intensity.

"Is this where you always fight it?" Bale asked.

"We've tried setting traps, spreading out, attacking from different positions, attacking from the buildings, hiding, charging up the hill, ambushing it outside the cave, and none of it worked. Now, instead of tiring ourselves out by doing all those things, we wait for it to come to us. The death count is lower this way. If it has to hunt for its victim, it tends to kill whoever it comes across until then," Tusks said.

"It must weigh two ton," I said as it rounded a bend and vanished; the steady shaking of the ground told of its continued approach.

And then it was coming around the corner of another building and standing at the end of the street. I adjusted my grip on the spear as the moonlight spilling over it revealed all its repulsive details; my heart galloped like a runaway horse.

Standing on its legs, it was at least ten feet tall and the size of a small house. Its chest was the size of five men put together and broader than any tree, and its shoulders were more like battering rams. Though it had the body of a man; it was like no man I'd ever seen.

And then there was its head. I'd expected the head of a bull, but I hadn't anticipated the glowing, sickly yellow eyes or the pulled back muzzle revealing razor-sharp teeth no bull possessed. Two black horns curved out two feet from either side of its head before twisting over, so the lethal ends aimed ahead of it. Turned toward us were its two pointed ears.

Three-inch-long claws tipped the foot-long fingers of its massive hands, and its black, cloven hooves also looked like they could eviscerate a person. Fine brown hair covered its entire body, but the etched muscles of its chest were visible beneath the hair.

A chill ran down my spine, and I gulped as I tried not to let the size of this monster intimidate me, but it was almost impossible not to edge away from it as it grinned at us. And then, it was running toward us.

The thunderous beats of its hooves rebounded off the buildings. Someone cried and threw themselves to the ground where they started to weep. Hawk stepped protectively closer to me and hefted the battle ax he'd selected from the weapons. I forced myself to keep breathing as the minotaur closed the distance between us.

When it was only ten feet away, it dropped to all fours and charged at us like a bull. Feeling like the pin in front of the bowling ball, I darted to the side seconds before it would have gored me.

My foot caught on a broken piece of asphalt, and my ankle twisted out from under me. Unable to get my hands out in time, I fell to the side. Taking the impact on my shoulder, I rolled before leaping to my feet.

I spotted Hawk across the road as the minotaur barreled over two women before stopping at the end of the street. One of the women was still alive and clutching her stomach. The other was sprawled across the road like a broken rag doll while blood seeped out beneath her.

"Look out!" someone shouted.

Randy grasped the injured woman's arm and started dragging her off the road as the minotaur came back toward us. He didn't get her out of the way fast enough as the minotaur speared her with a horn, tore her from Randy's grasp, and tossed her in the air. I didn't look to see where she landed as the beast veered and came straight at me.

CHAPTER THIRTY

Aisling

My body reacted like a deer caught in the headlights, but my training overrode my instincts, and I braced myself to leap out of the way. My vision pinpointed until all I saw was the glow of its eyes as the gigantic beast barreled toward me. I wanted to run screaming from it, but I had to wait until it was closer or it would veer off course and kill me anyway.

I leapt to the side at the same time as Hawk grabbed my arm and yanked me out of the way. He pushed me behind him, and grasping his battle ax with both hands, he smashed it into the minotaur's back. When I plunged my spear into its side, it tore from my hands. The ax also pulled away from Hawk.

The beast charged by us before rearing onto its back legs to grasp at the ax. As if it were no more than an annoying splinter, the minotaur stretched its arm over its back and plucked the ax free. As it studied the thing, a gurgled chortle issued from its throat before it threw the ax.

"Watch out!" Corson shouted.

Hawk and I flung ourselves to the ground as the ax flew so close that a breeze ruffled my hair when it soared over our heads. Someone screamed, and I looked up to see a demon staggering back with the ax embedded in her chest.

The minotaur plucked my spear free next, but before it could do anything with it, Lix raced forward with his sword raised while he released a savage battle cry. Corson, Bale, and Wren followed as Lix dodged the hand the minotaur swung at him and leapt onto the creature.

With the agility of a monkey, he dodged the minotaur's grasping hands as he clambered up the front of the creature before swinging around to its back. Raising his sword, he clasped it with both hands before plunging it through the creature's neck.

The minotaur's muscles were so thick the blade embedded halfway through before catching on sinew and refusing to budge. The creature slapped at Lix like he was a flea, but the skellein dodged the blows as he yanked on his sword to free it.

Corson leapt off the ground and plunged his talons into the beast's throat. Before he could pull his talons free, the minotaur's nostrils flared, and it seized Corson. The beast's hand swallowed half of Corson's body.

"No!" Wren shouted as she ran behind it and sliced open its Achilles tendons.

The minotaur roared and tossed Corson aside as Bale plunged her sword into its chest and more demons ran forward to spear it. Hawk and I scrambled to our feet and ran to join the others as more humans and demons leapt into the battle.

Blood oozed from the minotaur's wounds as it swung its claws down. The powerful blow eviscerated one woman and cleaved a demon in half. I recoiled and closed my eyes when warm blood sprayed my face.

Before I could clear the blood from my eyes, something hit me so hard, it lifted me off my feet and tossed me aside. I couldn't see where I was going or how high I flew as wind whipped around me.

"Aisling!" Hawk bellowed.

My breath burst out of me, needles of pain pierced my body, and my lungs compressed when I crashed into the side of a building. Wood splintered, and something gave way against my back, but I didn't go all the way through the wall. Instead, I hung for a moment before sliding to the ground.

I struggled to gasp in air, but my lungs refused to accept it until, finally, the pressure in my chest eased and oxygen rushed in. I tried to open my eyes, but the blood caking my lashes made it impossible to see. Wiping frantically at them, I listened to the screams and grunts of the battle; not being able to see made it more terrifying.

Hawk! I scrubbed at my eyes and peeled them open again.

I found Hawk immediately as he darted out of the way of the minotaur's horns. The beast was back on all fours. As it swung its head back and forth, it shoved and threw aside anyone close to it before rising onto its legs again and reaching over its back for Lix.

When it grasped Lix, another demon ran in and thrust a sword into the creature's stomach. The minotaur ripped the sword free and plucked Lix off its back before tossing him aside. Then it fell to the earth with enough force it dented the asphalt and rattled the glass in the windows beside me.

I pushed myself further up the side of the building when those yellow eyes swung in my direction. My heart plummeted into my stomach as it turned and raced toward me. My hand fell to one of my guns, and I pulled it free. Shooting this thing would be like firing at a freight train, but it wouldn't take me alive.

My first two shots struck it in the chest and blood spilled free, but it never slowed. The third bullet hit it in the center of the forehead. Its head jerked back a little, but that was the only reaction it revealed to being shot in the *fucking head.*

My ears rang as I continued to fire until my gun emptied, and I tossed it aside. Lifting my hands, I willed fire into them. My terror must have fueled them as the flames burst free and encircled my wrists. If bullets and axes weren't any good against this thing, my fire wouldn't do much, but I'd make this thing scream.

When Hawk raced after the minotaur, the fury on his face propelled me to my feet. I couldn't let him get himself killed trying to fight this beast. If this thing was going to take me, then so be it, but Hawk would make it through this.

Still a little disoriented from hitting the wall, I stumbled more than ran toward the minotaur, but it was closing the distance between us fast. Three feet away from me, the creature came to a halt and plucked a motionless demon off the ground. I recognized Tusks as the minotaur lifted him and rose onto its hind legs.

Skidding to a halt, I staggered back as the minotaur examined Tusks before throwing the unconscious demon over its shoulder. On the other side of the minotaur, Hawk stopped running toward the beast and ran behind it toward me. The minotaur smacked another demon out of its way and strolled down the road as if it wasn't bleeding from a hundred different wounds.

I gawked after its fading back as it disappeared around a corner before reappearing on the trail to the mountain. Then, it ducked to enter the cave and vanished.

What remained of my adrenaline rushed out of me, and I nearly went down. I hated the relief that washed over me, but I'd been so sure that thing was coming for me. Instead, it chose Tusks, who would most likely die. I disliked myself for feeling grateful, but I couldn't help it. I was going to live another day.

Then, Hawk was before me and wrapping his arm around my waist. Unable to stand on my own anymore, I sagged against him. He easily kept me up as he cradled my head with his other hand and kissed my forehead.

"Are you okay?" he demanded.

I couldn't form words yet. I'd never seen or experienced anything as unstoppable as that *thing* before. Everyone had warned us, but none of us were willing to listen. Unless we came up with some new way to defeat it, that thing would pick us off one by one, but what could we possibly do to destroy it?

"Aisling, are you okay?" Hawk inquired as he pulled my head from his shoulder and brushed back my hair to look at me.

I opened my mouth to tell him I was fine; I would have told every other living creature I was good, but this was Hawk, and the truth slipped from my lips. "No. I thought it was coming for me."

"So did I."

"And when it took him instead..." My voice trailed off.

"I understand," he said as I'd known he would. "I was glad it wasn't you too. Come on, let's get you inside and somewhere you can relax."

Neither of us would ever relax again in this town, but I didn't resist as he led me back toward the library.

"What about the dead?" Wren asked.

"They'll still be there tomorrow," Randy said.

CHAPTER THIRTY-ONE

Hawk

I finished tying the rope onto one of the beams in the attic of the home and gave it a gentle tug. "Can you feel it?" I shouted down the stairs to Aisling.

From the first floor, I heard her distant shout of "Yes!"

I plucked the string one more time before walking away and climbing down the ladder to the second-floor hallway. With my forearm, I wiped the sweat from my brow while I gazed through the open door of the bedroom across from me and out the window.

Through the glass, I saw the woods and the sun creeping toward the horizon. Would the minotaur return tonight?

If it did, we would be better prepared for it, though everyone said traps were useless against it. I wanted to tell them they were wrong, but after last night, I suspected they weren't. That thing had stormed in here and slapped us around like annoying gnats it was determined to squash.

They told us it would happen, but I was so certain we could kill it. We'd survived the falling of the seals, escaped Hell, destroyed

Lucifer, battled the jinn, and destroyed five of the eleven horsemen; one overgrown cow couldn't be that tough to kill.

I hadn't expected that cow to be the size of a small house and nearly impervious to injury.

However, it didn't matter the minotaur seemed unbeatable; I *would* find a way to stop it. When it went after Aisling last night, I was sure she was the victim it was going to take, and I was helpless to stop it. I'd always known I'd do whatever it took to keep her safe, but in that instant, I realized how much she meant to me.

I was falling in love with her, and if I had to find some way to kiss the minotaur to stop it, I would do it.

"Hawk?" Aisling asked from the bottom of the stairs leading to the first floor.

"I'll be right down."

I tore my gaze away from the window and bent to lift the stairs going into the attic. They creaked as they slid into place. I plucked the string again, and it remained secure—one more trap set for the thing.

A squeak from one of the stairs alerted me Aisling was climbing them before she turned the corner of the hall. My heart skipped a beat when my gaze met hers and a sad smile curved the corners of her mouth. Her limp from last night was already gone, but the horror of the night lingered in her eyes.

When she glided toward me, I opened my arms and enveloped her against my chest when she stepped into them. She fit so perfectly against me that her body melded to mine. My chin rested on her head while she played with the buttons on my shirt.

She undid a couple of buttons, and her fingers slid inside my shirt to rest against my flesh. She sighed when her palms flattened against my skin. Sliding my fingers through her hair, I clasped her nape and held her closer.

"When I thought it was going to take you..." My voice trailed off when she lifted her head to look at me.

Her beauty robbed me of my breath, and releasing her nape, I clasped her cheeks in my hands as I kissed the tip of her nose. I stifled my resentment over not being able to really kiss her and show her how much I'd come to love her, but I settled for telling her.

"I'm falling in love with you, Aisling," I admitted as I released her face.

My mouth hovered near the corner of hers as she remained unmoving against me; her increased breaths warmed my cheek. Then she removed her hand from my shirt and rested it against my cheek. Leaning back, she released my face to trace her finger over my mouth; I turned my head away.

Rising onto her toes, she kissed my cheek before taking my earlobe into her mouth and nipping at it. My hands constricted on her when her fangs grazed my flesh and her breasts pressed against my chest. I lifted her off the floor and carried her into the bedroom to set her on the bed within.

When dust rose around her, I lifted her again and yanked the blanket off before setting her down. I gripped the bottom of her shirt, and she sat up as she lifted her arms into the air for me to tug it over her head.

I threw it on the floor before running my fingers over the delicate curve of her collarbone. Bending my head, I kissed the hollow beneath her throat and listened to the increased beat of her heart as I unhooked her bra and tossed it aside. I stroked the curve of her breast before rising over her again.

She leaned back and set her hands on the mattress while watching as I untied her boots and pulled them off; they hit the floor with a thud. I pulled her socks off before unbuttoning her pants.

A sexy smile curved her mouth, and she lifted her hips so I could tug her pants down. I admired the smooth curve of her legs while I ran my palms over her silken skin and shapely calves.

Unable to take being apart from her, I released her leg and rose to remove my boots, socks, and pants. She moved back and lay down when I climbed onto the bed to join her. Settling beside her, I propped my head on my elbow and simply stared at her. She was achingly lovely, and she was mine. She gripped the edges of my shirt and pushed it back until I shrugged it off.

Shifting my weight to one side, I rested my hand on her hip before sliding it to her thigh and running it down to her knee. Her hips rose and her legs spread when my fingers glided up the inside of her thigh. She gave an impatient little wiggle when I moved from one thigh to the other instead of sliding my fingers inside her. I skimmed my hand down her other leg as I memorized every inch of her body.

"You're exquisite," I murmured.

"You're a tease," she replied, and I grinned at her.

She smiled back at me as she rested her hands on my shoulders and pushed me back onto the bed. Pressing my shoulders into the mattress, she climbed on top of me and bent to kiss my neck before working her way down my chest. She used her teeth and tongue to leave a trail of kisses and nips across my flesh as she moved steadily lower.

I sucked in a breath when her breasts brushed against my rigid cock, and then she was hovering over it. She licked the head of my shaft while her hands ran down the inside of my thighs. Then she slid lower and nipped at my inner thigh.

My fingers twisted into the sheets as I waited for her to take me into her mouth, but she continued to run her hands over my legs as she kissed my inner thigh. Rising over me again, she ran her tongue down my dick before kissing my stomach. She leisurely made her way back up my body while her belly slid tantalizingly along my dick.

She leaned over me to whisper in my ear, "I can tease too."

I growled as I grasped her arms, lifted her, and flipped her over.

Her sweet laughter rang in my ears as I came down on top of her. Biting her lip, she lifted her arms over her head while she wiggled enticingly beneath me. My gaze latched on to her pert nipples, and I bent my head to suck one into my mouth.

Her fingers entwined in my hair as she held me close. "Mark me," she whispered.

I sank my fangs into her breast, and she cried out as she arched beneath me. The sound and scent of her set off something wild in me, and I rested my hands on her thighs as I pushed them apart. She lifted her hips to me.

"I need you inside me," she pleaded.

Unable to resist anymore, I thrust into her. Her tight wetness enveloped me, and I groaned against her breast as I buried myself inside her. For a second, I couldn't move as everything in me became centered on her.

I could spend another thousand years making love to her and still never get used to the way she fit me so perfectly or the right-ness of her in my arms. Her mouth nuzzled my cheek as she lifted her hips.

I licked her nipple before releasing her breast and kneeling between her thighs. She ran her hands down my chest, tracing every muscle there as her eyes followed her movements. When she reached the junction of where our bodies joined, she hesi-tated for a second before her hands fell away and her eyes met mine.

She locked her legs around my waist and dug her heels into my ass. She stared at me as she lifted herself and slid down my shaft again. Grasping her hips, I guided her movements while savoring every second of this. And then, she turned her head and sank her fangs into my arm. Her hips bucked against mine as her nails raked my flesh.

I felt something unraveling inside her, and it set off something in me that I couldn't stop. I'd planned to take my time, but I couldn't control myself. As I absorbed some of the sexual energy she released, I couldn't think beyond simple words.

Need.

Claim.

Mine.

And when she bit me again, and I sank my fangs into her, we became almost animalistic as we fucked like it might be the last time. And then she was crying out as her sheath clenched around me and her head fell back. Unable to hold back anymore, I plunged into her and came so hard my whole body shuddered with the release.

I almost collapsed on top of her but managed to turn to the side before falling onto the bed and drawing her into my arms. Hooking my leg around hers, I locked her against me. I was never going to let her go.

CHAPTER THIRTY-TWO

Aisling

I was pleasantly sore after what I could only consider a thorough claiming from the man sleeping against my back. I didn't think he meant to fall asleep, but his soft breaths stirred my hair, and I felt the rhythmic rise and fall of his chest.

Careful not to wake him, I wiggled around until I faced him. Relaxed in sleep, he looked five years younger, or maybe that was because he'd fed from me. I rested my hand against his cheek as his earlier words replayed in my mind. *"I'm falling in love with you, Aisling."*

I'd opened my mouth to tell him I loved him, but the words froze in my throat. He'd said, *I'm falling in love,* not *I'm in love with you.*

It was such a small difference, but it seemed as big as the Grand Canyon considering I *was* in love with him. He'd stolen my heart, and I couldn't leave myself vulnerable by letting him know that; instead, I'd remained silent while I took my need out on his body. And what a magnificent time it was.

I squirmed as recalling the details of what we did to each other aroused me again. I wanted to push Hawk back, climb on him, and take him once more, but I couldn't stop staring at him as I ran my thumb over his full lips. I'd never yearned for anything as badly as the claiming heat of his mouth on mine while I branded myself onto every inch of him.

When I first realized I was bound to him, I'd considered screaming as I ran away. The idea of being tied to someone I didn't know terrified me, but now that I knew him better, I couldn't consider the idea of living without him. I was so in love with him that the idea of being enslaved by his kiss didn't cause my legs to so much as twitch with the urge to run.

"The kiss of a canagh demon enslaves their lover," I recalled him saying, but what if that lover was already lost to the canagh demon? Would it matter then?

I was insane for considering it, but could we spend an eternity dancing around each other's mouths? A kiss would happen one day; either by accident or out of sheer frustration.

His lashes fluttered open as my thumb stilled on his lips before I leaned closer to him. He smelled of the earth and brownies, and his breath was sweet. When he turned his head away, I grasped his chin and pulled it back to me.

"Aisling—"

Before he could speak, I pressed my lips to his. He recoiled and knocked my hand away as he swung his feet to the floor; before he could get out of bed, I grasped his wrist to halt him. When he spun on me, rage filled his eyes.

"I won't be responsible for destroying you!" he spat.

"This is *my* decision to make." *And it might be the worst decision you ever make!*

But I found myself stubbornly insisting I could handle this. I was his Chosen; demons were specifically designed to do only certain things with their Chosen. I had to believe withstanding the kiss of a canagh was one of those things.

You're insane. But I'd always suspected that.

"No, it's not," Hawk said.

He tried to turn away again, but with a speed I didn't know I possessed, I locked my leg over his waist and twisted so I straddled his lap. His eyebrows rose, and I'd shocked myself, but my demon DNA must still have a few tricks up its sleeve. I suspected the growing strength of our bond was unraveling those tricks, which only reaffirmed my belief I could survive his kiss without becoming a mindless sex slave.

"I'm already bound to you, branded by you, and claimed by you. My existence is tied to yours." The words hadn't come earlier, but I had to say them so he would understand. "I'm in love with you, Hawk; I can't get any more enslaved than that."

The burst of air that escaped him tickled my mouth and only made me more determined to kiss him. I clasped his cheeks and held his gaze as I lowered my lips to his. He watched my every movement with rapt attention until our mouths touched and a mixture of ecstasy and anguish shone in his eyes.

Still, I didn't stop as I ran my lips over his before tasting them with my tongue. At first, he remained rigid against me, and then his body started to relax though he didn't kiss me back. I licked his lips again and slid my tongue partially into his mouth. He emitted a tormented groan as his hands fisted in the sheets.

"Shh," I murmured as I caressed his nape.

Despite his determination not to give in to me, his cock lengthened against my thigh. Shifting my hips, I centered myself over him and took him inside me again. The sheets tore in Hawk's grasp, and I felt him throbbing inside me, but I didn't move. I simply needed to feel connected to him right now.

I bit his lip and drew it between my teeth before nipping it with my fangs. He was mine; I would have him in every way, but instead of becoming frustrated that he wouldn't kiss me back, I kept working to break his steely resolve.

When I circled my hips on him, the sheets tore further before he released them to grip my arms. He started to pull me away, but when I nipped his lip again before soothing it with my tongue, he froze.

He kept his mouth closed as I tasted him again, and just when I was about to scream in frustration, I felt his wall crumble. His mouth parted, and his tongue met mine. I didn't experience a surge of victory; instead, unexpected tears filled my eyes.

His kiss was everything I'd dreamed it would be—deep, penetrating, consuming...

Soul shattering.

The last piece of a puzzle clicked into place as our tongues entwined and the searing passion of his kiss shook me to the core of my soul. I didn't realize I was crying until he wiped the tears from my cheeks, but I refused to let him stop.

He enveloped me in his arms as he turned me on the bed and came down on top of me. I refused to let him stop kissing me while he slowly made love to me.

CHAPTER THIRTY-THREE

Aisling

"How do you feel?" Hawk asked for what had to be the hundredth time over the past three days.

"I'm fine," I assured him impatiently. "And if you ask me again, I'm going to show you how unenslaved I am from your kiss by kicking you in the nuts."

He grinned at me, which made me tempted to kick him. If I'd known kissing him would turn him into a nervous wreck, I wouldn't have done it. Well, no, I still would have, but he was making me nuts.

"Sarah definitely wouldn't have done that," he said.

I scowled at the reminder of his past lover but let it go. "You have to forgive yourself for that; it wasn't your fault."

"I may not have known better, but it was my fault."

When I rested my hand on his cheek, he stopped throwing wood onto the growing mound of it. "You have to let it go, and I'm fine. We've kissed numerous times over the past three days, and I still have all my senses. If I start following you around like a helpless puppy, you can put me out of my misery—and please do—but I'm okay. I think being your Chosen gives me a natural immunity to your demon charms."

He pressed my hand more firmly against his cheek. "I am pretty charming."

"Sometimes," I teased before focusing on the task before us.

We'd spent the past three days setting traps around town. I had no idea how good any of them would do, but I refused to simply sit and wait for the minotaur to return for its next victim. And I refused to fight the beast the same way as before; thankfully, Hawk, Bale, Corson, Wren, and Lix felt the same way.

They were on board with the idea for a new plan I'd set out for them after the first day of trap building. Everything we were doing was done before—as the others liked to incessantly remind us—so now it was time to try something new, even if that new was entirely crazy.

Some of the other demons and humans helped with the traps, but most retreated to the restaurant and library, or they aimlessly roamed the town. I tossed another piece of wood onto the pile and wiped my hands on my jeans.

We'd been gathering wood from the collapsed buildings on the other side of town and using it to build a giant pile of debris at the end of the road. The massive pile, which was meant to become a giant bonfire, might set every building around it on fire too, but I didn't care if this whole town burned.

Hawk stepped back and used his forearm to wipe the sweat from his forehead as Bale joined us. "I spoke with Caim and told him about our plan."

"What did he say, and any sign of Raphael or the horsemen?"

She brushed a strand of red hair over her shoulder and studied the pile while she spoke. "No sign of Raphael, and he said we're nuts. I didn't argue with his assessment. He wants to come into town and help us. I told him to stay out. If we don't make it through this, someone has to report to Kobal what happened."

"It's too bad; we could use his help," Hawk said.

"We could," Bale agreed, "but he has to stay out."

"I agree," Corson said as he and Wren emerged from the other side of the pile. "We're all set."

"Then it's time to retreat to the library; if it comes back tonight, we'll be ready for it," Bale said.

We were halfway to the library when we met Lix coming out of the restaurant; he'd gone there to convince the others of our plan. Judging by the slope of his shoulders and the lack of demons and humans following him, he wasn't successful.

"They're still against it?" Corson asked.

"I convinced a few to help, but the rest are being stubborn," Lix said as he tugged on his tie.

"Then they can die here," Wren said. "But we won't."

Hawk

I wasn't surprised when vibrations rattled the earth the next night; it was only a matter of time before the minotaur returned, but the demon with the tusks put up a good fight before being caught and killed.

Lifting my head from where it rested on top of Aisling's head, I looked out the glass doors of the library. Aisling kept her head on my chest, but I knew she was awake when a small tremor ran through her before she straightened her spine.

I kissed her temple before releasing her and rising to walk over to the doors. The minotaur was already out of the cave. We had to get out there if we were going to set our traps into action.

"Can you see it?" Aisling asked.

The hulking beast stood feet away from the exit of the cave; its head swung back and forth while it surveyed either side of the mountain. It must be searching for a trap as the others had said they'd once tried ambushing it outside its lair.

Seeming to decide no one lurked in the shadows, it rolled its shoulders and turned its head from side to side like it was cracking its neck. It wouldn't surprise me if it stretched its arms wide and yawned as if about to go for a Sunday stroll.

"I see it," I replied

"We have to go out there," she whispered.

"We do."

I held my hand out to her as I heard the others shuffling around in the main section of the library. It wouldn't be long before they joined us. Even those who weren't going to help with Aisling's plan would leave the building and meet the minotaur in the street like they always did.

She grasped my hand and squeezed it. The love shining in her eyes reaffirmed my conviction to do whatever it took to get her away from this town and the minotaur, even agreeing to her crazy plan.

I kept Aisling by my side as I opened the glass doors; we walked down the front steps and into the middle of the road. At the end of the way, the pile of debris blocked the street. The ground shook when the thing stalked away from its cave before turning the corner and vanishing.

It would encounter the first of our traps soon.

Corson, Wren, Bale, and Lix came to stand beside us on the road as the others filed out of the building. Anticipation and stress thrummed on the air as the beast stalked closer. Someone whimpered as a piece of wood leaning on a porch rattled against the railing before sliding to the ground.

"Are you ready for this?" Bale asked.

"The only choice we have is to be ready," Lix said.

Before the minotaur came back into view, a loud bang sounded, and a puff of smoke wafted into the air.

"The first trap," Wren said.

Aisling and I set what would become the first trap in the house with the attic. We'd run the string through the house and to the front door. Once on the porch, more strings were attached to the main one, so three of them ran across the road and into the neighboring house to the three guns propped in the windows.

The strings weren't wired to go off when pulled, but instead, they went off when something stepped on one of them. Once weight was applied, the strain pulled the trigger of the gun it was attached to on the other side of the road.

We didn't expect the guns to do much more than annoy the minotaur, but they might cause it to search for someone who wasn't there while Aisling set the pile at the end of the road on fire. Her fingers constricted on mine as the minotaur's roar rattled the windows of the library.

A thunderous bang resonated through the air and glass shattered; I pictured the beast tearing the front door off the home with the guns as another shot rang out. Another crash reverberated through the night as the minotaur tore the house apart.

"Are you ready?" I asked Aisling.

"As I'll ever be," she replied.

"Let's go."

Another loud crash shook the night, and a puff of dust burst into the air as what I assumed was the roof of the building collapsed.

"We have to hurry," Aisling said.

I squeezed her hand before releasing it and sprinting down the road toward the pile with her. When the ground trembled again, I realized the minotaur was on the move once more. The distraction with the guns and the house was over, but more traps lay ahead of it.

We were halfway to the pile when another bang sounded and another cloud of dust billowed into the air. The minotaur had fallen into the first trench we dug across the road and carefully covered again to make it blend in. The ground quaked so violently that I imagined the minotaur slamming its hands onto the ground or driving its horns into the earth.

"Oh shit," Aisling breathed.

"Just keep going," I told her. "We're going to get through this."

We skidded to a halt in front of the pile as the minotaur's claws emerged over the side of the trench. This thing could eviscerate us with one swipe of its hand, and blood still caked the wicked-looking talons. When its head emerged over the top of the trench and its yellow eyes met mine, I could tell that happy thoughts of wearing my intestines were dancing through its pea-sized brain.

Aisling's breath came faster as the minotaur began to pull itself out of the fifteen-foot-deep trench. The ground gave way beneath its weight, and with an enraged roar, it vanished into the ditch. The following silence was more unnerving than any of its reverberating bellows. And then those claws appeared again, and those yellow eyes blazed with a fury that lit the night around it.

With methodical precision, it worked its way free, rose, and took one step forward. Dozens of knives and spears exploded from the spring-release trap we'd set next for it. The minotaur reared back as the weapons embedded themselves in its side and one stuck into its neck. Aisling's hands shook as she knelt in front of the pile and held them over the wood.

I rested my hand on her shoulder. "Take your time."

Flames burst out of her palms. The intensity of it was so astonishing that Aisling fell away from the fire, which followed her as she landed on her ass. She gazed at her hands in amazement while she turned them before her. The flames followed her movements as they danced up her wrists and circled her forearms. The sleeves of her shirt fell away, but the rest of it didn't catch fire.

"What the...?" She marveled as she turned her hands before her. "It's getting stronger."

"It's the Chosen bond. You can withstand my kiss, and your fire has grown."

"It's made me faster too," she said as she held her hands over the wood. "I noticed the other day."

I'd noticed that the other day too when she pulled herself on top of me so fast, I'd barely seen her move before she was straddling me. I squeezed her shoulder again. "My touch probably helps to fuel it."

Her mouth formed an O before she replied, "Yes, it does."

Leaning forward, she placed her hands against the pile. The flames blackened the wood as the minotaur succeeded in pulling the last of the knives free. I kept one eye on the monster and the other on the smoldering pile as the beast dropped to all fours.

Come on. Come on.

Aisling gazed between the beast and the pile as her flames licked across some drywall. When the minotaur took a step toward us, her fire grew until a wave of it was streaming across the pile. Smoke filled the air as the minotaur charged toward us.

I thought the ground shook before, but now it was a full-on earthquake tearing the earth apart. Glass broke and fell from the windows closest to the beast. The minotaur was fifty feet away from the pile when another trench gave way, and it plummeted into the hole.

Its infuriated roar echoed through the night as the pile caught and flames leapt into the sky. Sparks shot off and rained over us as the crackling pop of wood drowned out the noise of the minotaur.

The heat forced me away from the fire, but awe filled Aisling's face and flames danced in her eyes as she sat before it. The fifteen-foot-high flames leaping into the air reflected off the windows closest to us and blocked my view of the minotaur. I didn't feel any vibrations beneath my feet, which meant it was probably still trapped, but it wouldn't stay that way.

"We have to go," I said.

Aisling rose in one fluid motion. Turning away from the fire, I clasped her hand as we ran back to the others. Corson, Wren, Bale, and Lix stood with those who agreed to go with us. The remaining dozen or so humans and demons were huddled together near the library.

"Are you sure you won't come with us?" Corson asked them.

Some of them exchanged looks while others backed further away. A few broke away from the crowd and joined us, but the rest remained where they were.

"Please," Aisling pleaded as she stepped forward. "There's no way of knowing what the fire will do if it spreads, or what will happen if the minotaur discovers us gone. *Please* come with us."

"No," one of the demons said.

"We're not leaving," a woman said.

"Let's go," Bale said.

She snatched the one bag of supplies we'd packed for the trip from the ground and put it on her back. Because we needed to move fast, there was only some water and a little bit of food in the bag. It wouldn't last the humans with us more than two days, and that was if they were lucky.

"We can't leave them here," Aisling whispered.

"We have no choice," I told her. "We have to go."

She hesitated, but when I gave her hand a small tug, she fell into step beside me as we turned away from them. The flames leapt higher, and smoke billowed into the air as the fire spread to the building closest to the pile. It was only a matter of time before the fire consumed the town.

Like wraiths, we slipped into one of the alleys between the stores and onto a side street. We didn't take that road but jogged across front yards and into the backyards of houses as we made our way over to the next street.

The faint vibrations beneath my feet alerted me the minotaur had worked its way out of the trench and was hunting once more. We didn't have much time before it found its prey or realized we were gone and returned to its cave.

We had to beat it there.

CHAPTER THIRTY-FOUR

Aisling

We were probably crazy for doing this, but there weren't any other options. Fighting the minotaur had proven useless, and we couldn't sit around and wait for it to come for us. We couldn't get out of the town, we couldn't hide, and we couldn't lay down and die like those we left behind.

Instead, we were going to try and escape by going straight into the monster's lair. The insanity of the idea wasn't lost on me. I'd been the one to suggest it, and when I looked at all of those who decided to join us, the weight of their lives rested heavily on my shoulders. They'd chosen to join us, but I'd offered a carrot they couldn't resist.

What if it all backfired?

I couldn't think about that now. It was already too late; there was no turning back. I'd seen the look in the minotaur's eyes; it would tear us apart if we went back.

Stepping into the shadowed interior of the minotaur's cave, I realized this might be the last bad idea I had. I didn't know why I'd suggested this, or why the others listened to me, but instead of keeping my stupid ideas to myself, or being told I was an idiot, I said them out loud, and after some consideration, they agreed with me.

I wasn't sure who that made dumber, them or me, but it made us all equally nuts.

A trickle of amazement ran down my spine as I stared into the shadowy interior of the minotaur's lair. I wasn't sure what I'd expected to find here, but it certainly wasn't this clean space. There should be bones or broken rocks from the creature's horns, or maybe victims chained to the wall. Instead, there was nothing.

For some reason, the nothing unnerved me more than if bones and bodies were strewn everywhere. Did that monster eat its victims whole?

Bile rose in my throat as I pictured that thing swallowing its victims in one gulp. It could probably unhinge its jaw like a snake too. Shuddering, I rubbed at my arms as I tried to get rid of the image of the man-bull holding a screaming, flopping person over its mouth and lowering them down its gullet. But once the image was there, it was impossible to erase it.

"Come on," Hawk said as he cupped my elbow. "We have to get as much distance between us and that thing before it returns."

Twisting my head, I stared down the mountain at the town nestled in the valley below. If it weren't for the toppled buildings and raging inferno, it would have been a peaceful place, and I imagine that, before the war, it was a tranquil place to live.

Now, I wasn't surprised to discover the flames had spread to consume more of the buildings. With nothing to put the fire out, it would soon encompass the library and town. A stab of guilt twisted in my gut, but there was nothing I could do for those we left behind. They'd made their choice, and we'd made ours.

I spotted the minotaur stalking down the first side street we entered after leaving the others behind. It must have taken the street to avoid the fire. Instead of slipping down the alleys, which it would never fit through, it went to the end of the road and turned right toward the library.

It was still on the hunt, which meant we should have at least fifteen minutes before it returned to the cave—hopefully longer if it decided to try to uncover Hawk and me first. I'd seen the way it looked at us, even if it didn't intend to hunt us tonight, it was eager to kill us.

Would it realize we weren't in town anymore or assume we were hiding and content itself with claiming its intended victim?

I suspected it might move on; it didn't strike me as the smartest creature, and it would never consider someone would be ballsy or stupid enough to enter its domain *willingly*. We also had to hope the others didn't rat us out, but I doubted we'd get much loyalty from them.

Still, I believed we had fifteen minutes on the minotaur. Perhaps we could get through the labyrinth without it knowing we were here—if there was a labyrinth. So far, all I saw was rock.

Turning away from the spreading fire, I focused on the cave as the others shuffled forward. Though only a faint amount of the moon's rays pierced the interior, I saw Oliver watching me over Nadine's shoulder. I smiled at the boy, and he smiled shyly in return.

I really hoped this was the right choice for him; I couldn't live with myself if this decision caused his death.

"Aisling," Corson said, "we need your fire."

Hawk and I made our way to the front of the group to discover Corson, Bale, Wren, and Lix gathered near a tunnel leading deeper into the cave. It was impossible to see more than two feet into the fifteen-foot-high tunnel leading into the bowels of the earth.

We couldn't go back, but I wasn't too thrilled about going forward either.

With no other choice, I lifted my hand and created a small ball of fire in my palm. The shadows slid back as the flames danced in the air flowing from the tunnel. The fire's glow revealed the chipped stones in the ceiling that were gouged out by the minotaur's horns as he carved his way through the rock. I frowned at the small pieces of metal and wood on the ground until I realized they were the remains of the tracks the carts once traversed.

"Maybe this isn't such a good idea," someone said from behind me.

"It's too late to change our minds now," Randy said.

It *was* far too late to change our minds now. We only had two options: keep going or die.

And I was not going to come this far to die without a fight.

With my flame illuminating the tunnel, I led the way deeper into the earth. In the beginning, cobwebs brushed my face, and then we reached a depth that was too much for spiders. I still didn't detect the potent reek of death I'd expected, but smelled the musky aroma of something feral mixed with the stench of wet dog hair; it was the scent of the minotaur.

We were a few hundred feet into the tunnel when it branched into two different directions.

"Shit," someone whispered from behind me.

"Now what?" someone else asked.

I tried not to let my mounting panic show as my brain stuttered for an answer. This was supposed to be a maze, but I'd been expecting bushes or something like those old-fashioned English mazes I'd seen pictures of in school. I had not expected the minotaur to carve out a maze within the mountain.

I turned my flame in the direction of the tunnel to the right before swinging it to the left. *Now what? Now what?*

The question looped through my mind as I swung my flame back again. Left or right? Life or death? *That* was the real question here because one of these tunnels would give us a chance while the other ended all hope.

When I swung my flame back again, I almost sobbed with relief. "Left," I said.

"How do you know?" Wren asked.

I swung my flame back to the right and watched as it burned in my palm before turning it back to the left. Once it settled down from the motion, the flames flickered and danced far more than they did from the tunnel on the right.

"There's airflow coming from this tunnel," I said before swinging it right again. "But there isn't from this one."

"Left it is then," Hawk said.

I was sure I was right, but a tendril of unease crept down my spine as we strode down the left-hand tunnel. Almost immediately, the broken pieces of track vanished, and the rocks became more jagged as we entered a section of the tunnel carved by the minotaur instead of miners. I didn't know how long it took for the creature to cut its way through the rock, but I suspected it spent a good chunk of time creating its new labyrinth after leaving Hell.

Would we be aware of the minotaur's return? I suspected we would know when it entered the cave again. The creature's footsteps shook the town when it left the mountain; they would definitely rattle the walls of this cave.

Would it know we were here when it returned?

I didn't know how intelligent the creature was, but I hoped it had the brain capacity of a mouse and wouldn't be able to scent us out over the stench of this place. Maybe we'd get lucky and it wouldn't know we were here at all; I didn't think that was likely as our luck had led us into this town.

We'd traveled at least five hundred feet into the tunnel when I detected a glow ahead of us. I squinted as I lifted the flame to see what lay ahead, but I couldn't quite make out what it was. The light grew brighter as we approached, and the tunnel came to an end with a circular opening.

I stepped through the entrance, and my breath sucked in at the same time gasps filled the air. My flame sputtered out as I gaped at what lay beneath us.

I'd expected twists and turns through the tunnel along with offshoots that would go nowhere or circle around or maybe lead to freedom. We'd encountered only one branch, but that was because the tunnel was nothing more than the entrance to the labyrinth.

Here was where the real fun began.

There were so many winding pathways I couldn't focus on just one of them. They intersected each other in a crisscrossing pattern that confused me, and I hadn't even stepped foot in the thing. I tried to follow one of the pathways, but it was impossible to stay with it for more than twenty feet.

I couldn't begin to decide which of those pathways might lead out of here before the rows of convoluted routes disappeared over a hill that blocked out anything on the other side of it. I bit my lip as I tried not to think about the possibility there was no way out of here.

There *had* to be an exit, or I'd led all these people to their deaths.

Despite the convoluted pathways, the labyrinth was amazingly beautiful. Like the old English maze I'd expected to find, rows of hedges created the hundreds of corridors beneath the earth. Overhead, a dome of hewn rock arched over the labyrinth. That dome stretched at least two hundred yards and arced over the section of the maze I couldn't see.

The sun couldn't shine down here, but golden light illuminated the labyrinth and chased away the shadows of the cave. Before me, a rocky, winding pathway led down to the entrance of the maze. Once we walked down it, we'd have no idea which way to go or where we were in the maze.

We'd be as lost as a bird in a tornado the second we stepped foot in those hedges.

For a moment, I feared I might throw up as bile rose in my throat and my head spun. Part of the plan was to get enough of a head start that maybe we could find our way out of the labyrinth before the minotaur realized we were here. That was probably impossible.

When Hawk rested his hand on my shoulder, I glanced at him. I saw apprehension in his eyes, but there was also a steely resolve that straightened my spine.

"Now what?" the blue-haired demon asked.

"Now we keep going," Hawk said.

"Into that?" a human asked.

"Do you want to turn back?" Corson inquired. "Because there is nowhere for us to go back there."

"Except into the mouth of the minotaur," Bale said.

I glanced into the shadows of the cave. I wasn't sure which was worse, wandering into the maze or returning to fight the monster who so easily defeated us the other day.

Turning back is worse.

There was no way to know how much time we'd spend trapped in the labyrinth, but we wouldn't have much time left in the town before it came for us. And now that the town was burning, we'd have less time there.

"We have to go," I said.

Before anyone could stop me, I started down the side of the mountain. Here the rock walkway was at least ten feet wide and open all around me.

"How is this place possible?" I asked as I led the way down the winding path. "How did that beast create this world? How are there *bushes* growing under the earth and in this rocky ground?"

"The same magic the minotaur used to trap us in the town was also used to create this," Bale said. "The labyrinth is the minotaur's home and its creation."

"If this is its creation," Randy said, "then can it change it around us?"

I shuddered at the possibility and realized it might happen. If that creature had built this world, then it might be able to do anything with it, which meant we had no chance of escaping this maze.

CHAPTER THIRTY-FIVE

Aisling

I had no idea where we were in the labyrinth. We'd been wandering for what felt like hours, but it could've been minutes or a day. All I knew was my feet hurt, the humans were exhausted, and the minotaur had returned to its cave.

I didn't know how long ago that return was, but the bushes in the labyrinth had shaken like an earthquake was rattling them. No screams accompanied its return. I didn't know if that meant its victim or victims were unconscious like Tusks when taken, or if the beast decided to eat them already. Either way, the minotaur was back, and it didn't know we were here or else it would be hunting us.

"Do you think the horsemen could have hidden their army in here?" I asked to distract myself from my surroundings. "It's big enough, and if they teamed up with the minotaur and came and went out of the other exit, no one would have known they were here."

"I don't think the minotaur would let anyone in its domain that it didn't plan on eating," Corson said.

"And it doesn't strike me as the type to share its territory," Bale said.

"With as big as this place is, it's not big enough to house the kind of army the angels and horsemen came at us with," Lix said.

"True," I muttered.

A sudden breeze caused the bushes over my head to sway; the rustle of their leaves reminded me of the cornfields I'd play in as a kid. My friends and I would laugh as we plunged through the rows, losing and finding each other in a game that was a mix of tag and hide-and-seek.

"That's new," Wren said.

And it was new. Up until now, the only thing moving the bushes were our arms brushing against them as we walked and the stomp of the minotaur's feet. I gulped down the lump in my throat.

It was difficult to remain calm when every twist and turn had me feeling increasingly claustrophobic. I kept waiting for the fifteen-foot-tall bushes to uproot themselves, close in, and suffocate us beneath their shiny, green leaves.

Or maybe they would uproot themselves and twist all around until we had even less of an idea of where we were going.

"Maybe we should have let Caim come," Lix said. "At least he could have flown over the top and told us which way to go."

"It's too late for that," Bale said. "And we couldn't risk him getting trapped in here too."

I tilted my head back to gaze at the dome as I tried to figure out our position by the change in the light. When we first entered the maze, the light was dimmer, but as we got closer to the center, it grew brighter, but I still didn't see anything to explain it.

"What if I torch the plants?" I asked.

"And if the fire gets out of hand?" Hawk inquired.

"Or if it alerts the minotaur to our presence," Corson said. "We know its back, but it doesn't know about us."

I had no answer for them, but my frustration mounted as row

after row of endless green stretched before me. Usually, I loved plants, but I wanted these things out of my way so I could see more than five feet ahead and ten feet to the side of me.

"We know there's a way out," Bale said. "Otherwise the beast couldn't have returned to the town when the mining exit was blocked. Right now, that's what we have to focus on finding."

I didn't ask her how we were supposed to find it when we had no idea where we were. I'd never been pessimistic before, and I wasn't about to start now, I glanced back at the cave leading into the minotaur's domain. Going by the light and the distance to the cave, we were in the center of the labyrinth. We were also about two hundred yards to the right of where we first entered.

That information didn't do me any good when I had no idea if the exit was ahead or to the left or right, or nowhere.

Just keep going.

Because that was our only option.

I turned a corner and smacked straight into a row of hedges. The branches and leaves knocked me back a step but not before it also added insult to injury by shoving a stick up my nose. "Motherfu..."

My words trailed off as I wiped at my wounded nose and came away with a smattering of blood. Fire filled my clenched hands, but I smothered the flames instead of unleashing them on these awful things.

I rubbed at my nose as I tried not to scream in frustration. We'd tried shoving our way through the plants, but though they were made up of sticks and branches, they were as unyielding as a concrete wall and would not let us pass through.

In the magical light, the green leaves shone, and I took a couple between my fingers to rub their silky texture. Releasing the leaves, I stepped back to survey the plants. It was impossible to see over the top of them or through them.

I glanced up at the dome; *where* was that light coming from?

Before I could think about it too long, a shrill scream pierced the air.

My heart lodged in my throat as I spun back toward the mountain. At the entrance to the labyrinth, a man and a woman came into view as they burst out of the cave and sprinted down the path toward the maze.

I didn't know if they'd seen us, but I had no doubt the minotaur would as soon as it arrived.

"Can we hide somewhere?" I whispered frantically.

"This whole place is somewhere to hide," Corson said, "and nowhere to hide."

The cryptic words only escalated my anxiety. My heart was pounding too fast, and my palms were so sweaty I kept expecting water to drip from them. If I wasn't immortal, I'd be a little concerned I was about to have a heart attack.

That thing was coming, and we were surrounded by row after row of green bushes, and I'd been the one to suggest this *stupid* plan. I was the one who led all these people and *Oliver* into the heart of the minotaur's labyrinth, and now it was coming.

Deep breaths, Ash; panicking isn't going to get anyone anywhere.

I tried to regain control while examining the wall ahead of me. I wanted to torch all the plants, but Hawk was right; there were too many of them, and the fire could easily get out of control. Because I was a fire demon, I could withstand the flames, but the others couldn't.

"Come on," Bale said.

She started back through the maze. I stayed close to Hawk as we navigated our way through the plants once more. I brushed my fingers against his and closed my eyes when a small thrill ran through me. We'd get out of this; I would not lose him.

When we came up against another dead end, we headed back only to walk smack dab into the middle of more bushes. Pure frustration almost caused me to kick them, but I managed to restrain myself as we headed in a new direction. We'd turned around so much that I was at the back of the pack with Hawk.

"Dead end," Randy said from ahead of us.

We were back at the head of the pack as everyone turned back toward us. When I glanced at the mountain, the man and woman were off the pathway and in the labyrinth. Any minute now the minotaur would arrive, and I suspected once it realized we were here, it would make us its priority.

"Are we going in circles?" Wren asked.

"It sure feels like it," Nadine said.

I looked at the dome again and craned my head to see where the light was coming from, but it remained a mystery. I had no idea why this mystery obsessed me so much; probably because it was easier to focus on something *outside* the maze than to remain centered inside it. I suspected most people who survived for any length of time in the labyrinth went mad from the sameness and hopelessness of it.

And then, I felt the vibrations beneath my feet.

I didn't have to look to see if the minotaur had arrived, I felt its insidious yellow eyes boring into the back of my head.

Hawk

Aisling's arm brushed against mine as she faced away from the cave to focus on the maze. The minotaur stood at the top of the mountain with its shoulders hunched up and its head lowered. Its nostrils flared as its yellow eyes glowed.

Then it scuffed its feet against the ground like a bull about to charge and launched itself straight off the cliff.

"Run!" Bale shouted as the minotaur hit the ground with a thunderous crash.

Though it was at least a hundred yards away, the impact caused the bushes to sway around us, and I was sure it dented the ground. Aisling gripped my arm, and I hugged her against me before she pulled away to survey the sea of green surrounding us.

"This way," she said and plunged down another corridor.

Everyone ran behind us, but there was nowhere to run as we rounded a corner and smacked into another dead end.

"Son of a bitch," Corson snarled and unleashed his talons.

He hacked at the bushes, but as the leaves fell around his feet, more regrew on the plant. He couldn't cut through them fast enough to keep them from regenerating. Loud cracking noises filled the air along with the thunderous thumps of the minotaur's hooves.

The high bushes blocked my view of what was happening, but I didn't have to see to know the minotaur was plowing through the hedges it created. Discovering us inside its lair had caused it to throw all rules out the window, and now it was hell-bent on destroying us. But if it was charging through the bushes at us, that most likely meant it could not change the labyrinth around us. Otherwise, it would have pinned us in.

"It's coming," Aisling whispered.

"Aisling," Bale said as the noise grew closer. "Torch them."

"What if it gets out of control?" she asked.

"If we don't get through this maze, that thing is going to squish us," Wren said.

"What if the fire doesn't work?" Randy asked.

We all knew the answer to that. The minotaur had found us in its nest; it would *not* make our deaths pleasant.

Aisling gulped and stepped forward to rest her palms against the hedge. I settled my hand on the small of her back, in the hopes of calming her while offering her strength. Small tremors raced up her spine as flames encircled her wrists. I held my breath while I waited to see what the fire would do; would it be like Corson's talons and the hedge would regrow as she was setting it ablaze?

The leaves crinkled and shriveled as smoke streamed from beneath her palms. I could see the hedge trying to regenerate itself, but unlike Corson's talons, the fire ate through the leaves too fast for the bushes to completely regrow.

A strange, almost keening sound emanated through the air, and I realized it was coming from the bushes as smoke wafted in the air. The bushes swayed in an unseen breeze, and the minotaur's bellow bounced off the dome until it echoed around us and filled the rows. The hedges swayed faster as the keening rose to meet the bellow before silence abruptly descended.

The unnerving stillness was broken only by the crackle and pop of Aisling burning through the bushes. If those hedges could come alive like the calamut trees, they'd go for her first. But if they were anything like the calamut trees, she'd be dead already. Still, I wanted to rip her away from the hedges, tuck her against my side, and...

And what? We were trapped in this place with that monster and nothing but endless green before us. There was nowhere for us to go and nowhere for me to take her. *This* was our only option, and I had to let her do it.

"What the fuck?" Lix muttered when the strange wailing started again.

I had no idea what was happening, but as the fire spread over the bushes, the inhuman keening increased until it drowned out the sound of the minotaur's approach. I recalled the hounds once covering the noise of Kobal trying to break free of a trap and wondered if these bushes were doing the same. However, it was impossible to mask the minotaur's approach as its heavy steps caused my teeth to chatter.

The leaves crumpled and fell around Aisling's feet; then the branches burst into flame and smoke filled the air.

"Go!" Bale yelled when enough of the bushes burned away and the fire arced like electricity across the top of the plants.

CHAPTER THIRTY-SIX

Aisling

When the next set of hedges fell apart, I staggered through them and out the other side only to come across another row of hedges. I set my fiery palms against the next set of bushes. That awful shrieking noise grew louder as the fire spread, and I burned my way through the next barrier.

"The fire's going to get out of control," I whispered.

"We don't have any other options," Hawk said. "We'll get out of this."

A roar resonated behind us. When I looked back, I couldn't see the minotaur, but the sound of the hedges came from a different direction than before. The spreading flames had caused it to veer off course, and it sounded like it was coming up on our left now instead of heading straight for us.

"Hurry," someone urged from behind me.

I gritted my teeth against an angry retort; did they think I was about to order a margarita and sit down to enjoy the view? I placed my hands against the next set of hedges and watched as the leaves crumpled before falling away. Did they think I was taking a stroll through this place?

"There!" someone shouted.

I looked where they were pointing to discover a row of hedges toppling over. If we could see the bushes falling, then it was too close. The fire lancing across the tops of the hedges was heading toward the minotaur, but I didn't know if it would be in time to head the thing off.

"Stay here." Bale removed the bag from her back and shoved it into the arms of a human.

"Where are you going?" Corson demanded.

"To lead it away."

"You can't do that; the fire is spreading," Randy said. "You'll be trapped in here."

"I'm part fire demon," Bale said. "I have no fire, but I can withstand the flames. I'll be fine."

Before anyone could reply, she vanished into the thickening smoke.

~

BALE

I pulled my sword from its sheath as I sprinted through the rows of hedges. I had no intention of fighting the minotaur, that would be useless, but I would irritate it and keep it distracted while Aisling worked to get the others free of this place.

Flames arced over my head and sparks rained down on me, but I didn't feel them and they didn't burn me. To me, the fire was freeing, and I thrived on the power it emitted as I ran faster.

I dashed through a group of burning bushes and burst out the other side where I almost collided with the minotaur. I managed to skid to a halt before I crashed into the beast, but it caught my movement from the corner of its eye. As it turned toward me, I swung my blade against the creature's ankle and sliced it open before plunging back into the maze.

This time, I stayed away from the burning hedges; it would be less likely to follow me through the fire. I glanced back to make sure it was coming after me. It bounded down the passageways with more grace and speed than I would have expected from the monstrosity.

And it was rapidly closing the distance between us.

I made a left and crashed into a wall of bushes.

"Shit," I whispered as the impact knocked me back.

I spun and doubled back ten feet before plunging down another corridor, but the move brought me closer to the minotaur, and it was only twenty feet behind me. I compelled my legs to move faster as my feet thudded across the ground. I had to buy the others enough time to get free, which meant I couldn't stop moving. However, that was probably impossible in a maze filled with dead ends.

But dead ends didn't prove to be the issue as the minotaur burst through a row of hedges only five feet in front of me. My feet skidded on the ground and slipped out from under me; I got my right hand down in time to keep from hitting the ground. A breeze blew over me as the beast swung out a massive hand, missing my head by mere inches.

With my toes digging into the rocky ground, I scrambled away from the beast and into another corridor. My sword swung in front of me and my heavy breaths filled my ears as I pumped my arms while sprinting toward the flames. The fire might deter the mino-taur from pursuing me, but if I didn't make it into the flames, it would flatten me.

I was almost back to the flames when the minotaur burst through the bushes again. It blocked my way toward the fire as it charged into the corridor on all fours. I recoiled as its horns sliced through my shirt, skimmed my stomach, and caused blood to trickle from the cut it delivered to my flesh.

Gripping my sword, I leapt up and sliced off the tip of its ear. The monster let out a bellow that blew my hair back from my face and filled my nose with the rancid stench of decaying flesh. I didn't bother to attack it again but ducked the claw it swung at me, threw myself forward, and rolled into the fire on the other side of it.

The flames enveloping me turned my clothes and boots to ash. Orange and yellow snapped in front of my face; my hair billowed out as the inferno whipped air currents around me. I rested my hands on the ground and pushed myself to my feet as the flames parted to reveal an opening.

I stepped into another corridor as the minotaur exploded out of another section of hedge. Before I could retreat into the flames, it slammed a claw-tipped hand into my back, and I hit the ground.

CHAPTER THIRTY-SEVEN

Aisling

Everywhere I looked, fire surrounded us. I didn't feel the heat of it, but sweat poured down the faces of the others, terror shone in their eyes, and burns marred their skin and clothes. I had to get them out of here; I couldn't be the one who destroyed all these people.

Tears from the smoke burned my eyes, but I didn't dare let up on my onslaught against the hedges for fear they'd regenerate. I'd never used my power so much before. I'd trained with it for the past two years, learned how to keep it leashed, but I'd never set it free for so long. I didn't feel depleted; instead, the inferno fueled my ability as did Hawk's hand on my back.

The crackle of the fire and the strange wail made hearing anything else impossible. I didn't know where the man and woman who entered the maze were; I hoped they'd seen the minotaur leap into the labyrinth and run back toward the cave entrance. If they hadn't, they would die in here.

I stumbled through the next set of hedges and nearly fell when

I tripped over a flaming branch; Hawk caught me before my knees hit the ground.

"I'm going to get you out of here," I whispered.

"I know," he said.

I realized he had complete confidence in me, and that unwavering belief only made me love him more. Resting my hand against his cheek, I took a second to gain strength from him before turning and setting the next set of hedges on fire.

I had no idea if we were heading for the exit, but I kept going straight ahead and toward the golden light. When the roar of the minotaur pierced the air, I glanced back to discover fire in place of the hedges.

"Bale," Corson murmured.

Wren rested her hand on his arm. "She'll be okay."

I kept waiting for open-air, space, and freedom, but the next hedge burned away to reveal another wall of bushes. Ashes and sparks rained down as wall after wall of green shriveled and died. The others slapped at their arms to smother the sparks and ducked the flames, but I didn't feel the golden embers eating through my clothes and leaving small, pink spots on my arms that faded as soon as they appeared.

My increasing urgency to break free of the maze and get the others to safety drove me onward. Then, just when I was sure we were never going to break free and the fire would consume everyone behind me, another wall gave way, and I stumbled into an open area.

The elation that came with the rush of open-air that blew the smoke away from my eyes vanished when my gaze fell on the thousands of bones piled before me. The pile was so high I couldn't see the hedges behind it as it rose halfway to the domed ceiling. It must be located over the hill that blocked my view of the maze; otherwise, I would have seen it from above.

There were all different kinds of human and demon bones

while others could only be the smaller, delicate bones of animals. Despite the death piled before us, it didn't reek of rot as there was no flesh left on the bones. They'd been picked cleaner than my father picked a chicken wing at the annual Volunteer Day picnic.

The minotaur didn't swallow its victim. No, it skinned them, feasted on their organs, and picked their bones clean before tossing them into this horrible graveyard.

At the very top of the pile, a single skull faced us, and I couldn't help thinking it was watching us and reporting our location to the minotaur.

~

Hawk

The fire licking at my heels caused sweat to roll down my back. The heat of the flames and the thick smoke made moving difficult. Some of the humans were starting to lag, and the pile of remains hadn't boosted their energy.

Aisling turned a corner around the pile and briefly vanished when a billowing cloud of smoke rolled between us. I ran to catch up and nearly collided with her as she stopped on the other side of the bones. The hedge ahead of us was free of fire, and the air through here remained cleaner, but that wouldn't last.

When Aisling took my hand, hers trembled slightly before she steadied it. "There are more bushes up ahead!" she shouted over the crackling fire.

From behind us, someone let out a startled cry, and a woman collapsed. She kept her head bowed before stretching her hand out to the demons in front of her. For a second, they didn't react; then one of them turned back and lifted her off the ground.

The demon hefted her over his shoulder and started after the others as we followed Aisling back into the maze. She burned her way through another section of bushes and kept going until we were almost directly beneath the strange light illuminating the labyrinth.

Then, Aisling broke free of the hedges and stumbled back as her hand flew to her mouth and she gazed at the ceiling.

BALE

Claws raked across my back and bit into my flesh as the minotaur lifted me off the ground. I almost lost my sword, but my fingers clamped around the handle as the beast plucked me off the ground. When it swung its horn at me, I deflected it with my blade and threw myself forward.

I couldn't withhold a scream as its claws shredded my flesh, and hot blood spilled down my back as I tore free of it. The minotaur tried to catch me before I hit the ground, but I twisted to the side as I fell. When I hit the ground, air burst out of my lungs and stars popped before my eyes. Unable to see, I rolled toward the heat licking at my back.

The flames enveloping me burnt away the blood on my back as my skin stretched to cover my gashes. I came to a halt within the fire and lay with my arms spread out beside me while I stared into the inferno and took strength from the fire.

I would have liked more time to recuperate, but the vibrations against my back told me I had to go. Rolling over, I pushed myself to my feet and sprinted through the flames. I had no idea where the minotaur was, but I had to return to the others.

Bursting out of the flames, I gasped in the fresh air enveloping me as I ran down an open corridor. To my left, the minotaur trampled bushes as it ran in a row parallel to mine.

Ahead of me, a wall of fire consumed the hedges, and I charged back into the flames. The earth shook so forcefully I knew the minotaur was close, but I had no idea where it was anymore.

Faster!

I pushed my body to the brink of endurance as I sprinted into another fire-free corridor. Smoke clogged the air while I ran heedlessly forward and into another wall of fire. This one must have been set more recently as some of the hedges remained standing. I threw out my hands and shoved aside the branches slapping at me.

To my left, I spotted more bushes crumbling beneath the weight of the minotaur; we were on a collision course with each other, but it didn't know that. As the distance between us narrowed, I reduced my speed, so I didn't come out ahead of it.

When it barreled past me, I jumped out of the hedges and swung my sword down. The blade sliced across the back of its knee; the creature howled as its leg gave out. My blood dripped from its claws when it swung a hand at me. The wind whistled past my ear as one of its talons sliced it off. It took a few seconds for my body to register the missing part and then a searing pain lanced through my head.

Tit for tat. I smiled grimly, over taking a piece of its ear and losing all of mine to it, but if I made it out of this, my ear would regenerate.

Blood spilled down the side of my face as I darted back into the flaming hedges. A blast of air followed me, and when I looked back, I saw the minotaur's gigantic hand crushing what remained of the bushes I'd run into.

Turning to my right, I stayed parallel with the beast as it rose and started shoving bushes out of its way again. When it traveled another twenty feet, I dashed out of the flames and brought my sword down across the back of its other leg and ran for the fire.

I was almost in the fire when its hand connected with the side of my head and sent me reeling into the flames. Scrambling to my feet, I pushed myself off the ground as my head spun and stars danced before my eyes. I only made it thirty feet before I fell to my knees and bent my head against the dizziness assailing my body.

I had to get up, but I was pretty sure the minotaur had rattled my brain. Inhaling deep breaths, I lifted my head to stare into the inferno while the fire renewed my strength. Feeling like I could stand without falling over, I planted the tip of my sword in the ground and pushed myself to my feet. I steadied myself before running to catch up with the minotaur.

CHAPTER THIRTY-EIGHT

Aisling

I gawked at the dome and the radiance it emanated while I tried to understand what I saw. It was like glass as it reflected the labyrinth in the smooth silvery surface. Flames consumed more than half the maze.

Back toward the entrance, green bushes remained, but the fire was spreading toward them. The smoke drifting across the surface of the dome made it difficult to see everything about the labyrinth, but I could make out enough of it.

"What the...?" Hawk's voice trailed off as the question died on his lips.

"I don't understand," one of the humans said.

"Is it a map?" I asked.

"It's something," Lix said.

There had to be something important about it, but I couldn't figure out what. Closing my eyes, I rubbed at my temples while I tried to puzzle out what the mirror image of the maze could mean.

Opening my eyes, I studied the ceiling version of the labyrinth more intently as a yellow, magical sun shone down on the maze.

That mirror sun illuminated our labyrinth; I didn't know how, but a lot of the impossible had proven to be possible since the gateway opened.

As I studied the reflection more closely, I discovered the entrance to the minotaur's cave, but that didn't make it easier to locate where we were in the labyrinth.

"Look," Corson said and pointed at the maze above us. "There's the minotaur."

It took me a minute to see where he was pointing, and then I spotted the hulking creature smashing through the hedges. The minotaur was cutting through a section that wasn't yet on fire, but it was only a matter of minutes before the fire reached it. If I could see the minotaur, then we had to be somewhere on there too.

My eyes narrowed as excitement pulsed through my veins; it was like a giant game of Where's Waldo, except we were Waldo. Then I spotted the pile of bones and straight ahead of that...

There we were!

The height of the bushes made seeing us difficult, but a cluster of what looked like ants grouped near a dead end only twenty feet away from the encroaching fire. I searched for the man and woman the minotaur brought into the maze, but I didn't see them anywhere. I hoped they managed to avoid the flames.

"There!" Wren shouted and pointed at the dome. "It's the exit!"

I followed her finger and saw the opening of another tunnel carved into the other side of the mountain. It *had* to be the exit, and it was only a hundred yards to our left.

"Why is there a map on the ceiling?" Hawk asked.

"Maybe it's a reward for those who made it this far," Randy suggested. "Because I doubt many do."

"The minotaur doesn't strike me as the type to reward anyone."

"He's right," Corson said.

He was right, but I couldn't think of why else a mirror image of the maze would be on the ceiling. And then, it hit me.

If it *was* a mirror image, then it was reversed.

And suddenly, I understood why the minotaur rewarded its prey for making it this far; it wasn't rewarding them at all. Worried that if its prey made it this far, it might break free, the beast added this little trick to the labyrinth so it could confuse them and ensure they didn't make it out alive.

The creature probably added the sun not only to offer light in the maze but also to get its prey excited by the possibility of almost being free of this place. This mirror maze and the sun was meant to distract them from thinking about what they were seeing.

"The exit isn't over there," I said and pointed to our right. "It's over there. It's a mirror, and it's meant to disorient the minotaur's captives if they make it this far. It's just one more trap."

"What makes you say that?" Lix asked.

"It's a mirror image, which means everything is reversed. So instead of the exit being to our left, it's actually to our right."

Their heads went from the dome to the left and then to the right as they tried to decide what to believe.

"I think she's right," Wren said.

"So do I," Hawk said. "If someone made it this far, the minotaur is going to do everything it can to keep them from escaping. And giving them the hope of freedom, only to tear it away, is one more cruelty the minotaur can deliver."

"I agree," Corson said.

"What about Bale?" Lix asked.

"She'll find the way out," Corson said, but I saw the apprehension in his eyes when he glanced over his shoulder. "But we have to go; the fire and minotaur are getting closer."

I hesitated before turning to my right. I hated leaving Bale behind, she'd run into the fire for us, but if we didn't get out of here, the humans would die. We hadn't come this far only to lose half our number now.

While we jogged down an open corridor, I followed our movements through the labyrinth in the mirror overhead. The mirror effect was confusing, but we had to be right as winding our way through the hedges, we got closer to the exit. I tried not to use my fire, but whenever we encountered a dead end, I burned my way through it.

The minotaur stayed away from the flames, but it was gaining on us. With a sinking heart, I realized breaking free of the labyrinth didn't guarantee us freedom from the creature.

"What do we do if it follows us out of the maze?" Wren asked.

That was a damn good question as fighting it had proven to be useless already.

"We'll deal with it if the time comes," Corson said.

I appreciated him saying *if*, but I suspected the beast would be hot on our heels when we reached the other cave.

"One more row to go," I said as we skidded around a corner and came face-to-face with the last bushes separating us from freedom.

Resting my hands on the hedge, I willed the fire forth and watched as it spread from my palms to my hands. That awful keening started up again as the bushes fell away to reveal the tunnel leading out of the labyrinth.

I couldn't recall a time I'd ever been so excited or apprehensive as I raced out of the hedges and toward what I hoped was freedom and not another trap.

Hawk

I kept close to Aisling's side as we ran through the tunnel. The fire encircling her wrists was the only source of illumination in the cave. The flames bouncing off the rock walls and stony floor cast shadows all around us as our feet pounded across the ground.

Though the air was fresher here than in the labyrinth, the smoke choking it made breathing more difficult as it wafted past us in thick plumes. After the searing heat of the fire, the cooler air of the cave was a welcome balm against my blistered skin. The humans were suffering far worse than any of the demons, and I didn't know how much longer they could go on.

A flutter of wings drew my attention to the ceiling as I waited for a bunch of bats to break free and swoop down at us, but there were no bats. Instead, Caim soared overhead before turning and sweeping back towards us.

"The horsemen are coming!" he shouted as he flew overhead before turning and coming back. "The horsemen are coming! The horsemen are coming!"

"He's the fucking Paul Revere of angels," I snapped.

We'd just broken free of the labyrinth, we had no idea if we'd evaded the minotaur, and now the fucking horsemen were back. What else could go wrong?

I probably shouldn't ask the question; since the gateway opened, I'd learned anything could go wrong, and it often did.

"Where are they?" Corson demanded.

Caim landed in front of Aisling. She skidded to a halt to keep from plowing into the angel and bent over to rest her hands on her knees. Stopping beside her, I placed my hand on her back as her breaths wheezed in and out. Her exhaustion beat against me, but when her eyes met mine, I saw the determination in them.

"They were headed for the town," Caim said.

"So they could be trapped in the town?" Wren asked.

"They could, but it's doubtful," Caim said. "The smoke will probably draw them here like it drew me. It's how I found you."

"Shit," Corson muttered.

"We have no choice; we have to keep going," Lix said.

"Caim, can you see if you can find Bale?" Corson asked. "She's still in the labyrinth behind us. The flames won't hurt her, but she has to get out before the minotaur finds her."

"I'll try," Caim said. Unfolding his wings, he lifted himself into the air.

I watched him disappear into the tunnel before turning my attention back to the freedom and danger ahead.

CHAPTER THIRTY-NINE

*B*ALE

I had no idea where I was in the labyrinth anymore. I stumbled blindly ahead, or at least I assumed I was going forward. I might be going behind or back or left or right; it had all become the same.

I stopped to examine the dome and saw the labyrinth reflected there. *What the...?*

The ground vibrated with the minotaur's heavy footsteps, but where it was in the maze was as much of a mystery to me as to where *I* was. Then, it released a bellow of rage and agony. Its thundering footsteps became heavier, and the ground lurched beneath me as the bushes to my right suddenly parted.

I leapt back and raised my sword as I prepared to battle the beast again, but it barreled past me on all fours. The flames trailing it snapped at the air as it howled while charging heedlessly forward. I felt no sympathy for the suffering it radiated. I'd seen its pile of remains; this thing had never shown an ounce of compassion for anything.

I should probably keep going, but since I had no idea *where* I was going, I decided to follow it. The minotaur turned a corner and reeled back as fire shot toward its face. Then it spun and came straight back at me.

Gripping my sword with both hands, I darted out of the way and swung the blade up and into the minotaur's belly. The creature grunted as I yanked the blade out, but it barely paid attention to me as it vanished into the flames again.

I followed it with the hope it would lead me out of this place. We ran back beneath the dome, but I didn't bother to look at the ceiling as the minotaur charged forward. The fire consuming its body revealed patches of muscle, and on one section of its ass end, bone showed through.

It shook its head back and forth and tried swatting at the flames with one hand, but there was no avoiding the flames surrounding us. At one point, it stopped to roll over to smother the fire, but that exposed its belly, and the fire greedily took advantage of the new fuel.

Rising, it staggered before thundering forward again with another bellow. I didn't see the rock wall until the minotaur ran headfirst into it. The rock indented before a chunk broke off over the minotaur's head and fell to hit it.

The beast shook its head before staggering back. It hunched up and released a keening wail that echoed the forlorn noise the hedges made when the flames started devouring them.

The minotaur's skin crackled and popped as the flames dug into its flesh. The stench of burning meat filled the air as more of the minotaur's skin peeled back to reveal the muscle and bone beneath. It stumbled to the side before collapsing with a thud that fanned the flames into my face.

I studied its side as I waited for the telltale rise and fall of its chest. Minutes passed without any movement, and more of its skeleton became exposed until the flames ate its heart. The thing was obviously dead, but I cut off its head to make sure it didn't return.

Slipping away from the minotaur, I placed my hand against the rock wall and ran my fingers over the jagged edges as I followed it. The smoke clouding the air made seeing difficult, but there had to be an exit somewhere in this place. I'd prefer not to wait until the fire went out to locate it, but I was beginning to fear that might be my only option.

A blast of air from above caused the flames around me to die down before surging up again. I shaded my eyes with my hand as I looked up to discover Caim hovering thirty feet above me.

"This way!" he shouted.

I sprinted after Caim as he led me through the fire.

"It's right up here!" he yelled. "I have to get back to the others; the horsemen are here."

"Of course they are," I muttered though there was no way he heard me over the fire.

I ignored the burning of my lungs and the exhaustion creeping into my bones as I ran. My hand tightened on my sword as I braced myself for the next battle. Unlike us, the horsemen would be well-rested, but that didn't mean I couldn't slice them to bits.

Through the rolling flames, I spotted the opening leading out of this place as Caim swooped into the tunnel. A fresh burst of energy caused my legs to move faster, and I sprinted across the hundred feet separating me from the exit.

Hawk

We were almost to the end of the cave when three of the horsemen appeared. It wasn't until they blocked out the sunlight streaming through the entrance that I realized we'd spent most of the night in the labyrinth.

I didn't know if the bastards had managed to get behind us after the fog and been stalking us the whole time or if the smoke had drawn them here, and it didn't matter. They were here now, and like when they attacked the wall, they were arriving when we were exhausted.

"What do we do?" Aisling asked.

"We kill them," Corson said.

And that was exactly what we had to do to get free. There was no turning back; the flames effectively blocked any chance of escape behind us. The exhaustion of the others beat against me, but I had a feeling the horsemen would regret coming at us now. We were all too pissed off for their shit.

As we got closer, I recognized Pestilence because of the hundreds of flies buzzing around his head. Quarter-sized, blistering sores covered his cheeks; he was missing the tip of his nose, and something black festered on the skin around what remained of his nose. His horse was the greenish-brown color of snot, and the blistering sores on it had eaten through its hide to reveal ligament and bone in some areas.

Pestilence's fingers were the same black color, and I speculated that he had leprosy or gangrene. He wore no clothes, and his flesh rippled as if blowing in a breeze. And then I realized the movement wasn't from a breeze but something moving *beneath* his flesh.

Lust sat beside Pestilence with a smug smile on her luscious mouth. Her white hair spilled past her waist and across the ass end of her gray horse. Her emerald eyes twinkled in amusement as she threw her shoulders back to reveal more of her bare, voluptuous body.

Unlike the last time I saw her, I only experienced a small stirring of desire, but it wouldn't be the same for most of the others. Because of the Chosen bond, Aisling and I had a better chance of withstanding these monsters, and so did Corson and Wren, but their effect would be a lot stronger on everyone else.

I didn't know who rode the third horse, but judging by the

scarlet color of the mount and the unnatural rage clawing at my chest, I assumed it was either War or Wrath.

As we got closer to the horsemen, some of the humans fell back while a couple of the demons stopped. Then one demon leapt onto the back of another, took him to the ground, and punched him in the face. We were already losing our fighters to the horsemen's effects, and the one on the scarlet horse was more powerful than the other two.

I almost grabbed Aisling and told her to run back into the fire. As long as she avoided the minotaur, she would be better off in there, but it would be a waste of time as I knew she wouldn't leave me.

We were a hundred feet from the end of the cave when the scarlet horse broke free of the other two and charged into the cave. Its hooves rang against the steel as it galloped toward us.

"Look out!" I shouted and pulled Aisling out of the way of the rider.

I hugged her against me as the horse thundered past us. Some of the others couldn't get out of the way in time, and the rider ran them over. As the rider swept us, I realized it wasn't trying to attack but was spreading its maliciousness through the cave. I still wasn't sure if it was Wrath or War when the others turned on each other like a pack of rabid dogs.

"Oliver," Aisling whispered.

Randy and Nadine stood away from the others, but the shaking of Nadine's shoulders and the clenching of Randy's fists indicated the horsemen were affecting them too.

"I have to get Oliver," Aisling said.

I was reluctant to release her, but I had to let her go; it was impossible to fight the horsemen with her in my arms.

Aisling sprinted across the cave and took Oliver from Nadine's arms. She cradled the boy against her chest as Nadine practically salivated while eyeing her. "You try anything, and I'll torch your ass," Aisling promised her.

Enough reason remained in Nadine that she didn't turn her hostility on Aisling but focused it on the brawl growing inside the cave.

"Close your eyes, baby," Aisling told Oliver as she pushed his head onto her shoulder.

The boy stuck his thumb in his mouth as Nadine and Randy jumped into the fight.

"I *hate* the horsemen," I snarled.

"You and me both," Wren said.

She was paler than before, and her lower lip quivered, but she didn't wade into the fight to separate Nadine and Randy from it; she must have known it was useless. The effects of the horsemen wouldn't ease until they were dead or gone from here, and fighting our allies wouldn't help achieve either of those goals.

"They're not making it out of here alive," Lix said.

Lifting his sword, Lix charged forward. With a loud battle cry, he leapt into the air and sliced Pestilence's horse's head straight down the middle. The sickly-looking creature didn't move as the two pieces of its head bobbed awkwardly before starting to fuse themselves back together.

"Holy shit," Aisling breathed.

Lix's movements slowed with every passing second, but he didn't stop attacking Pestilence. When his head bowed and his shoulders slumped, I realized Pestilence was doing something to him.

I removed one of the guns strapped to my waist, and before Pestilence's horse could completely heal, I fired a series of bullets into it and its rider. The shots did nothing to stop whatever the horseman was doing to Lix as his sword tip fell to the ground and he stumbled back.

Corson charged forward, leapt into the air, and buried his

talons in Pestilence's leg. Wren ran in from the other side and sank her talons into Pestilence's other leg. The hundreds of flies buzzing around the monster's head became frenzied. Their wings beat so loudly, their noise drowned out the sounds of the battle.

When my gun emptied, I slid it back into my holster. Two demons beat at each other as they rolled past me. One of them had a battle ax strapped to its back. Stepping forward, I planted my foot on the demon's hip and pulled the ax free.

"Stay with Oliver," I told Aisling before charging into the battle.

CHAPTER FORTY

*B*ALE

Fresh, cooler air caressed my skin when I stepped into the cave and took a deep breath. I had only a second to enjoy my relief over the minotaur's death and the destruction of the labyrinth before the reverberating sound of hoofbeats filled my ears.

My eyes flew open, and I lifted my sword as I leapt away from the wall. I glimpsed a scarlet horse before it hit me in the chest, lifted me off the ground, and carried me into the cave. When I punched the horse's face, it captured my arm and flung me into the flames.

I soared twenty feet through the air before I crashed onto the ground. My lungs seized as air flooded out of them, and none returned. Knocked from my hand, my sword clattered against the rocky terrain as it bounced a few feet away from me. My fingers clawed at the ground as I tried to grasp the handle while my lungs still screamed for air.

A fiery wave of heat filled my lungs as I finally breathed in what little oxygen there was in the inferno. The approach of hoofbeats had me rolling to the side in time to avoid the hooves that would have trampled me.

As the beast and rider disappeared into the flames, I glimpsed broad shoulders and a sword strapped to the rider's back.

Wrath! I realized when mind-numbing rage coursed through my veins. I didn't know how I knew it was Wrath and not War, but I felt the identity of this rider deep in my bones.

Kill him! Kill him! Kill! Kill! Kill!

I rested my hand against my forehead as I tried to regain some control over the rage pulsing in my temples while I struggled to recall whose head I wanted to chop off.

It's Wrath; you want to kill Wrath!

My breath hissed in through my teeth as I pushed myself to my feet and staggered over to reclaim my sword. The familiar weight of it in my hand helped steady me further as I searched the flames for the rider.

Through the fire, I spotted Wrath turning and charging back toward me. The flames licked at the sides of his legs and horse, but neither of them caught fire.

This bastard's immune to the inferno.

Lifting my sword, I braced my legs apart as I waited for them to draw closer before dropping suddenly. When I acted like I planned to take out the horse's legs, Wrath jerked up on his reins to steer the horse away, but at the last second, I leapt up and plunged my sword into his thigh.

He grunted as he clutched his leg, but keeping hold of my sword, I jerked it to the side and yanked him from his steed. As Wrath hit the ground, he wrenched his leg back to free it from my blade. I went to plunge my sword into his heart, but it crashed into stone as he rolled into the fire.

I shifted my hold on my sword and lifted it above my shoulder as I searched for him in the inferno. The second he reemerged, I was going to use every ounce of the fury he'd created to chop his head off.

The ring of hooves against rock turned my head as the red horse came back at me. At first, I thought the flames got the best of the beast and it was on fire, and then I realized it *was* fire. Either it possessed the ability to make the inferno encompass it, or it could make flames sprout from its body.

"Shit," I whispered.

Shifting my stance, I prepared to take the beast out, but before I could chop off its head, something hit me in the side. I somehow managed to retain my weapon as I was thrown to the ground.

Twisting beneath the weight of whatever was on top of me, I found myself gazing into a set of red and orange eyes that looked like they mirrored the inferno. But as they searched my face, I realized that *was* the color of Wrath's eyes.

Despite my hatred for this bastard and his kind, a sense of awe stole through me. He was a magnificent, lethal, killing machine. And if I didn't stop staring into those eyes, I was going to be his next kill.

Pulling my arm back, I hammered my left fist into his face and smiled when I felt his cheekbone give beneath the blow. The red in his eyes blazed hotter, but before he could punish me for what I'd done, I lifted my knees and somehow managed to wedge my feet between us.

He scrambled to hold on to me but failed to do so as I put all my strength behind my legs and shoved him away from me. He flew backward and disappeared into the inferno. I didn't kid myself into thinking it was over; he'd be back soon. Rolling over, I searched for his horse but didn't see it anywhere. That beast was as lethal as its rider, maybe more so.

Through the flames, the opening of the cave beckoned me, but I couldn't leave here without destroying this monster. I'd cut off his head and stick it on my sword to show to his friends.

Rising, I gripped my sword with both hands and stalked a few feet into the fire. I couldn't go too far, or I'd allow him to slip up behind me, so I stayed close enough to see the exit. Motion to my left caused me to turn in that direction. I blinked as flames rolled within flames to create a spinning ball of fire.

It can't be...

And then the flames parted.

No... that wasn't right. The flames didn't part; they coalesced into a figure.

A figure that was coming straight at me. I barely managed to keep from croaking out a holy shit as I saw that, like his steed, Wrath could become fire too.

And then, he vanished.

~

Aisling

"You have to stay here," I said to Oliver as I set him inside the crevice I'd discovered in the cave.

"They're going to kill us," he whispered.

I rested my hands on his shoulders. "No, they're not. You're going to be safe, but you have to stay in here until I come to get you. Do you understand?"

Oliver gazed over my shoulder and toward the continuing sounds of a brawl, but we were too far into the crevice for him to see what was happening. "Yes," he murmured.

He stuck his thumb in his mouth as he gazed at me with sorrow-filled eyes. He'd already been through so much; he shouldn't have to endure this too, but the only way to stop it was to kill the horsemen.

I didn't know why he wasn't affected by the horseman who'd turned the others into bloodthirsty monsters. He was probably too young to understand the emotion, but thankfully, he wasn't a spitting, kicking, demon child. I didn't know if I could handle that.

"It will be over soon," I said and really hoped I was right. I ran my hand over his cheek. "Close your eyes, baby."

He settled on the ground and closed his eyes as he rested his head against the stone. He had to be exhausted; maybe, just maybe, he would sleep through all of this. I doubted it, but I held on to that hope as I ruffled his brown hair.

"I'll be back," I promised and bent to kiss the top of his head. I wished I could stay with him, but the others needed my help.

He didn't respond as he kept his eyes closed and huddled deeper into the shadows. It took everything I had to back out of the small hiding place. I kept my eyes on him until I rounded a corner and he vanished from view. Tears burned my eyes when I turned away from him.

I didn't care what I had to do; I would make sure he got away from this place. Stepping out of the alcove, I was confronted with a group of fighting and gagging people and demons. Some of them were on their knees puking out wretched green bile while others were punching each other even as they groped at one another and tore at their clothes in a rage and lust-fueled frenzy.

The smell and sounds permeating the cave made my stomach turn, but so far, I was still withstanding a fair amount of the horsemen's effects, though I couldn't look at Hawk.

When I looked at him, all I could think about was tearing his clothes from him and screwing until we were too exhausted to move.

Lifting my forearm, I wiped away the sweat from my brow and felt the warmth of my skin. I knew that heat had nothing to do with the fire we'd left behind and everything to do with the nausea twisting in my stomach. Saliva flooded my mouth along with the coppery taste that often preceded vomiting. I could *not* start spewing up green bile; if that stuff came out of me, I'd never stop.

Before the horsemen, I would have believed it impossible to be horny while trying not to vomit, but these assholes were a whole different ballgame.

I ignored the churning of my stomach and focused my attention on Corson and Wren as they battled Pestilence. My eyes kept trying to go to Hawk, but I couldn't control myself enough to look at him.

Deep breaths. Stay in control. Don't give in to the urges. You can do this.

Finally feeling in control of myself enough to look at Hawk, I felt like someone punched me in the gut as he ran at Lust.

No! Not alone! You can't fight her alone!

But that was exactly what he was going to do.

CHAPTER FORTY-ONE

Aisling

Forgetting all about the sickness churning inside me, I leapt over a group of humans and demons rolling around on the floor. I snagged an abandoned spear from the ground as I ran toward the others. Near the front of the cave, Lix sat with his hands on his knees and his head bowed as he spewed green bile.

A flutter of wings drew my attention to the ceiling seconds before Caim burst free of the cave and crashed into Lust. The impact tore Lust from her saddle, but before Caim could rise into the air with her in his arms, she grabbed one of his wings and yanked it down.

The motion threw off his ascension; they tumbled to the ground in a jumbled heap of white hair and black wings that blended as they rolled with each other. When Lust settled on top, Caim tossed her off and braced his arms under him. He staggered to his feet and steadied himself as his face changed.

Slack-jawed, he grasped the sides of his head as he staggered away from the cave. Nonsensical words I suspected might be the angelic language spilled from his lips as he started hitting the sides of his face.

Then, he turned into his raven form and released a loud caw before taking flight. I had no idea where he was going, but after enduring Lust's touch, it was probably better if he got away from here.

Hawk ran at Lust, but before he could get close to her, her horse inserted itself between them. Hawk dodged the striking hoof of Lust's horse, and throwing himself to the ground, he rolled beneath the animal. My breath caught when he came up on the other side of the beast and Lust grasped his ankle.

Hawk jerked at his leg, but she didn't release him, and the longer she held on, the more sluggish his movements became. He lurched to the side as, with its ears pinned and mouth open, her horse lunged for him.

"No!" I shouted as I sprinted toward them.

The horse seized Hawk's arm and ripped him off the ground. He spun and launched a punch at the animal, but before it could land, the horse tossed him away like a rag doll. I couldn't breathe as I watched him flip through the air before hitting the ground. He bounced across the rocky earth and underneath the striking feet of Pestilence's mount.

"No!" My scream left my throat raw as Pestilence's horse struck again and again.

Hawk avoided most of the blows and rolled out of the way in time to prevent the horse from crashing onto him, but not in time to keep a hoof from striking down his back and tearing his flesh open. When blood flowed down his back, red filled my vision and fire flowed from my palms.

I dropped the spear before I torched it and stopped running to plant my feet as a wave of fire erupted from my palms. Not even my astonishment overseeing such a thing could bury the fury pulsing through my veins. They'd *hurt* him!

I'd kill all of them for that!

I couldn't get at Pestilence without setting Corson on fire, so I unleashed my vengeance on Lust. The blast hit her in the chest and threw her back five feet. Her screams reverberated off the mountains as she slapped at herself to smother the flames devouring her flesh.

When her horse lunged at me, I dodged a hoof that skimmed my forehead and sliced it open. Blood slid into my eye as I ran at Lust and tackled her flaming figure to the ground. She was still screaming as her nails gouged the flesh from my arms, and blood spilled free to sizzle on the flames enveloping her.

The stench of her burning hair and skin filled my nostrils as she rolled on top of me. She wasn't so pretty now, and when I shattered her perfect nose with my fist, she became even uglier. The punch infuriated her further as her hands flailed at me. Flames still erupted from my palms to fuel the ones consuming her.

Over her shoulder, Hawk appeared and ripped her off me. Fire rolled up his hands, and I cried out when his flesh blistered. When he threw Lust across the ground, she crashed into the mountain beside the cave.

Hawk turned to me and extended his blistered hand. Afraid to burn him; I hesitated to take it. "Aisling—"

He didn't get to finish speaking as Lust's horse galloping toward us pulled his attention away from me. I didn't have a chance to extinguish my fire before Hawk threw himself on top of me and rolled us out of the way. I smothered my flames, but though he didn't make a sound, I knew I'd burned him before I put the fire out.

No! My moan died away when he stopped rolling. He lay on top of me with his breath tickling my ear as I turned my head into his. My heart ached for the pain I inflicted on him, and I needed a second to savor him and everything he meant to me.

When he walked into my life, I wasn't ready to be tied down; now, I couldn't imagine my life without him. I'd never expected to experience the love I felt for him; I was immortal before meeting him, but *he* was the one who brought me to life.

I *wouldn't* lose him.

"I love you," I breathed.

"I love you too," he whispered.

He kissed my temple before rolling away. I stared up at the clear blue sky and gathered my dwindling strength before launching to my feet. Wren and Corson had succeeded in pulling Pestilence from his horse. They circled him while he turned to face them. Wren kept her lips clamped together as sweat poured down her face; she looked ready to throw up, but somehow, she kept moving.

The swarming flies were so thick it almost looked as if they were wearing a helmet made up of the creatures as they bounced angrily off their heads. My stomach rolled at the sight of those insects, and saliva filled my mouth; I swallowed to keep from throwing up. Lix had regained his feet and was staggering toward them, but he went down to one knee before pushing himself up again.

Rolling across the ground, Lust succeeded in extinguishing her flames. She didn't stop until she came up against the rocky mountain. With hands that were more bone than flesh, Lust grasped the rocks and pulled herself up before turning to face us. Badly burnt, she slumped against the rocks while she glowered at us from her one remaining eye.

Lust's effect on me was gone, but I was done with the horsemen, the minotaur, and Hell. I was finished with these bastards trying to destroy my world, my life, my friends, and Hawk. I recalled Oliver standing in the shadows of the cave, and my rage returned to bury my nausea.

Hawk

Most of Lust's influence faded when Aisling torched her, but the lingering effects of Lust's touch made my skin hypersensitive. Having Aisling beneath me for those brief seconds hadn't helped, but I was regaining most of my control and could walk again without extreme discomfort.

Lust's mount trotted toward her, but before it reached her, Aisling released another wave of fire. The flames hit Lust, and she threw up her arms in a useless attempt to protect herself as Aisling pinned her against the wall. Her mount reared back and spun toward Aisling.

Ignoring the blisters on my palms, I hefted the ax and ran at Lust. Unable to move, Lust screamed as Aisling's fire melted away what remained of her flesh. When I was only feet away, the flames abruptly cut off. I swung the ax down to sever her head from her body.

Thundering hoofbeats pulled my attention away from her rolling head as her mount charged at me. The beast was only five feet away when it burst into a cloud of ash that blew straight into my face as it rained over me.

Releasing the ax, I wiped the debris from my eyes and blinked them open as Pestilence's horse charged toward Aisling. "Aisling, look out!" I shouted.

She lunged to the side but not in time to avoid the horse clipping her in the back. Knocked off balance, she fell beneath the animal as Corson succeeded in severing Pestilence's head with his talons. The horse vanished into a cloud of dust.

"Aisling," I breathed as I ran toward her.

She was pushing herself to her hands and knees when I fell beside her and rested my hand on her back. I gently felt for any broken bones while reassuring myself she was okay.

"I'm fine." She winced as she gripped my hand and pulled it away from her back before smiling. "They're dead."

"They're dead," I agreed.

I brushed back a strand of her hair and tucked it behind her ear before wiping away the smoke and soot streaking her face to expose her pale skin. Her eyes were shadowed and bloodshot from exhaustion and smoke, but they shone with happiness.

"Where's the other horseman?" Corson asked.

I looked back toward the cave, but there was no sign of the horseman or Bale. The others had stopped fighting each other, so did that mean the other horseman was dead? Or maybe because he was in the fire the effects of his powers weren't as strong?

"We have to help Bale," Aisling said.

Before I could stop her, she pushed herself up and staggered to her feet. I rose beside her and gripped her arm when she winced. Her hand went to her ribs as she leaned against me. Pestilence's horse had done more damage than I realized.

"Are your ribs broken?" I asked as I wrapped my arm around her waist and she leaned against me.

"No, they're just bruised."

"You have to rest."

"Oliver!" she cried and winced again when she stumbled forward.

I pulled her back and tucked her securely against my side. "You're going to be fine, but you're not going to heal if you keep pushing yourself," I told her. "We'll find Bale and get Oliver."

"If Bale is still in the labyrinth, you won't be able to go into the fire like I can," she said.

"We'll figure it out, but you can't go back into the fire like this either. We have no idea where the horseman or the minotaur are, and you can't face them wounded. Sit and allow yourself to heal for a few minutes."

She opened her mouth to argue with me, but then her legs gave out and she sank to the ground as Nadine emerged from the cave with Oliver in her arms. Bruises marred Nadine's face and arms, but she looked otherwise unharmed. Oliver pulled his thumb from his mouth and smiled at Aisling.

CHAPTER FORTY-TWO

BALE

I kept my sword high and my eyes on the fire as I edged toward the exit. I had no idea where Wrath went, but I sensed him stalking me. The flames crackled all around me as they fueled my power, but I suspected they fueled his power too.

A shift in the flames drew my eyes to the left as Wrath strolled from the fire like he was walking through the park. I half expected him to clasp his hands behind his back and start skipping toward me while he whistled, but he smiled as he sauntered like he had all the time in the world.

This bastard had no idea who he was dealing with, and I'd wipe that amused expression off his too handsome face if it was the last thing I did.

The inferno had eaten away his clothes. I refused to admire the breadth of his broad, bare shoulders or how chiseled the muscles of his large, powerful body were. The man was a wall of steel.

In his hand, he held the sword that was strapped to his back when he first entered the maze. Flickering flames filled his orange-red eyes. Fire encircled his sword, and he lifted his hands at his sides to push the flames toward me.

Before I could react, the flames surging toward me whipped my hair back and momentarily blinded me. I didn't try to see or fight through it as instinct told me to *move*. Ducking, I threw myself to the ground, but I didn't roll away like he probably expected. Instead, I went toward him and popped up a few feet away from him.

He leapt back as I swung my sword out. The blade cut through the flames, and the tip skimmed his chest to spill his black blood. Before the blood could trickle too far down his chest, the fire ate it away.

Wrath glanced at his chest before smiling at me. I didn't know if his presence was fueling my fury or the fact he kept *smiling* at me, but my temples throbbed, and it took all I had not to swing my sword viciously at him. He wanted me to lose control, because once I did, I would die.

Gritting my teeth, I kept my temper leashed as I lunged at him. He parried fast enough to knock my blade aside, but I didn't stop pressing him. I was strong and fast, but Wrath was an ancient demon with more power than I possessed. His strength would eventually wear me down, and when it did, he would kill me.

The only advantage I had against him was my agility and speed. If I deflected the head-severing blows he swung at me, I might get the chance to dart past his defenses and injure, if not, kill him.

When he jabbed at my belly, I sucked it in as I arched back enough to keep my intestines from spilling free. With a turn of my wrist, I caught the tip of his sword with my blade and slammed it into the ground.

When he lifted his head, his smile was gone, and his eyes narrowed. I kept his sword pinned to the ground as I punched him in the face. Bone crunched, blood spilled free, and his head snapped back. His hand flew toward his face, but before he grabbed his battered nose, he dropped his palm to smash my wrist aside when I tried to bury my blade in his stomach.

The flames leapt higher when he swung his sword up in a move that would have sliced me from groin to gullet if I didn't deflect it with my blade. The steel of our swords clashed, and sparks flew from our blades as we pushed each other forward and back while dancing around each other.

Despite his bone-crushing blows and our lethal dance, a smile curved the corners of his thick lips. I would wipe that smile off his face by slicing him open, but every move I made, he countered. Despite my inane hatred for everything this monster represented, I couldn't deny my grudging respect for his talent with a sword.

As much as I hated to admit it, the way he danced was beautiful. He was almost as fluid as the fire and just as deadly. This horseman knew how to kill, and he thrived on it. But then, he was Wrath; he was born to leave misery in his wake.

My hands and arms ached from his blows as steel kissed steel over and over again as the exertion of our fight started wearing me down. I nearly missed deflecting his next blow before it took my other ear off. When his smile grew, I bit back a scream; this fucker was *playing* with me.

Our blades kissed against each other and slid down. He twisted mine over and pushed down until I had no choice but to save my wrist from breaking by yielding to him. With my sword pinned to the ground, I launched another punch at his face. He caught my hand before I could break his jaw and jerked me forward.

I tried to yank my hand free of his powerful grasp, but he wouldn't let go as he pushed me down until my knees smacked off the rock. He pulled his blade away from mine, but before he could kill me with it, I jerked as far back as I could and got my feet out from under me.

I swept my leg against his and knocked his feet out from under him. When he hit the ground on his back, his sword tumbled from his grasp and clattered against the rock as it bounced a few feet away.

The fire parted, and the head of his mount materialized while the rest of its body remained hidden in flames. I expected it to charge at me, but it stayed where it was while its eyes danced with fire. I didn't know why it chose not to come after me, but I would take this small favor.

With his hold on me broken, I gripped my sword in both hands and rose on my knees to plunge it into Wrath's belly. I drove it down as he rolled out of the way and reclaimed his sword. The tip of my blade crashed into the rock, and a chunk of stone broke away as sparks shot up.

No!

I'd made a huge mistake and wasn't prepared to block his blow. Somehow, he'd anticipated it. My heart pounded, and all my senses honed in on him as time slowed. The sound of the fire died away as the whistle of his sword arcing toward my neck became the only noise I heard.

Somehow, I managed to swing my sword up too. I couldn't deflect his sword, but as his steel pressed against my neck, my blade cut into the skin beneath his ear. A hot trickle of blood crept down my flesh and his blood beaded on the tip of my sword while we knelt, staring at each other.

Cut off his head!

I'd probably lose mine too, but it didn't matter. I'd fought my whole life to keep things like him from taking over Hell and now Earth. I'd accepted the fact I would perish in a fight and would proudly do so.

But something kept my hand from pushing my sword deeper into his throat and ending the suffering he rained down wherever he went.

The fire faded from his eyes as they became a deep, fathomless black. And then, instead of killing me, he grasped the back of my head and dragged me toward him. I stiffened against whatever he intended but didn't pull away.

And when his mouth crushed mine, I realized why I hadn't resisted him... I'd known what he planned all along, and a part of me *craved* it.

His kiss was rough as it mashed my lips against my teeth, but I didn't care as my body reacted like lightning struck it. My heart hammered, goose bumps covered my flesh, and my back bowed as desire seared through my veins. It was *so* wrong, yet it felt so incredibly right.

It wasn't until I heard the clatter of steel against rock that I realized my blade had fallen from his neck to hit the ground. I couldn't feel his sword against my skin anymore. I should break away; I should run. I should kill him now. Instead, my fingers entangled in his thick, black hair as I pulled him closer.

My nipples hardened when his bare chest met mine. Tendrils of pleasure spiraled through my veins while the rigid evidence of his arousal rested against my belly. Then he did the most destructive thing he could to me; he softened the kiss.

My body melted into his as the pressure of his mouth eased, and his tongue teased my lips until they parted. I actually *sighed* when his tongue touched mine, and I sank deeper into him as our tongues entwined.

I'd been with countless demons in my lengthy life, but I'd never been kissed before or even *had* the impulse to kiss someone. Demons didn't kiss; we fucked, and we moved on. Had I been missing something this whole time by not kissing the others?

And when his kiss softened further, I realized I'd missed a whole lot of something. However, no other demon could have given it to me because *this* man was what I'd been missing.

He was *so* right against me, and he made my body come alive in a way it never had before. When his grip on my hip eased and his hand slid around to cup my ass, I stopped myself from squirming while I rubbed against his erection. Seeming to feed on our sexual energy, the fire grew around us.

I wanted—no, I *needed* more.

I needed this man.

My Chosen.

The realization of what he was rocked me enough that my euphoria vanished. *No! No! No!*

My mind reeled as horror swelled within me. I'd spent my whole life battling monsters who sought to destroy everything in their wake. Now, a cruel twist of fate had made one of them my Chosen. I didn't rail against the unfairness of it all; life was unfair, and that's all there was to it, but I would *not* be taken down by this. I would *not* give into this.

I continued to kiss him while I lifted my sword and plunged it into his belly before tearing my mouth away from his. Shock filled his eyes, his mouth slackened, and then fury blazed from him. That fury was like gasoline on the flames as they surged around us.

Leaving my sword where it was, I staggered to my feet and fled into the fire.

CHAPTER FORTY-THREE

Hawk

Corson and I were almost to the end of the cave when Bale burst from the flames and sprinted toward us. "Run!" she shouted.

We skidded to a halt. I'd never seen Bale so panicked as her feet slapped against the stone and her hair flew behind her naked form. She bolted past us. I glanced at Corson who gaped after her before turning and following her through the cave.

"Is the minotaur coming?" Corson asked when we caught up to her.

"It's dead," Bale panted. "The fire and a headfirst run into the mountain officially ended its life."

"Good," I said.

"Where's the other horseman?" Corson asked.

She glanced nervously over her shoulder, and despite the reddish hue of her skin, she paled visibly. *What the...?* I looked back to the flames as I waited for the horseman to emerge, but there was no sign of him. He had to be a formidable opponent if he'd rattled Bale this much.

"Wrath's still in the fire, but he'll come," Bale said.

288 BRENDA K DAVIES

"And we'll kill him," Corson said.

Bale shuddered but didn't say anything as we ran.

"Are you sure it's Wrath and not War?" I asked.

"I'm sure," she said as we reached the end of the cave.

Everyone had moved outside where they sat on the ground holding their heads or huddled in small groups. About half the humans and demons were bloodied and bruised from fighting each other, and the other half still looked a little green.

Scattered amid the ashes of the horses and the bodies of the horsemen were thousands of dead flies. Even though they were dead, I could still hear the buzzing of their wings; I'd hear it in my nightmares for the rest of my life.

Aisling leaned against the wall of the cave with Oliver curled against her chest and her arms wrapped protectively around him. Nadine and Randy stood nearby as Wren helped them clean their wounds.

"Pestilence and Lust are dead," Corson said to Bale.

"I see that," she murmured, but she still didn't seem to focus on what was happening here. "Seven down, four to go."

"Unfortunately, one of those four is Death," Lix said as he walked over to join us.

"And he's been beaten before," Corson said. "He wouldn't have been behind the seal otherwise. We'll destroy them all."

Bale bit her lip and glanced toward the town nestled in the valley below. Fire still danced over some of the buildings, but the smoke choking the air masked most of the town.

"You okay?" Lix asked Bale. When she gave him a blank stare, he pointed to the side of her head. "You're bleeding."

"Oh." She pushed her hair back to reveal her missing ear. "The minotaur got one in on me, but it will grow back."

"Move faster next time," Corson teased.

"Yeah," she muttered. "I never should have stopped fighting."

We all frowned at her as she looked back toward the town.

Corson gave me a questioning look, but if he didn't have any explanation for her strange behavior, then I sure didn't. He'd known her a lot longer than me.

"We'll go back inside and wait for Wrath to leave the labyrinth," Corson said. "He'll be easier to take out now that he's alone, and we should be able to kill him before he gets close to everyone else."

Bale closed her eyes before replying, "Yes, that will work."

"Do you need Aisling and me for that?" I asked.

"Why?" Lix inquired. "What do you have planned?"

I pointed toward the town. "I want to see if the minotaur's death brought down the barrier. There could also be survivors."

"I think me, Wren, Lix, and Bale can handle Wrath," Corson said.

"I agree," Lix said and rested his hand on my shoulder. "Be careful not to get too close until you know the barrier is down."

"Believe me, I'm not getting trapped in there again," I assured him.

"We'll see you soon," Corson said.

I nodded before walking away. Nadine had taken Oliver back from her and was sitting against the mountain while he slept on her lap. I stopped to kneel beside her and brushed the hair back from Oliver's face. He was so exhausted his eyelids didn't flicker.

"We'll find some food soon," I told Nadine.

"We're okay." She rested her hand on Oliver's nape. "He's free."

"So are you."

"So are *all* of us."

I rose and walked over to Aisling. Shadows rimmed her eyes, but she smiled when I extended my hand to her. "What about the minotaur?" she asked as she took my hand and rose.

"Dead," I told her. "The fire was destroying it, and apparently it couldn't run through the mountain."

Her shoulders slumped, and she swayed toward me. "Thank God."

"The others are going to wait for Wrath to emerge, but I want to see if the barrier has fallen and if there are any survivors."

"I hope there are," she whispered. "I feel like we abandoned them."

"They made their choice."

"I don't think they expected the *whole* town to burn."

"They know it was a possibility, and they could have come with us. They were too scared to enter the labyrinth though."

"Do you blame them?"

"Yes, because one way or another, they were going in there; it was either going to be with us or the minotaur, and they refused to fight for their chance at freedom."

"They chose to cling to their lives for as long as they could," she said.

I draped my arm around her shoulders and pulled her close to kiss the top of her head. Her hands dug into my back as she rested her forehead against my chest. I still considered them cowards, but it wasn't worth arguing over it.

"Do you want to come with me?" I asked.

"Yes."

She rose onto her toes to kiss me. Her fingers lingered on my cheek before she stepped away. I reluctantly released her before walking over to reclaim my ax. Aisling retrieved her spear and waited for me to join her by the entrance of the cave.

When I glanced inside the cave, I spotted Corson, Wren, Bale, and Lix striding toward the distant glow of the fire. A row of demons stood in front of the cave. Some of them faced outward while the others faced inside the cave. The demons would see any threat coming and alert the others.

Taking Aisling's hand, I led the way into the trees and down the rocky terrain of the mountain. Pine cones and dried pine needles crunched beneath our feet, as did some of the smaller stones littering the ground.

The trees were sparse through here and consisted mostly of scraggly pines. When the descent became too steep, I released Aisling's hand, and we went sideways to keep our balance as we moved from tree to tree and boulder to boulder.

We were halfway down the hill when Caim landed beside us. He transitioned from a raven before shaking out his wings.

"Are you okay to be around her?" I demanded as I pulled Aisling closer. I'd come to like Caim, but I'd destroy him if he tried anything with her.

"Yes," Caim said as he settled his wings against his back. "Lust's effect on me vanished when she died."

"Did you see anything in the town?" Aisling asked.

"The smoke blocked most of my view," he said. "When you get further down the mountain, you're going to have trouble seeing."

"Great," she murmured. "Where are the hounds?"

"When I saw the smoke coming from the cave, I left them at the edge of the barrier to see if I could find you. They'll stay there until we return for them," Caim said. "Is the minotaur dead?"

"Yes," I said.

"Olé!" he shouted and put one hand on his hip as he threw the other in the air like a bullfighter. "Too soon?" he asked when Aisling and I stared at him.

Then Aisling started to laugh. "No, it's not too soon. We should celebrate the death of that monstrosity and two more horsemen."

We should, but there was no time to celebrate now.

"When this is over, there will be lots of celebrating," I promised as I brushed back her hair and kissed her temple.

She leaned against me for a second before pulling away and starting down the hill again. Caim hesitated as he looked to me before glancing at Aisling.

"What is it?" I asked.

Aisling stopped and turned to face us as Caim ran a hand through his hair. "The fog is moving closer," he said.

"The fog with those *people* in it?" Aisling demanded.

"That's the one," Caim replied.

Aisling paled visibly. "How close is it to us?"

"About a mile."

"Too close," she whispered.

"We have time to go to the town and leave again before they reach us," Caim said

Aisling's jaw clenched, but she didn't say anything more as we started down the mountain again. When we were halfway down the hill, a flash of something across the valley and on another mountain caught my attention.

I squinted while I tried to ascertain what it was, and then I realized a ball of fire was climbing the mountain across from us. It wasn't until the fire rose higher on the hill that I realized a horse and rider were within the flames.

"Wrath," I muttered.

Before Wrath arrived at the top of the mountain, the fire engulfing him went out. He paused to look over his shoulder as he pulled something from him. It wasn't until he lifted it in the air and the sun glinted off the blade that I realized Bale had been missing her sword.

Instead of tossing the sword aside, he laid it across his lap and continued up the hill before vanishing into the woods.

CHAPTER FORTY-FOUR

Hawk

"If Wrath left through the other cave entrance, he had to go through the town, which means the barrier *is* down," I said.

"We have to see if there are survivors," Aisling said.

"We will," I assured her.

The closer we got to the town, the more the smoke billowing into the air blocked out the sun and burned our eyes and lungs.

"Where did the other three horsemen go?" I asked. "Why weren't they with Wrath, Lust, and Pestilence?"

"Maybe they're hiding wherever they were before they attacked the wall," Aisling suggested.

"They could be, but why wouldn't they all return to hiding?" Caim wondered.

Only the horsemen had an answer for that, and since I didn't plan on talking to them before killing them, the question would never have an answer.

"Maybe they had a falling out," Aisling suggested.

"Anything's possible with those crazy pony riders," Caim said.

A few minutes passed before Aisling spoke again. "It's the four worst ones left—or at least, I think they're the worst."

"Pride, War, Wrath, and Death are the most destructive," Caim agreed.

Aisling took my hand and squeezed it. I felt the tremor in her fingers before she released me to grasp a tree branch while she climbed over a boulder. Our progress slowed when the smoke grew so thick it was impossible to see more than ten feet in front of us.

And then it started dissipating as we moved beneath the cloud and the dwindling tendrils of smoke, and the ruined town came into view. None of the buildings avoided the flames, but a few of them still stood while flames devoured what was left of them.

The remains of the toppled buildings glowed from the diminishing fire and hot embers beneath them. The charred stench of burnt wood permeated the air, and the smoke choking the sky created an unnatural dusk as it blocked out the sun.

"It's awful," Aisling murmured.

"It was necessary," Caim said.

From the shadows of the trees outside the town, figures prowled through the smoke and slithered through the woods. At first, I couldn't tell what they were; then the hounds materialized. Vivid against the unnatural dark, their amber eyes were luminous as they stalked toward us.

"Puppies!" Caim exclaimed and skipped over to the hounds.

Aisling gawked after him. "The last thing I'd call them is *puppies.*"

"Caim's not exactly normal," I said.

"No shit."

We were almost to the edge of the barrier when a dozen humans and demons emerged from the smoke and trees. They froze when they spotted us, but then their shoulders slumped, and some of them smiled as they came toward us. I waited for them to walk into the invisible wall of air, but nothing hindered their progress.

"The barrier is down," one of the women said.

"Good," Aisling breathed.

"Where is everyone else?" I asked as I rested a hand on Aisling's waist.

"Most of the survivors have gone their own way," a man replied. "The minotaur took two into the mountain after you left the town."

Aisling squeezed her hands as she clasped them before her. "Did they come back out?"

"Not that I know of," a demon said.

"I don't think they survived," Aisling murmured and bowed her head.

"The minotaur killed them, not you," I told her.

"The fire probably killed them," she said.

Grasping her shoulders, I turned her to face me before taking her chin and lifting her face so she had to look at me. "That *thing* brought them in there. And if they hadn't been too cowardly to help us"—I flicked a pointed glance at the newcomers; some of them had the grace to look away, but a few were unperturbed by my words—"they'd be alive now. Their deaths are *not* your fault."

The sorrow in her eyes tugged at my heart before I embraced her. Resting my chin on her head, I held her close as I stared at the remains of the town. She dug her fingers into my back as she hugged me back.

"Is the minotaur dead?" the man asked.

"Yes," Caim confirmed while he scratched one of the hounds behind its ear. When the hound turned into his touch and its tongue lolled out, I expected it to start thumping its hind leg in rhythm with the scratching.

"Good," the man said.

"No thanks to you," Caim said with a smile.

The man shrugged before speaking. "We didn't think it could be defeated."

"Everything can be defeated," Caim replied. "You just have to be willing to fight, and you were a coward who let others fight your battles for you."

The man's face turned red as he started to sputter a response, but when Caim unfolded his wings and embedded his bottom silver tips in the ground, the man shut up. The steely look on Caim's face made it evident he was fighting for the palitons now, but he would kill anyone who fucked with him.

"Do you want to join us?" Aisling asked them.

"Yes," a different woman breathed. She shot the man a look as she hurried toward us.

"Now they're all so eager to be around you," Caim said and closed his wings as he returned to petting the hounds.

Aisling shot him a look, but I agreed with him; these people and demons were not ones I'd trust to watch my back. However, they may be cowards, but I wouldn't leave them here.

"We should get out of here," I said as I kissed the top of Aisling's head. "With the barrier down, the fire might spread, and we have to tell the others Wrath is gone."

"Shouldn't we try to find more of the survivors?" she asked.

"They're gone," a demon said. "There's no one left in town."

I wondered if he was telling the truth or was eager to get away from here, but it didn't matter as Aisling said, "The fog people."

My head jerked in the direction she was looking. A thick fog had spread to block out the trees on the edge of town; tendrils of fog slithered out as it explored its surroundings. Those feelers reminded me of a pit of snakes slithering over each other while they sought out prey. When one of those tendrils came up against something hot from the fire, it would jerk back, and the fog would shift away.

"It's so... *awful*," Aisling said.

"What *is* that?" one of the humans asked.

"A pit of monsters," Caim said.

"Amber and her cohorts must have known the barrier and minotaur were here," Aisling said. "That's why they stayed in the valley and why they weren't trapped in the town. I bet those tendrils sensed it."

"And now they've come to scavenge whatever they can from the remains of the town," I said.

"They *have* to die," Aisling stated.

The steely look in her eyes was so different than the one of moments ago. No matter what I said, she'd always blame herself for the death of those people in the labyrinth, but she'd tear these fog people apart with her bare hands and never regret it.

Caim stopped petting the hounds and walked over to stand beside us as muffled screams erupted from the fog. Some of the survivors must have wandered into its treacherous depths.

"We *are* going to stop them," Aisling said.

She pulled out of my arms, threw back her shoulders, and stormed toward the fog. I caught up to her and grasped her arm to halt her. "Wait!"

Her eyes flashed red when she rounded on me. "They can't be allowed to live!"

Afraid she'd take off into the fog, I didn't release her arm as I spoke. "I understand, but you can't run in there without a plan."

"I have a plan." When she lifted her other hand, fire danced across her palm. "I'm going to torch them."

"You can't go into the fog again." I didn't care how badly she wanted to kill those people; I wouldn't let her back in there. They had too much of an advantage against us in there.

Caim strolled over to join us. "Might I suggest sending the hounds in after them."

"And if something happens to one of them?" Aisling asked.

"Their senses and ability to hunt is far more attuned than any of ours. They're far less likely to be caught by one of those people than we are," Caim said. "If you start a ring of fire around the fog, we can stop them from retreating and send the hounds in to destroy them."

"But the fire will hurt the hounds," Aisling protested.

"The hounds were born from the fires of Hell," I said. "They'll be okay. The fire might flush the fog people out before the hounds go in."

She turned to study the fog before giving a brisk nod. "It could work."

Caim sniffed. "It *will* work. Those puppies won't leave anyone behind and can hunt down anything. I'll get them."

Caim walked away while the fog edged closer to us, and I pulled Aisling against my side. I wanted to beat the shit out of this mist and everyone in it, but I wouldn't put her at risk by going back in there. She would follow me.

I gazed up the mountain toward where we left the others. Halfway up the hill, the wall of smoke obscured my view, but they were still up there. "Come with me," I said and nudged Aisling toward the survivors.

She glanced at the fog as we walked, but she didn't try to enter it again. I stopped in front of the survivors who were gazing nervously at the mist. "Shouldn't we leave?" a woman asked.

"That's exactly what you're going to do," I told her. "The rest of our group is further up the mountain. Keep going straight until you get above the smoke; once you do, you'll see smoke coming from a cave further up the mountain. Head for that. When you find them, tell them Wrath is already out of the labyrinth and he's gone. Also let them know the fog is here and we're going to take care of it."

One of the men frowned as he stared at the mist. "How can you take care of fog?"

"We have a plan."

"But... it's... *fog*," he said slowly.

"It's not just fog," Aisling said. "And the others are aware of that."

"Tell them we're taking care of it," I said impatiently. "But you have to go." When they remained staring at the fog, I barked the word, "*Now!*"

They all jumped before bowing their heads and scurrying up the mountain. The screams issuing from the fog died away, and silence descended.

CHAPTER FORTY-FIVE

Aisling

Hawk stayed by my side as I remained on the outskirts of the fog, setting fire to anything that would burn. A solid ring of flames rimmed most of the mist, but on the far side, the scorched earth left little for me to torch.

Hawk and Caim went into the woods and returned with some fallen logs, but they weren't enough to keep the fog pinned in. Fire danced across the logs and sparks flew into the air as Caim arrived with more wood, but already the fog was shifting toward us.

Prowling restlessly around, the hounds raised their hackles as they growled at the fog. I kept expecting the mist to devour the land it traversed, but when the ground it covered was exposed again, it was the same as before the fog took it over. Still, I couldn't help seeing this thing as a black hole consuming everything it encountered.

I jerked my hand back when a cold tendril of fog brushed against it. A sick, dirty feeling twisted in my stomach as I recalled the monsters with human faces and hideous souls who resided inside this mist.

When the fog shifted toward me, I felt the ravenous hunger emanating from it as more tendrils brushed against my cheek and neck. I stepped away from it and swore it made an eager chattering noise as fresh wisps searched for me.

It knew I was here, and it was not going to give up as more threads slid free. Hawk stepped in front of me, and some of the fog encompassed his bicep. I rested a hand on his shoulder, but he nudged me back as he edged away from the mist. It chattered again as more of the mist split off to search him out.

"It must sense our body heat," Hawk said.

"I don't care what it does," I said. "It has to be destroyed."

The crunch of debris jerked my head toward the mountain, and flames shot up my wrists as I prepared to torch any monster approaching us. Corson held his hands up and stepped in front of Wren.

"Easy," he said. "We're here to help. Lix and Bale stayed to protect the others in case Wrath returns."

"Sorry," I said as my flames went out. "We're trying to establish a fire barrier, but there's nothing here for me to burn."

"Then we'll establish ourselves here and kill anything that comes out of the fog," Hawk said.

"And if the fog rolls over us?" I asked.

"We'll make sure it doesn't."

"Then it's time to send in the hounds," Caim said.

I gulped as I rested my hand on the head of the hound standing beside me. Its eyes were focused on the fog as it bared its teeth and vibrated with barely leashed power.

"Be careful," I said and lifted my hand.

"Achó," Caim said, commanding the beasts to attack.

I swear the hound grinned at me before bounding into the fog. Standing on the edge of the mist and within the unnatural twilight created by the smoke, everything around me stilled. All I heard was the thump of my racing heart pumping blood through my veins.

I barely breathed as I braced myself for one of the hounds to scream in pain. I wouldn't be able to take it if something happened to one of them, but the silence stretched until the seconds became minutes, and still the only sound was the thump of my heart.

I opened my mouth to ask where they were, but I couldn't get the words past the lump in my throat. If one of the hounds cried out, I'd cry with them. The beasts had taken great joy in running all of us into every obstacle they could find. They'd given me a few headaches and bruises, but I really liked them.

Please let them get through this.

And then screams pierced the silence. Muffled by the fog, it was impossible to tell exactly where those screams originated from, but they grew louder as they mingled with snarls from the hounds.

I yearned to throw my hands over my ears and block out the noise, but I forced myself to listen. We'd sent the hounds in there; I had to know if one of them was hurt.

As the screams continued, the fog shifted and rolled faster toward us. Tendrils of it snaked rapidly on the air as it tried to ascertain where to go. Even as the sounds of death emanated from the fog, it rushed toward us and excitement radiated from it when those tendrils encountered us.

I wished there was some way to take a knife or sword to the fog and slice it to pieces, but it was as tangible as air. As we backed further away from the questing tendrils, a clammy sweat coated my body and stuck my shirt to me. I tried not to think about the possibility this might not work and these monsters would escape to hunt others.

When a tendril touched my cheek and another caressed my hand, I yanked my arm away and edged further back with the others. Another wisp grazed my neck while the screams abruptly ended.

The abrupt absence of noise confused me; for a second, I assumed my senses had gone haywire and I couldn't hear. Then,

Wren's foot crunched on the burnt earth and sound flooded in again.

I held my breath as I waited for the screams to restart or for one of the hounds to howl. I didn't realize I'd clenched my jaw and fingers until my teeth began to ache and blood filled my palms. The longer the silence stretched, the more my tension mounted until I was on the verge of screaming.

Then the fog rolled back like the sea before a tsunami.

I gaped as the vanishing fog revealed the charred land and the bloody bodies scattered across it. With a woman dangling from its jaws, a hound trotted out of what remained of the mist and dropped the body at our feet. Blood coated her face, and her throat was missing, but I recognized Amber when the hound sat beside her.

"Good boy," Caim said and patted the hound's head. "She must have been the one who created the fog."

"That's not surprising," I said.

The rest of the hounds came into view as the last of the mist vanished. A few survivors tried to run, but the hounds took them down before they got far. I didn't cover my ears, but I did turn away from the screams. Every person in that fog deserved to die, and the world was a far better place without them, but I'd seen enough death recently.

When the last scream ended, relief rolled through me and, with it, came exhaustion. Now that there was nothing left to fight and no adrenaline fueling me, my knees trembled, and I almost sank to the ground. Hawk cupped my elbow to steady me before bending and sweeping me into his arms.

"You don't have to carry me," I protested. "You must be exhausted."

"Nowhere near as exhausted as you, Ash," he said and touched my hands. "You've used your ability a lot recently."

"More than I ever have," I admitted as I cuddled against his chest. "But I could use it again."

"I know, but I love having you in my arms."

And there was no way I could protest when I loved being there.

CHAPTER FORTY-SIX

Aisling

The next day, I leaned against the rocks near the entrance of the cave as I watched the humans and demons from town prepare to leave for the wall. Sometime during the night, while I was sleeping, Raphael arrived with word that the others were fine; they lost their telepathic demon when he kicked a calamut tree that kept blocking his way. The tree had not taken kindly to it.

During the night, they decided Raphael would take the survivors to Magnus and Amalia, who would make sure they made it the rest of the way to the wall. Raphael would return to us.

"I never thought I'd leave the Wilds," Randy said to Wren as he finished tying his boots.

"I never thought I'd be a demon," she replied.

He chuckled as he rose and embraced her. "Neither did I, but it works for you."

Wren laughed and stepped away from him as Corson walked over to join them.

"It's best for Oliver," Wren said as she took Corson's hand.

"Even after what happened with the attack, he'll still be safer at the wall, and the queen has a brother about his age."

I turned my attention to Oliver as he lifted his head from Nadine's shoulder. I wanted to go with them and make sure he made it safely to the wall, but if we were ever going to have any peace, we had to destroy the last four horsemen. We may not know where they were, but we *would* find them.

I wasn't ready for another battle with them, but I yearned for peace and would do everything necessary to achieve it. I'd spent my whole life dreaming about being somewhere else. Now, all I wanted was to see my parents, to have a regular place to lay my head, and to wake up beside Hawk every morning.

Apparently, my wanderlust wasn't as strong as I'd believed.

No, that wasn't true.

My wanderlust hadn't changed; *I* had. I was so different from the girl who used to dream of standing in the shadows of the pyramids or exploring the Colosseum. That girl planned to explore the Catacombs of Paris before taking a train through the Alps. But now, I didn't know how many of those places still existed, and if they did, I'd one day see them with Hawk.

However, I'd seen enough of this new world to know I preferred a house at the wall with Hawk. I didn't want a tent anymore; I wanted a place to hang pictures and play games with friends. A home with a room for my parents to stay when they came to visit.

I wanted a home.

When he rested his hand on my shoulder, Hawk pulled me from my reverie. "They're leaving," he said.

I pushed myself away from the rocks and walked over to join the others. I didn't know any of them well, but I wanted to say goodbye to Oliver. Taking his small hand in mine, I bent to look into his eyes. I blinked away the unexpected tears burning my eyes when he smiled at me and used his other hand to pat my face. This resilient, beautiful, loving child was a brilliant hope for all our futures.

"Be safe," he said.

"I will," I vowed. "You're going to be okay." I shouldn't make him any promises when I didn't know if they would come true, but I had to believe he would make it to the wall. "And they're going to protect you."

At least I knew that much was true. Nadine and Randy would fight to the death for him. He *would* make it to the wall.

I hugged him and kissed his forehead before releasing him and stepping away. When I was sure no one was looking, I wiped tears from my eyes. Hawk slid his arm around my waist and pulled me against him as the survivors started down the mountain with Raphael soaring through the trees ahead of them.

"He'll be okay," Hawk said.

"I know," I muttered, but my voice was raw with emotion.

"We should go."

I turned to gaze up the mountain. With no idea where to find the four horsemen, we'd decided to move further up the mountain where we would rest until Raphael returned.

The still-rising smoke would probably deter a lot of things from coming this way, but it would attract others. We planned to be further away from the town and cave before those things started arriving.

Plus, after the exhausting events of yesterday, we needed a few days to recoup and formulate a new plan. What that plan would be, I didn't know, but I had no doubt we would find the remaining horsemen, or they would find us.

Resting my head against Hawk's chest, I listened to the beautiful, reassuring beat of his heart as I closed my eyes. In the beginning, I didn't want to be tied down by this man, but now I couldn't imagine my life without him, and I would fight to the death for him. I was madly and hopelessly in love with him, and I was never going to let him go.

"When this is over, I want to start a family," I said.

"I thought you didn't want kids," he said.

"I was wrong." I tilted my head back to smile at him. "Because I want *your* kids."

～

Hawk

My heart skipped a beat when she uttered these words; not because she was willing to give me something I'd always dreamed of, but because I could *not* wait to see her holding our child. I stroked her cheek as I closed my eyes and savored the softness of her skin.

"But only if our kid is as cute as Oliver," she said.

I laughed as I leaned back to look at her. "They'll be cuter."

"Especially if they take after me." She playfully bumped my hip and smiled before bending to lift a scavenged spear from the ground.

She was so different than the woman I first encountered. Then, she looked ready to bolt from me or throw up when learning she was my Chosen. But then, I wasn't the same man either. It was impossible to hate myself as much over what happened with Sarah when Aisling was looking at me with so much love.

She didn't see me as the monster I'd seen myself as for so long; she saw me as the man she loved.

"Thank you," I said.

"For what?"

"For loving me."

She opened her mouth to reply, but I silenced her with a kiss;

something I couldn't have done before she walked into my life. Lifting her against me, I deepened the kiss until I had to break it off before we gave everyone here a show.

When I set her on her feet, she swayed before she broke into a beautiful grin. "I'm going to make you finish what you just started later," she said.

"You better," I told her and lifted an ax from the ground as the others started up the mountain.

We fell into line behind Corson and Wren as Lix and Bale walked beside us. Bale still seemed distracted but determined as she stalked over the terrain. We'd scavenged clothes from the dead fog people, but most of them didn't fit well.

I kept Aisling's hand in mine while we picked our way over the rocks and further up the mountain. I didn't know what the future held with the horsemen, but when all this was over, I knew it would contain only joy and love for Aisling and me.

In her, I'd found my home, and she was my family. One day, we would have children, and they would grow up knowing how much their parents loved them and how loved they were. We would put an end to our enemies and give them the secure future they deserved.

When I squeezed Aisling's hand, she looked at me and smiled. Love swelled in my chest as I bent to kiss her.

The End

***The Edge of the Darkness* (Hell on Earth, Book 4) will focus on Bale and Wrath:**
brendakdavies.com/EODwb

Stay in touch on updates and other new releases from the author, by joining the mailing list.

**Erica Stevens/Brenda K. Davies Mailing List:
brendakdavies.com/ESBKDNews**

FIND THE AUTHOR

Erica Stevens/Brenda K. Davies Mailing List:
brendakdavies.com/ESBKDNews

Facebook page: brendakdavies.com/BKDfb
Facebook friend: ericastevensauthor.com/EASfb

Erica Stevens/Brenda K. Davies Book Club:
brendakdavies.com/ESBKDBookClub

Instagram: brendakdavies.com/BKDInsta
Twitter: brendakdavies.com/BKDTweet
Website: www.brendakdavies.com
Blog: ericastevensauthor.com/ESblog

ALSO FROM THE AUTHOR

Books written under the pen name
Brenda K. Davies

The Vampire Awakenings Series
Awakened (Book 1)

Destined (Book 2)

Untamed (Book 3)

Enraptured (Book 4)

Undone (Book 5)

Fractured (Book 6)

Ravaged (Book 7)

Consumed (Book 8)

Unforeseen (Book 9)

Forsaken (Book 10)

Relentless (Book 11)

Legacy (Book 12)

The Alliance Series
Eternally Bound (Book 1)

Bound by Vengeance (Book 2)

Bound by Darkness (Book 3)

Bound by Passion (Book 4)

Bound by Torment (Book 5)

Bound by Danger (Book 6)

Bound by Deception (Book 7)

Coming 2021

The Road to Hell Series

Good Intentions (Book 1)

Carved (Book 2)

The Road (Book 3)

Into Hell (Book 4)

Hell on Earth Series

Hell on Earth (Book 1)

Into the Abyss (Book 2)

Kiss of Death (Book 3)

Edge of the Darkness (Book 4)

The Shadow Realms

Shadows of Fire (Book 1)

Shadows of Discovery (Book 2)

Shadows of Betrayal (Book 3)

Coming Winter 2022

Historical Romance

A Stolen Heart

Books written under the pen name
Erica Stevens

The Coven Series

Nightmares (Book 1)

The Maze (Book 2)

Dream Walker (Book 3)

The Captive Series

Captured (Book 1)

Renegade (Book 2)

Refugee (Book 3)

Salvation (Book 4)

Redemption (Book 5)

Broken (The Captive Series Prequel)

Vengeance (Book 6)

Unbound (Book 7)

The Kindred Series

Kindred (Book 1)

Ashes (Book 2)

Kindled (Book 3)

Inferno (Book 4)

Phoenix Rising (Book 5)

The Fire & Ice Series

Frost Burn (Book 1)

Arctic Fire (Book 2)

Scorched Ice (Book 3)

The Ravening Series

The Ravening (Book 1)

Taken Over (Book 2)

Reclamation (Book 3)

The Survivor Chronicles

The Upheaval (Book 1)

The Divide (Book 2)

The Forsaken (Book 3)

The Risen (Book 4)

ABOUT THE AUTHOR

Brenda K. Davies is the USA Today Bestselling author of the Vampire Awakening Series, Alliance Series, Road to Hell Series, Hell on Earth Series, and historical romantic fiction. She also writes under the pen name, Erica Stevens. When not out with friends and family, she can be found at home with her husband, son, dog, cat, and horse.

Made in the USA
Middletown, DE
18 December 2022

19315277R00186